Daniel Mornin was born in 1956 in Belfast and left school at the age of fifteen. He tried out a variety of vocations including ship yard apprentice, anti-submarine operator and part-time diver in the Royal Navy before deciding that the Cod War was not for him. He cycled off to France, Austria and Turkey and later hitchhiked to Africa and Nepal.

His first play *Mum and Son*, was produced in Hammersmith in 1981, and since then he has written *Short of Mutiny*, *The Murderers*, *Weights and Measures*, *Scuttling Off* for radio 3, and the film script *Border Country* for Channel Four. He now lives and writes in London.

ALSO BY DANIEL MORNIN

PLAYS FOR THE STAGE
Mum and Son
Kate
Short of Mutiny
Comrade Ogilvy
The Murderers
Build on Sand
Weights and Measures
By the Border

PLAYS FOR THE RADIO
Scuttling Off

SCREENPLAY
Border Country

ALL OUR FAULT

A novel

Daniel Mornin

ARROW

This novel is a work of fiction and the events described in it do not necessarily reflect the specific dates in real life.

Published by Arrow Books in 1996

1 3 5 7 9 10 8 6 4 2

First published in the United Kingdom by
Hutchinson
Random House UK Ltd.
20 Vauxhall Bridge Road, London SW1V 2SA

Random House Australia (Pty) Limited
20 Alfred Street, Milsons Point, Sydney,
New South Wales 2061, Australia

Random House New Zealand Limited
18 Poland Road, Glenfield
Auckland 10, New Zealand

Random House South Africa (Pty) Limited
PO Box 337, Bergvlei, South Africa

Random House UK Limited Reg. No. 954009

A CIP catalogue record for this book
is available from the British Library

Papers used by Random House UK Limited
are natural, recyclable products made from wood grown in
sustainable forests. The manufacturing processes conform to
the environmental regulations of the country of origin

ISBN 0 09 996140 7

Printed and bound in Great Britain by
Cox & Wyman Ltd, Reading, Berkshire

For AINE

ONE

It is a warm summer's evening in Belfast, the full moon hangs low in the cloudless sky, seemingly about to touch the maze of slate roofs which radiate out from the ship-yard. The yard is busy this evening, filling the air with the dull sound of hammered steel. The moonlight reveals two gigantic yellow cranes standing like a couple of football posts, bestriding the yard, dominating the huddled houses and even the surrounding city, as slowly, imperceptibly they lift another giant segment of an oil tanker into place. Beneath the false daylight cast from the arc lamps under the cranes' corners, men scurry about in the gloom of the ship's guts burning, welding, thumping metal into shape, metal turned velvet by the light of the moon. Everywhere a thousand coloured lamps flash like so many lights on a shapeless Christmas tree.

The houses in the tight little streets are quiet, hushed, apparently at peace under the moon. The inhabitants of the houses lie in their beds, most of them soundly asleep; those few lying awake perhaps feel alone, frightened, or perhaps excitedly triumphant as they go over the evening's violent events in their minds.

Debris from the recent battle lies over the broad main road that bisects the area, lying thickest at the focus of the battle, a moonshadowed church standing some four hundred yards up from where the road crosses the river. The church stands as it seems always to have stood, mean-ing what it has always meant to those living within its precincts, indifferent to the superficial wounds inflicted upon its crumbling sandstone.

To the left of the church there is a small street with a row of houses sinking slowly into the sand on which they sit. Sand which had once formed the river bed. Across

1

the street the church railings stand like so many spears ready to be thrown. Where the street joins the main road a flimsy barricade has been flung down to mark territory and issue a warning: a warning the attackers had initially ignored. Though eventually the two sides had obeyed the marker of territory: there are rules even in a Belfast riot.

Half-way up the row of houses there are signs of life in one of the upstairs bedrooms. A window is wide open and a boy, Liam Kelly, hangs out, silhouetted by a dull light at his back. He looks down at his once familiar street and finds its transformation unsettling. The pavement upon which he had spent many long days playing with his friends has been ripped up to reveal the soil beneath. Across the main road, at another street junction, he can see the carcass of a car smouldering; the wispy smoke drifts from the car's heart into the warm night air. In no hurry to be gone from its source, the smoke hugs the ground, pushed by a gentle breeze towards the church.

'Are ye friggin' mad, wee boy?' asks Kathleen in a hushed voice, reaching over her brother to pull the curtains across, shutting out the dangers of the night. From the bed young Liam can see that her face has a silvery sheen as it is briefly caught in the moonlight.

'You been cryin' again?' he asks.

Kathleen straightens herself up so that she can gaze down on him.

'Do you blame me?' Quickly she turns away from her brother's bed to sit on the edge of her own. There is little space to manoeuvre in the box-like bedroom. From the sleeve of her frayed cardigan she takes a squashed piece of toilet paper and wipes her eyes and blows her nose.

'He's havin' a drink somewhere,' says the boy.

'What would he use for money?' asks the girl with an almost violent anger. She stuffs the toilet paper back up her sleeve before brusquely standing. 'Are ye hungry?' Her brother looks into her eyes. How she hates to wait for him to answer. She can almost see the thoughts flick through his brain under his dark, tangled hair as she stands passively by. She makes a note in her mind to tell him to switch off his bedside light.

'Aye,' he finally answers.

'I haven't much food left so don't expect a feed. We'll be lucky to find a shop open tomorrow.' He does not respond. Instead he picks up a thick book and opens it at his marker.

'Turn the light off, Liam, it's dangerous.'

'I'm readin' a story,' he answers without looking up.

'Never mind your story!'

'I'm readin' m' story, Kathleen,' says Liam with soft determination.

Giving up her battle she turns to the grubby door and the tiny darkened landing. Every step she takes down the stairs seems to sound out into the night and to draw attention to her vulnerability.

TWO

EGG SHELLS. WHITE spotted egg shells in my bed. So warm. So comfortable. Even without her next to me. Soon the alarm clock will sound off and I'll be out in the cold morning. Mouth dry. Need water. Too frigging lazy to go downstairs and get a drink. Though Kathleen will be up soon enough. Might get a cup of tea before she goes to school. What's that rancid stink? Oul chip fat and rotten tea leaves.

A draught of wind blows up Liam's trouser leg and he raises a foot to scratch his calf.

Shoe? I've come to bed with my shoes on my feet? Oh, you drunken pig. Oh, you drunken scut. That's why your mouth's so frigging dry. Stale stout. Where were you? Jesus. Can't remember. Who was it you were with? Can't remember that either. Oh, will you never learn?

Liam lifts his head and pain shudders through his body. Then again he feels a gentle breeze ruffle the hairs on his legs and he is immediately fearful.

Opening an eye he sees white egg shells nestling in a bed of tea leaves, potato peelings and milk bottle tops.

THREE

GINGER IS FINDING it hard to get the engine of the old Ford to start. He pulls hard on the choke as he presses down on the accelerator and twists the key, but still the engine stubbornly refuses to start. Ginger is infuriated. He feels an almost murderous hatred for the machine.

'Come on, you fucker!' screams Ginger, smacking the dashboard with his fist. His abuse seems to do the trick. The engine roars into life and emits a dirty black cloud of smoke at its rear. Ginger thanks his lucky stars and rests his forehead against the steering wheel. He has never been able to control his anger. He keeps his foot down on the accelerator until he remembers the promise to be quiet he had made to his wife while they were still in a sweaty embrace. His foot comes off the pedal. The engine dies away until it is idling softly. How well he has it tuned. How well he has it running. What a wizard he is with cars. He smiles to himself. Gently he turns the steering wheel and slips into first gear. The car rolls off the pavement, its powerful potential sounding in the depth of its drone.

Ginger looks up and sees that the moon is full. A sniper's moon, he tells himself. He rests back into the soft leather of his seat. How the street is transformed by the light of the moon low above the roofs. The cement of the roadway acts as a long mirror and throws reflected light into parked cars, doorways and windows. Surely he could read a newspaper in this light. Yet he is disturbed by it. He presses down on the accelerator for reassurance and the car moves faster along the street. His street, the street in which he has spent almost every day of his life. He takes out a heavy automatic pistol from his belt and slips it into the glove compartment. A feeling of power sweeps over him, warming his heart. Turning left, he leaves his street; immediately he feels as if he has been released, let loose from his family, friends, neighbours. Soon he will be far away from them all. Sticking his foot down on the accelerator he sweeps past the familiar boundary markers of his world until he comes to a junction. Across the street lies less familiar territory. He glances upwards at a huge Union Flag painted on a gable wall; it has been there for thirty years, its paint refreshed every year. His eye catches the full moon: never has he seen it so low, so full, so much a presence. Taking his foot off the accelerator he allows the silence of the street to envelop the car. Only the soft hum of the engine and the loud metallic click of the car's clock break into the quiet. He feels unsettled. Why? Is it because not more than three hours before the same street had been filled with running, screaming, shouting men? Now it lies utterly desolate under the moon's light. He shudders. Is he to die? Is that why he feels so uneasy? He dismisses the thought and presses again on the accelerator. The beer he has longed for all evening is a few minutes away.

FOUR

KENNY IS REACHING a climax. How? He wakes to find a figure bending over his crotch. Thrusting his body up from a supine position, he sees the figure move from the dull pool of light into the room's shadows.

'Who's that, for God sake?'

'It's me,' says the figure in the gloom.

'Betty?'

'Aye.' Betty giggles and steps back into the light. 'Wha's the matter, Kenny? Don't you like it any more?' Kenny is on his feet and adjusting his trousers. He is angry. He feels vulnerable, slightly humiliated. The girl had been around when he had needed relief. That is all. She is still giggling, a drunk fifteen-year-old. Raising his hand to strike revenge he moves towards her; his left hand holds his opened trousers closed. Her laughter dies away to be replaced by a silent acceptance. She waits to be slapped. She expects it. Always has. Kenny drops his hand.

'You shouldn't come in here 'less I tell you to. Okay?'

'Okay, Kenny.' She smiles weakly, her thin lips disappearing into her mouth. Her face is long and thin, her skin blotched; her hair drops down either side of her face, long, fair and greasy. She is flat-chested and pale and far too skinny, her thinness a result of malnutrition, her pallor the result of being imprisoned by walls, of never having lain in the sun.

She looks about the room until she finds what she wants.

'Kenny, can I have a drink of your vodka?'

'You're too young to drink.'

'Can I?'

'Aye, go ahead.' The girl quickly finds a glass and pours herself a large measure of vodka. Looking about the table

7

she finds a quarter-full bottle of coke and mixes it with the spirit. With a childish slurp she takes a gulp. She looks over her glass waiting on Kenny to speak.

'Just don't do anythin' like that again 'less I ask ye to.'

'Okay. I'm really sorry, Kenny,' she says with a defenceless humility. Something in her voice causes Kenny to look up. He is for a second sorry for the girl and almost puts out an arm to take her in an embrace, but the moment passes. Instead he reaches down for his socks and highly polished shoes.

'That's all right, just don't do it again.' He slips on a sock. 'What are you doin' in here at this time anyway?'

'It's only twelve.'

'Don't you have a school to go to in the mornin'?'

'We're off on holidays.'

'Oh, aye,' sighs Kenny, remembering that he will have to go down to his ex-wife's house to see their children. Perhaps drag them down to the sea at Donaghadee for the day.

Kenny mutters a curse as music starts up in the main hall of the wooden hut into which the club has been roughly fitted. It is a heavily rhythmical pop record he has heard a hundred times and he hates every second of it. Some time soon he'll smash it to pieces.

'Away home. You should be in your bed.'

'M' ma's here drinkin' with m' da.'

'Well, that doesn't –' He thinks. 'Did they see you come in here?'

'Naaa . . . Nobody saw me, Kenny.'

'Well, thank God for that!' He slips on his other sock. 'Look at this friggin' room!' he cries with a profound loathing for untidiness and dirt gained as a soldier.

'Want me to tidy up, Kenny?'

'Don't you bother. Not your job. I'll get one of the men to do it. You away an' have yourself a dance with some wee boy.' His eyes are now more used to the gloom and he can pick out the cigarette butts and spilt beer that cover the wooden floor. 'I'm probably infested with lice.' He stands up and looks back down at his bed. It is a plastic-covered sofa that has seen its best days. Its webbing lies on the floor as if it has been disembowelled.

The glasses in the room start to jingle as the music booms out more loudly.

'In the name of God turn that music down!'

'I'll go an' tell disc jockey, shall I?'

'Aye,' says Kenny, glad to be rid of her. The girl smiles brightly, pleased to serve.

'Kenny, I really love you,' she adds before leaving.

She leaves him to shake his head in disbelief and to pull a comb through his dirty blond hair. His hand hits the light bulb, sending it spinning upon its flex.

Sticking the comb into the back pocket of his jeans he strides to the door of the room and out to the darkened passageway which joins the back room to the body of the hall. He walks with authority and power; he is in control. He walks as a man with a purpose in life, a reason for living.

FIVE

TOMMY TAPS HIS foot to the beat of the music as he lifts his beer glass from the black vinyl table top to take a few sips of the stout. His eyes dart about, fixing briefly on each of his drinking companions. The other four young men, none yet twenty, start to join in on the beat with their feet or with the base of their glasses as the music is turned up still further. He smiles broadly at Joe and Joe returns the smile.

'Good 'un, eh?'

'Aye,' replies Tommy. He places his glass on the table, letting it glide through the beer drips, making larger and larger circles.

'I've got the LP,' adds Joe. Joe, kind and thick, smiles again at his friend. He has always liked Tommy more than his other ex-classmates. 'Want to tape it?'

'Aye,' replies Tommy, not looking at Joe. His gaze is fixed on the black space next to the oblong slash of light that marks out the bar-hatch. Down the passageway lies the room in which Kenny has gone to sleep, exhausted by that evening's events and a day spent drinking. Tommy watches as Betty emerges from the passageway to cross the hall to a platform on which a tall, unbelievably thin, long-haired fella sits with a few adoring girls surrounded by piles of records. Betty leans over to shout at the disc jockey, who waves her away with contempt; when she shouts again he replies by turning up the volume. She gives up and walks to the back of the hall where she rejoins her parents.

'Want another drink?' Joe waits by his side for a reply. When none comes he follows Tommy's gaze to the back of the hall. 'Aye, Betty Lawson, she's a desperate wee girl. I wonder if her oul ma knows what she gets up to?'

'Ach,' replies Tommy, wondering what it is she could get up to. Betty is being ignored; her parents look off

10

into the distance and sip their drinks as if she were not there.

'D'ye want another drink or what?'

'Aye, ta,' responds Tommy.

Joe heads for the bar-hatch. A crush of people besiege the bar-hatch – fighting with elbows and raised bank notes to catch the solitary barman's eye. Joe pushes into the crowd and shouts over their heads. 'Two bottles of Harp in a pint glass an' a bottle of Red Hand by the neck, Jimmy!' Jimmy looks up from the customer he's serving to wave acceptance. The lesser mortals turn to gaze at Joe in anger and mocking awe.

'Can you walk on water an' all?' asks a man with a ten-pound note gripped in a sweaty fist.

'Aye,' says Joe as he reaches up to grab the drinks out of Jimmy's outstretched hands. 'Stick it on the slate, Jimmy. Get one yourself!'

By the time he sets the beer on the table with a triumphant thump he and Tommy are alone, their friends gone to interrupt the choreographed dance of a group of girls. The girls protest against the interference but, split up by insistent pleas, they accept the inevitable. The one girl who persists in refusing her suitor's requests has to push him away several times before he heads to the bar in defeat.

'Gloria McCann, she's a cracker.'

'Aye, she is,' answers Tommy. They study the girl closely. She releases a bright smile to no one in particular, but Tommy decides it is aimed in his direction.

'I tried for her last bonfire night. Not so much as a kiss, Tommy.' Joe smacks his lips together in an act of disgust. 'I tell you, Tommy, I'd give m' right arm to spend half an hour with that wee girl.' He takes a consoling sip of his lager, looking at Gloria through the glass, marbled by the lights.

'Who wouldn't?' asks Tommy. He feels an intense longing for the girl as he watches her gyrate across the improvised dance floor. Her short skirt lifts to reveal her stockinged thighs which are luminescent in the gaudy oranges and yellows of the disco lights. Her breasts are large and heavy for her tiny frame and move loosely in her black sweater. Her face is pale and fleshy, with overly red lips

11

and very dark eyes. She is rarely without a smile or an ironic grin.

'Tommy! There's Kenny!' Tommy looks up to see Kenny emerge from the blackness of the passageway and cross the hall towards the disc jockey.

Kenny clears the girls away from the platform before climbing up to have a word in the disc jockey's ear. The grin on the disc jockey's face vanishes, his hand goes out and the pick-up arm lifts off the record. Kenny swings round and snatches up the record, breaking it in two. A cry of approval goes up in the hall as Kenny tosses the record to the floor and hands a pound note to the disc jockey to cover the damage. Next he turns his attentions to the chaos around the bar-hatch, ordering the drinkers into a queue as a ballad starts to play and the older men and women rise to take their turn on the dance floor. In a minute Kenny has brought order and a bit of justice to the club and most of its occupants feel a little safer knowing its commander is there again.

'Good on ye, Kenny!' cries a neatly turned-out pensioner as he heads for the queue with an empty glass in his hand.

'That's right, Kenny! Get them oul boozers sorted out! Man dear, you need to be a heavyweight champ to get a drink in here!' cries Annie, a bejewelled forty-year-old, her laugh breaking into a nervous cackle.

'Where's your oul man tonight, Annie?'

'Out for the count in yon corner!' replies Annie, pointing to a distant table. 'Too drunk to move his arse!'

'So he'll be no good to you tonight!'

'He's no good to me drunk or sober, Kenny. Couldn't find a key-hole on a dark night.' She pushes herself against Kenny and the surrounding men and women burst into laughter. Kenny gives Annie's bottom a playful pat and kisses her cheek before setting off across the dance floor.

Kenny's progress is watched intently by Tommy: Tommy longs for him to look his way, to acknowledge his presence, his existence.

SIX

EDDIE HAS NEVER really enjoyed copulation with a woman, but he knows that his friends would ask uncomfortable questions if he never indulged. So he kisses the heavily lipsticked lips and pushes his way into Lizzie's vagina. He gains some satisfaction when she emits a little cry; it does not occur to Eddie that she may be false in her sounds of enjoyment.

'Now go easy, you big pig! My arse is hittin' the ground! Go easy!'

'Aye,' replies Eddie, absent-mindedly. His dilated nostrils are filled with the woman's perfume; it smells to Eddie like rotten apples. He begins to beat her buttocks against the grass and cinders in time to the music drifting across the waste ground from the wooden hall.

'What did I tell ye?' says the woman, now with considerable anger. 'Take it easy. If you can't do it right, don't bother. I'm not a punch bag, you know.'

He slows down somewhat. To his surprise the music coming from the hall slows down, too. He can faintly make out the words: it's one of his favourite ballads. Lizzie laughs and wraps her legs around Eddie's hips and starts to moan with pleasure.

'You're a lovely big fella, Eddie. You can have this anytime you like. As long as my oul man doesn't find out.'

'Aye,' replies Eddie. His mind is focused upon a face. The face is marked with rivulets of blood. It is surrounded by an absolute blackness. He towers above the face. He wants to push the face into the blackness, wants to obliterate it.

'Eddie, a wee bit harder.'

Eddie obliges.

13

'Not too hard.'

'Aye.'

'That's just right. That's lovely.'

'Aye.'

The face has disappeared into the blackness. Where has he seen the face? He thrusts his penis deeper into Lizzie and takes pleasure in watching her gasp.

'Oh, Eddie!' cries Lizzie, her voice throatily taut.

'Wha'?' says Eddie.

'Oh, Eddie!'

'Aye,' says Eddie. He decides to get it over with. He grips Lizzie's buttocks and concentrates upon finishing it. He musn't be away from the door of the club much longer.

SEVEN

JAMES STANDS IN his dressing-gown by the large, ceiling-high window, looking out over the castle's grounds. He cradles a glass in his right hand and swills a mouthful of whisky before letting it slip down his throat. His wife is away in London this evening, and when she is gone he prefers to spend as little time as possible in bed by himself; so he takes a gulp of the whisky and hopes it will take him through the night.

His gaze is fixed upon the giant trees which stand in a long line down the hill on which the castle looms. He thinks the trees even more ethereal in the moonlight than they are in daylight. He is obsessed with their grandeur. Their presence, their timelessness, though the thought occurs to him that he could not put a name to the trees if asked. He had first caught sight of the trees as he swung into the castle grounds seated in a large helicopter. The trees had been stirred into an almost sexual frenzy by the rotor blades. He had been so transfixed by them that he had stumbled through the formalities of meeting his ministry underlings. He smiles to himself as he takes a sip of the whisky, enjoying the coolness of the iced liquid and starting to feel its effects. He hears a click at his back and turns from the window to see the door to the high-ceilinged room open and a young man in a pin-striped suit enter. The man registers the whisky in James's hand before he looks at James, who receives the silent rebuke with a smile.

'Yes?' asks James sharply, mockingly putting his aide in his place; if he wants to get drunk he shall get drunk.

'Cup of coffee, sir?' asks the tall, powerful, young man who seems uncomfortable in his suit.

'Coffee? Yes, please.'

The aide gives James a bow which starts at the crown of his head and ends at the shoulders.

'Steven, do you have anything good to read? I've got through everything.'

'I've got a rather good thriller I could let you have, sir. It's very fast; clever ending. Heavy body count. Smashing.'

'Oh, good.'

'Would you like some sandwiches, or something, sir?'

'No, thanks, Steven.'

'Right.'

'Anything happening?'

'Quiet, sir. Very quiet. Thank God,' Steven replies.

His tone has the resonance of eight hundred years of English condescension; a bored indifference bordering on out-and-out contempt for the whole mess.

'Good.'

Steven opens the door to the high-ceilinged room and is gone as quietly as he came. James turns back to the window just in time to see a black-clad man emerge from the blackness of the shrubbery to cross a gravel path illuminated by the moon. Someone come to slit my throat? Or a member of the praetorian guard? James's heart suddenly chills and he feels utterly alone. His hand stretches out to the bottle of whisky. The more he has, the sooner sleep will come. Why is he stuck in a country he does not care for one way or another? A country he is meant to rule over. James sighs and checks his watch. It's almost twelve o'clock. Soon he'll crawl into bed and try to sleep. He is here because he became unfashionable, rebellious and old, he reminds himself. Resentment is never far away from his mind, but the whisky relaxes him and prevents an intense anger swelling up.

As he pours himself another glass of whisky he notices that the moon is intensely bright. Preternaturally so.

EIGHT

THE VOICE OOZES from the wireless to soothe Kathleen's nerves as she flicks hot fat over the spluttering egg in the heavy iron frying pan. The voice seems to speak to her and no one else, every word hits home and when the voice tells her that she will enjoy the next record she knows she will.

She flips the saggy egg over to cook the yolk before lifting it on to the plate, which already holds the last pieces of bacon and bread she has: it will have to do young Liam, she tells herself. No food 'til she finds a shop open in the morning. She looks up to an old tea caddy sitting on a high shelf: four pounds and sixty-four pence, she tells herself. Twisting off the gas she lifts the plate on to the red formica-covered table positioned by the pantry door. Tightness returns to her stomach, she remains absolutely still in the centre of the pantry; her hand feels round to her front and she imagines she can feel a bird flutter within.

'Liam. Come down,' she mutters up the stairwell. 'Don't turn on the hall light, whatever you do.'

'Why not?' Liam appears on the landing.

'Because it's dangerous, that's why.'

'Ach, nonsense,' protests Liam coming down the stairs.

'Not nonsense. You never know who's out there.'

Unsettled at having an argument with him at eye level, she puts out an arm to bring him off the lower stair and through the plastic strip curtain into the little pantry.

'Sit down an' eat,' she says in a whisper.

'I can't see a thing,' he complains.

'Wait a minute 'til your eyes get used to it.' Kathleen is already used to watching things by the light of the moon.

'I want the light on,' he persists.

'Oh, hold on,' she compromises. Her hand reaches out

17

and pulls the refrigerator door open. Light spreads across the brown linoleum floor and on to the table. Liam makes a sound of grudging acceptance of the strange world he finds himself in. His head goes down to eat the only food he's had in many hours. For a second or two Kathleen watches him with satisfaction.

'Our Kathleen, you're mad,' he says out of the side of his mouth.

'I'm not mad,' she replies weakly as she goes through the plastic strip curtain out to the unlit living-room. 'Eat your food.' The walls of the living-room seem very close to her as she stands in the centre of the room under the creamy brown light shade. Her eyes close as she listens for sounds leaking into the room from the outside world. Only the soft voice from the wireless and the scraping of knife and fork on china break into the absolute stillness. Her eyes open again and she finds herself looking at the curtains covering the front window. Through a chink in the curtain the familiar street appears warmly at peace until her eyes stray down to the devastated road and pavement. In front of the house she can see the remains of its guttering and downpipes lying across the kerb stone. They'd made useful missiles when the attackers looked as if they might drive back the defenders.

What would her mother do if she were here? Go looking for him? Or stay in the house and wait? Tears trickle down her cheeks as she turns away from the window. She trembles at the thought of even opening the door, let alone stepping out into the night. Softly she steps to the outside door which opens directly into the living-room. Her hand rises to the latch and with her heart working hard she eases the door back. The cool night air envelops her as she opens the door wide enough to stick her head out on to the street. Looking down to the barricade she sees no one. Looking up the street, again, no one. Yet she is sure she is being watched by hidden eyes, that the men are still about, keeping watch. Hurriedly she closes the door and steps back to the centre of the room where she feels safest.

'What's the matter?'

Her heart leaps.

'What's the matter?' asks Liam again. She turns to see

him standing by the stairs. 'Our Kathleen, do you want me to go an' look for him?'

'No!'

'He's havin' a drink somewhere,' says young Liam, bored with his sister's silly fretting. He leaves her in the living-room while he rushes to his bedroom to finish off his story. Kathleen bites her lip as she listens to his heavy footfalls on the stairs. How can he be so indifferent to their father's fate?

NINE

LIAM GATHERS UP his courage to defy the pain he knows he has to defy, if he is to be home before daybreak. What will Kathleen be thinking? That he's lying dead somewhere. He knows he could so easily be dead.

Against a crumbling, urine-stinking wall, he pushes himself upright using legs he is not absolutely sure can support his weight. They feel crushed, useless. What if he has to run? He turns to rest his back upon the wall. With his right hand he lifts his left, which feels numb, to his eyes. By the moonlight he can see his watch: it's just past twelve o'clock. Not so late as he had thought.

Pain returns as his head grinds round to the left. The alleyway stretches off into the distance. The long row of homogeneous houses seems quite lifeless. Dustbins are turned over, their rotten contents strewn over the concrete of the alleyway; it's been a while since the dustbins were last emptied. The stench fills his nostrils until he feels quite nauseated. The sooner he's out of the alleyway the better. He pushes himself off the wall, his legs give way and he falls to the concrete.

Jesus, what has hit me?

He can see a street thirty yards away to his right. The street will tell him where he is. That seems the most important thing. He already fears that he is nowhere near his own, safe territory. Up he gets, determined to get going. Swaying from side to side, until he finds the wall for support, he moves carefully down the alleyway, avoiding the mass of refuse as best he can.

Into his mind's eye comes a face. Teeth are bare, eyes wide open, nostrils dilated and a right hand is raised. He shudders at the image, causing him to stumble over an upturned bin; he falls heavily against the wall. As he slides to the ground his right hand scrapes against the old, weathered brick. Lying on the concrete he breathes hard to fight back the tears of pain. Why him? What had he done? He'd gone out to the street to do what he could to stop his house being attacked. Where had the Army been? The police? Why wasn't someone doing something? He felt desperately alone and angry. How could it have happened a few hundred yards from his own front door? He can only sigh and renew his determination to get back to his family. Trying his best to deny the pain he stands again. If he is going to pass out it's best he does so on the street, where he has a chance of a good Samaritan passing his way. His heart aches to be at home. To be in his own bed waiting on Kathleen to bring him a cup of tea before his walk to work. Work! Whatever happens he mustn't be late for work at the builders'.

TEN

GINGER STOPS THE Ford at a junction, checks that the road is clear and drives round the corner. The club sits on a large patch of wasteland lying between a long row of houses. He can hear music playing inside the hall. There are quite a few cars parked around the club, cars from many parts of the city driven by men in search of a late night drink. Putting his foot down he roars past the hall for fifty yards or so until he sees a place to park. He curses the fact that he can't park nearer: he may need the car in a hurry. As he reverses, the car headlights sweep over the wasteland: two pairs of cats' eyes are caught in the beam. He expertly squeezes the car into a space and lets the engine die. The music from the hall drifts down the street and he feels happy already. He jumps out and heads back down the street. Has he money? He checks. She had wanted something extra to buy the girl a pair of shoes, but he had protested that it wasn't available. He makes a mental note to grub up some money for the wife; she needs it and he must provide it. Ginger is beginning to feel warmly generous: a few beers and a good talk will only make him feel more so, he decides.

He pushes the wooden door open and enters the bluish-grey lobby. It's empty. There should be at least one man sitting behind the small wooden desk checking for weapons, drunks and troublemakers. Never mind, he decides, there will be no more trouble tonight. He pushes open a pair of frail wooden doors and enters the packed hall. He glances up at the hanging red, white and blue flags before sweeping his gaze across the faces looking to see who has entered. One or two of the faces look frightened, as if they expect some manner of danger to come in through the doors. A girl sitting near the entrance is smiling at Ginger and he nods and returns the smile before heading towards his desperately-needed bottle of beer.

ELEVEN

EDDIE WATCHES AS she lies on her back to pull her knickers up her legs.

'Act the gentleman and turn the other way, Eddie,' she demands. Eddie keeps on looking and gives her a smile instead.

'What's the matter, Lizzie, are ye shy?' he asks.

'I'll give you a good thump if you don't look elsewhere. Look at the moon while I make m'self decent.'

'Ach, all right,' he says as he turns to look at the moon; he takes out a cigarette and tosses it into his mouth. 'Want a fag?'

'In a minute,' she replies. She slips off her blouse and brassiere to rearrange herself. He turns back. Her breasts are large and still self-supporting. Eddie notices the goose-pimples.

'Give's a feel.'

'If you must.' Eddie's hand reaches out and over her right breast. He feels her nipple harden.

'You're well blessed there, Lizzie.' He removes his hand.

'So I've been told.'

'Your oul man have a good time with them in bed?'

'If I had a good time with my oul man I wouldn't be out here freezin' t' death, now would I?'

'You're right. You're right.' He lowers himself to the ground, finding it still warm from that day's burning sun. 'Men are walkin' about on the moon this very second, Lizzie. Doesn't it make you wonder?'

'Not much,' she replies, her voice showing dissatisfaction with Eddie's banter. 'Though sometimes I feel as if I'm walking about the moon down here.'

Eddie lets out a genuine laugh and feels a little more

24

comfortable with the woman. He takes his eyes off the moon to search the heavens for his stars, the stars his father used to show him when he was alive.

'Eddie, you go back to the club first. I'll wait a while before goin' in,' suggests Lizzie, showing considerable past experience with furtive love. She buttons up the last buttons on her blouse, pulls her handbag towards her and starts to redo her face with a nervous hurry.

'I'd give anything t' walk on the moon,' Eddie says. 'Anything at all. If somebody said I could walk on the moon, but would have to die doin' it, I'd say yes.'

'Then you'd be a bloody eejit.' She turns the mirror this way and that in an attempt to capture the moon's rays. Her skin looks ashen in the reflected image she holds in her hands. She combs back her dark hair, which she has long since given up trying to keep free of grey. She reminds herself to pluck her eye-brows, get rid of the hairs about her lip and buy a new pair of eyelashes.

'God, I look like a creature from the moon,' she cries, hoping Eddie will be just good enough to contradict her.

'You look okay. You look fine.'

At last, he's done something right. She puts her make-up stuff away and decides she'll just have to slip into the toilet and finish her make-up behind a closed door. Not that her husband's going to notice a smudged lipstick line, or question her excuse for being back at the house for so long. She starts to think of a good excuse.

'Did you know that Neil Armstrong's family come from Ulster?' asks Eddie.

'Who's he when he's at home?'

'Only the first man to walk on the moon.'

'Oh.' She uses a paper hanky to clean some black dirt from off of her tartan skirt. 'Do you think that fella in the car saw us, Eddie?'

'No way,' replies Eddie, hoping that he has been seen with Lizzie so that the story will go round.

'You sure?'

'Positive.'

'Well, I'm going back in. You wait a wee while before coming. Okay?'

'I'm not coming back in, Lizzie. I'm on the door.'

'Oh. That's right. That's right.' She feels a tear start to form in her eye. She finds a clean piece of the hanky and wipes it away without fuss. Why can't she control herself?

'Did you see that wee moon buggy they've got for drivin' about the craters?' asks Eddie.

'Ach, will you shut up about the friggin' moon?'

'What's the matter?'

'Dear Lord, why do I bother?'

'Because you like it.'

'Because I'm stupid.' She can feel more tears rising up behind her eyes.

'You're all the same. Always cryin' for no good reason.'

'Are you some great expert on women as well as the moon, Eddie?'

'I've known m' fair share.'

'Well, I hope you were better with them than you were with me.' She gathers up her belongings and brushes the loose grass, cinders and dirt from her clothes. 'I'm away back in here.'

'Maybe see you again, Lizzie.'

'You'll be lucky,' she replies; as she starts to make her way through the remains of that year's bonfire she knows she will regret having spoken to him so rudely.

Eddie watches her go. He has a smile on his lips as he puts out an arm to pick up his revolver. The moon seems so close, perhaps if he had a pair of binoculars he could see the men on the moon?

TWELVE

THE KERB STONES, painted red, white and blue, proclaim the loyalty of the street's inhabitants and confirm Liam's suspicions. He needs to know how far he has to walk before he's safely within his own familiar streets. He looks for a street sign on the houses opposite, but there isn't one. Not knowing where he is, or how he got where he is, disturbs him more than the pain of his injuries. He wants desperately to slip into his favourite armchair to await the attention of Kathleen's hands and the first-aid kit he keeps under the kitchen sink.

Frightened to go fully into the street, he pauses by the mouth of the alleyway. The houses nearby look much larger than any he has seen in his area. The houses look warm and friendly; their little front gardens all have various hedges and fences proclaiming their owners' independence and territorial pride. They are the kind of house Liam would love to own. He judges that they have at least three bedrooms each and a large parlour. If it weren't for the painted kerb stones, which somehow seem out of place, he'd simply knock on a door and ask for help. Then Liam reminds himself that he would probably have to face the police. Years spent in England had somewhat erased his childhood fear of policemen, but it had all flooded back on the first sighting of a heavily-armed RUC officer. Over the nearest privet hedge he can see the street stretching off in a slightly dipped rightward curve. To his left the street comes to a halt at a high warehouse or factory wall. Through his clogged-up nostrils he begins to catch the smell of baking bread and he realises the wall belongs to a bakery. On the wall an irregular box has been painted in white to serve as a goal. In the middle of the goal a cricket wicket has been roughly painted.

He smiles to himself: they never needed much to enjoy themselves.

As he limps along it feels as if his legs are made of steel and are somehow directly connected to his brain, allowing no fraction of elasticity. Every step is an effort. Somehow he must find the strength to keep himself upright and walking. He pauses by a gate to hawk up a mouthful of blood and phlegm before going on.

The houses that he passes seem so quiet, warm, peaceful. Each window is dressed with porcelain figures, horses, unicorns and ballet dancers, as if some rule demanded it and for some reason it makes him feel safe. If only he can conquer the continuing pain he will be home in no time at all.

THIRTEEN

TOMMY SCANS THE hall, carefully peering into the darker corners, until he sees Gloria, now with a fella called Geoff standing by the door to the women's toilets at the front of the hall near the entrance. Geoff leans over Gloria with his left arm raised above her head to rest against the wall. He seems to be in possession of Gloria, or would like those he knows to be watching to think so. She seems to be acquiescing, placidly waiting for the punch-line to a joke and then laughing loudly, moving her body in little ways which seem to be sending signals of acceptance, or interest. When he puts out his right hand to place it upon her waist she does not object as Tommy desperately wants her to. The warmth that had crept into his heart all evening is replaced by a cold hatred. He feels an immediate need to rush over and push Geoff away from her, to start a fight, to vent his rage. Then his rage is replaced by an acceptance of the inevitable. She has in fact shown him little encouragement. She's too good for him.

Lifting up his pint glass he gulps down half-a-pint of the stout. Through the wrinkled glass, washed in the reflected blobs of coloured light, he sees the couple illuminated by bright white light cast from the opening door of the women's toilet just as Geoff bends to make an attempt to kiss the girl. Gloria smiles and steps away from him, he grabs her hand and her smile dies away to be replaced by a strict 'no'. Undeterred, he attempts to pull her to the dance floor, but she braces herself and lies back on her weight: he will have to drag her. He gives up before too many people turn and notice his humiliating defeat. He spits out a few curses before walking quickly to the bar-hatch. If any fella could make a claim upon her, Tommy thinks, it would be Geoff. Geoff, tall, blond

29

and fashionably dressed, knows better than anyone how it is done.

'Tommy, will ye buy's a drink?'

He looks up and into Betty's glazed eyes which reflect the red and blue disco lights blinking on and off to the slow music. He looks around and realises that Joe has left him.

'Sure, what d'ye want?'

'Vodka an' coke.'

'Okay.' He stands.

'Thanks, Tommy. You're a real friend. Will you bring's it over t' th' one-armed bandit? I don't want m' ma an' m' da t' see's drinkin', you know?'

'Aye, I know.' He sticks a hand in his pocket to find his last remaining five-pound note. 'Where are they?'

'Dancin'.'

He looks to the dance floor and picks out a middle-aged couple dancing close together. The man looks as if he is keeping his wife on her feet. They are both thin and wiry, and have a general air of not being where their bodies happen to be. They dance round in a small circle almost completely ignoring the beat of the music and the other dancers attempting to dance round them.

Tommy nods to Ginger and Eddie as he passes them on his way to join the queue at the bar-hatch. They are huddled together as if they are discussing secrets, secrets Tommy would like to be in on: he would dearly love to be part of the inner circle surrounding Kenny, to experience the excitement he knows they experience.

He joins the queue by a table where Joe sits talking to an elderly man.

'Joe, what will you have?'

'Ach, you're all right, Tommy: I'm just after buyin' one. Here, Tommy, d'you know Charlie Moss?'

He looks down at the man.

'Can't say that I do.'

'Ach, Tommy, I'm an oul crony of your da's. I lived next door t' yez in Severn Street before youse moved.'

'Ach, aye,' says Tommy, looking elsewhere.

'You were a lot younger then.'

The man chuckles, coughs, spits and picks up his whisky.

'Will you have a drink, Mr Moss?'

'Ach, you're all right, son,' says Mr Moss, spitting on the floor for the second time. 'Your da on nights?'

'Aye, he is that. He loves it.'

'Ach, you get used to workin' nights, I suppose, but I hated 'em. Plenty of work for the night-shift these days, Tommy. Gettin' yon big tanker out on time. Th' cranes are busy: great t' hear it, too.'

Mr Moss nods to himself and drinks his whisky. He is pale and frail, not long from his grave and he knows it.

'Well, I'll see you later, Mr Moss.'

'Right, son,' replies Mr Moss.

Tommy turns to rejoin the queue and is immediately smiling at a woman's familiar face.

'Wasn't that trouble t'night terrible, Tommy?'

'Ach . . .' mutters Tommy, not knowing if it was terrible or not: it had excited him considerably.

'I hope you weren't out throwin' stones.'

'Ach, I don't throw *stones*, Mrs Anderson.'

'I hope not, Tommy. After all we're all God's people. We're all a wee bit good an' a wee bit evil: there's none of us that can claim t' be perfect. Live an' let live, that's what I say.'

'Aye,' says Tommy, wishing Margaret Anderson would go away.

He gazes around the hall, over the flags and bunting, over the pictures of dead and imprisoned comrades, over the picture of a smiling, serene Queen. His spirits lift a little. Gloria is dancing with a tall, raven-haired girlfriend. She is still there, still available.

'Have you heard from the yard, Tommy?' says Mrs Anderson.

'Naaaa . . .'

'I've heard they're not takin' any more apprentices.'

'Aye, so they say.'

'You'll have t' wait t' next time. The bakery isn't bad is it, Tommy? Sure you get free baps! What more do you need, Tommy?' He can see her blackened teeth and taste her breath in the shared air. 'There's little enough work in this town these days, Tommy.'

'The IRA aren't helpin' matters, Margaret.'

31

'Ach, you're right there.'

'I know I'm right.'

Something in his voice makes Margaret change her mind about this seemingly gentle, dark-haired, smooth-skinned boy; he has crossed some sort of line, has broken with the past; he is no longer the boy running off to school, satchel over his shoulder. When she speaks again her voice has dropped and she speaks to him as an equal.

'My Linda's emigratin' t' Canada. They need nurses over there, you know. She doesn't want t' go, but she'll get a better life over there than she'll ever get stuck here.'

'You'll not catch me thinkin' of emigratin', Margaret. That's what the IRA fuckers want, isn't it? They'll have to emigrate long before us. Either that or end up in wooden boxes.'

'Ach . . .' Margaret doesn't finish her sentence; it's no use talking to them, she tells herself. 'What are you drinkin', Tommy?'

'Ach, now, you're all right, Margaret, I'm buyin' a round.'

'Well you buy your round an' I'll buy you a drink! Now none of your nonsense! What will you have?'

'Get's a bottle of Red Hand by the neck, Margaret.'

'Right ye are, Tommy,' she says with a deep laugh and shake of her head that suggests a good-natured determination to get what she wants. 'Will you look at that wee girl! They won't leave her alone!'

Tommy looks across to the dance floor and sees a fat little fella he doesn't know grabbing hold of Gloria's forearm in an attempt to force her to dance. She is backing away from the fella as a record starts to play, shaking her head, determined to free herself. She twists her arm to release herself, but the fella aggressively persists. Gloria's raven-haired girlfriend begins to shout in her support and grabs the drunk's arm to pull him away.

'What're you waitin' on, Tommy?' Margaret says.

Tommy remains where he is.

'Away an' get that drunken eejit off the poor wee thing. G' on, for dear sake!'

She gives Tommy a sharp shove in the back which forces him forward. He quickens his pace, but is too late to stop the struggling pair from falling to the floor. Those surrounding them stop to laugh and stare.

'What's th' matter?' Tommy can hear the fella say, 'amn't I good enough for ye?' He attempts to kiss her, but she lashes out with her fists.

'Let me go! Get your filthy hands off me!'

'Can't you hear what the girl says?' asks Tommy, standing over the drunk.

'What's it to you?'

'Get up an' get out.'

'You an' whose army?' says the drunk as if it were an argument in a playground.

Tommy reaches down and takes a hold of the fella by the hair. To Tommy's surprise the fella jumps to his feet and starts to lash out with his fists and feet.

'I'll knock your fuckin' wine in, you cunt.'

The fella's head stabs towards Tommy, catching Tommy's forehead just above his right eye. With a fella like this, Tommy decides, he has to fight dirty. He can hear the cheers of encouragement coming from the little circle of people that has formed. The fella's punches are harmless, but then he kicks Tommy where it hurts. Tommy responds with both fist and foot. His fist smashes into the fella's face, causing blood to gush from the fella's nose. The fella falls back and Tommy follows up his lucky punch with a couple of hard kicks. The fella falls to his knees and bursts into tears, giving Tommy an even stronger impression of being in his primary school playground. He knows he's been lucky.

'Don't hit him again,' says Gloria, looking down at her tormentor. 'Is he all right?'

'He'll live,' says Tommy, as coolly as he can to give Gloria the impression that he does it all the time.

'The experience will harden him, Gloria love,' says a smirking Kenny at Tommy's back. 'Who let this stupid wee bastard in here? He's barred.' Kenny looks around the gathering crowd for an answer, but receives none. 'Who's supposed to be on the door?'

'Me,' says Eddie, weakly.

'Why'd you let him in?'

The silence created by the end of the record causes

attention to fix upon the argument between Kenny and
Eddie. The crowd waits: waits for another fight or another
humiliation.

'Did he come through the cracks in the floorboards?'
asks Kenny.

'He must've sneaked in when I was out th' back havin'
a leak.'

'Having a leak!' exclaims Kenny with an aggressive
laugh. 'You mean you were out th' back with some wee
girl!'

The crowd laughs and Eddie doesn't feel so bad. Could
he ask for a greater recommendation? Kenny, sensing the
crowd waiting for him to humiliate Eddie some more,
thinks better of it: best not to discipline your men in
public.

'Okay, ladies and gentlemen! Show's over! Now's your
chance t' get a drink at th' bar! Hey, put some music
on!'

Men and women turn away from the violent interlude
and they go back to their drinks, their talk and their
dancing. Tommy looks for Gloria, but cannot see her
about the hall.

'Pick that drunken eejit up and toss him out,' orders
Kenny. Eddie and Ginger willingly pick the eejit up and
Ginger propels him towards the door with a blow to the
back of the fella's head.

'You did well there, Tommy,' says Kenny, taking him by
the arm and leading him towards the bar for his reward.
'Watch out for your man, he's an evil wee pig: he'll stick
a knife in your back if he saw his chance.'

'Aye,' says Tommy, wondering if he should take Kenny
seriously.

'What will ye have?'

'Ach, a bottle of Red Hand, Kenny,' says Tommy, feeling
the eyes of the surrounding drinkers fixed upon him. He
feels uncomfortable, but exhilarated by the attention.

'I asked ye what ye'd like t' drink!'

'Ach, Black Bush, Kenny. Thanks.'

'That's better.'

Before Kenny can turn to the bar to shout his order
Gloria comes up to Tommy with a bottle of stout held

out in both hands as if she were presenting him with a trophy.

'Does he get a kiss as well?' asks Kenny.

Gloria merely smiles before turning away to rejoin her girlfriend at a table.

'Oh, she's worth fightin' over, is that one,' says Kenny, smiling, enjoying Tommy's embarrassment.

Kenny slaps the young man on the back before turning to the bar-hatch.

'Hey, Jimmy, a double Black Bush for the hero!'

Tommy takes a mouthful of stout from the bottle as the men surrounding the bar-hatch begin to laugh.

FOURTEEN

IN HIS MIND'S eye he can see Mary running up a steep hill
to a path on the brow. There are trees nearby, their leaves
turning from green to an orange brown; the sun is bright,
but watery cold. Mary stops on the brow of the hill and
turns to wave to him to come and join her, but try as he
might to run some unseen weight holds him down and
makes him slide in the sodden grass and mud. If only he
can be rid of the weight! If only he can be beside her
looking over the view from the top of the hill. What is it
she's shouting? He stops in the street to listen. What is it
she is shouting? She opens her arms and the weight he has
been carrying drops away and he sees Liam and Kathleen
rushing up the hill towards Mary. Tears run from his eyes.
He rests against a wall next to a window and starts to drop
to the warm pavement below. His eyes close, his legs draw
up, his hands form two fists. He curls up to cut off the
exterior world as he forces himself up the hill in his mind's
eye. Slowly, making sure of each foothold, he climbs up
the hill. He can see the children with Mary's arms around
them. Their backs are turned as if they have completely
forgotten him. Any second they will walk off down the
path and leave him to reach the path alone. He fights
hard. He digs his fingers into the sodden grass. He must
not slip. Her voice is carried by the wind as she speaks to
the children. He tries to pick out her words, is she telling
them to forget their father? A little closer. A little closer
and her words become distinct and innocuous. A little
closer until he is at the top of Parliament Hill, smiling,
as he stands by his family looking over the vast expanse
of London.

'You all right, love?'

He looks into the face of a youngish woman bending over

him. He starts to speak, but the words die in his throat as if they have come up against a ball of wool. He starts to get to his feet, and with the determined help of the woman is able to stand.

'Christ, somebody's given you a right kickin', haven't they.' He nods his head and again attempts to get some words out of his blood-dried mouth. 'D'you want me t' get an ambulance?' He shakes his head. 'You sure?' He nods, hurting his head in the process.

'I'm all right. Thanks. On m' way home.'

'Where d'you live?'

He doesn't answer.

'Well, you're not from round here, that's for sure.'

'Aye,' he replies. They understand each other.

'You better come in. I'll fix you up the best I can.'

For a second or two they stand in silence, not looking at each other, as the same thoughts go through their separate heads. Though they are a few feet apart they are locked within their own bounds, which stretch back hundreds of years.

'I'll wash your face, clean them cuts an' give you a cup of tea. Okay?'

'Okay. Thanks.'

She opens her handbag and finds the door key to her terraced house. She turns to the door and unlocks it with a twist of her wrist and a push from her right foot. Immediately Liam is thrown back to the first uneasy, embarrassed moments when Mary had asked him into her flat. The same half look she'd given him over her shoulder, the same tension between them, the same dread of the unknown. The woman flicks on a light in the hall and stands aside to let Liam enter. 'In there,' she guides him into the front living-room. He stands in the darkness for a second or two before she has closed the front door and switched on the living-room light.

'Sit down,' she commands.

'Don't want t' dirty your good chairs, Missus.'

'Never mind m' good chairs. Sit down before you fall down. My name's Ann. What's yours?'

'Liam,' says Liam softly. He reckons she is about thirty-four; very, very pretty. Her hair is an amazing bright copper, her face heavily freckled, her nose is small and her eyes are an intense blue. For a split second their eyes meet and they subconsciously, or consciously, register each other's presence sexually. She quickly dispels any possibility by an authoritative instruction for him to remove his coat and shirt. She disappears into another part of the house while Liam slowly takes off his brown jacket and unbuttons his shirt. He suspects that he has fallen into the hands of a professional.

'Are you a nurse?' he asks when she comes back into the room with a small plastic basin and a cardboard box filled with various medicines.

'Was a nurse 'til I got married.' She sets the box to one side and puts the plastic basin on his knee before squatting on the carpet to hunt in the box.

'I've no idea what I've got in here,' she mutters as she takes out various bottles and inspects their labels. Her hand sweeps back the shock of copper hair and she twists her head round slightly to let the light from the overhead bulb shine on a bottle. Liam is transfixed by her actions, she seems so graceful, so poised, so lovely. 'This will do,' she says brightly; she opens the bottle and immediately fills the room with an antiseptic smell.

'Here, wash your mouth out with this.' She pours a measure of the liquid into the bottle cap. 'Couple of times round the mouth an' then spit it out.'

'What is it?'

'It's just to wash out your mouth. Go on,' she urges; she waits for him to take the antiseptic, her eyes ordering him to do as she says. He lifts back his head and empties the liquid into his mouth. It burns. It stings. It must be doing him some good, so he fights against the impulse to spit it out.

'Spit it out,' she orders.

He spits into the basin, but to his embarrassment the liquid runs down his chest.

'Ach, I'm a dirty pig,' he complains when he sees the brownish slime slide down his chest and on to his trouser front.

'Don't worry about that. Can't be helped.' She hands him a piece of kitchen paper and he wipes his mouth.

'How's your ribs?'

'Sore,' he replies.'

'I bet,' returns Ann. 'Any difficulty in breathing?'

'Just the blood, you know.'

'Okay.' She starts to feel around his ribs. He looks down and sees a patchwork of bruises which suggest internal damage. 'Bend over so I can listen to your breathin'.' He brings his head down between his knees as she leans over to press her ear against his back. 'Okay, breathe deeply.' She listens. As she does so his gaze wanders to a framed photograph of two young women standing outside the Houses of Parliament.

'Okay, I can't hear anything wrong with your lungs. But you should really go up to the hospital, up to Dundonald.'

'Ach, I'm all right. You're bein' very decent. I'm better already just bein' able t' take the weight of m' feet, you know.'

'Aye, I know.'

'If you've got a couple of aspirins it'd be a great help.'

'Aspirins? An' have you bleedin' t' death inside?'

'Oh. Aye.'

'I've Paracetamol. I'll get you water and a cup of tea.' She walks briskly from the living-room, leaving Liam gazing at the photograph. The two young women seem happy and contented, obviously pleased with themselves to be standing in Parliament Square. The room is eerily quiet. He has a sensation of being watched; he turns to see a child of six or seven standing in the doorway.

'Hello,' he says warmly.

'Hello,' the little girl replies. 'What's your name?'

'Liam.'

The little girl forms the word in her mouth without pronouncing it. She looks about the room and then at Liam. He waits for her to speak, but instead the child silently stares into his eyes.

'What's your name?'

'Penelope.'

'Penelope?'

Penelope nods her head and looks about the room.

'Do you know where my mummy is?'

39

'Yes. She's in the kitchen.'

'Oh.'

'She'll come back soon.'

'Are you hurt?'

'Aye,' he replies.

'Is it sore?'

'Aye.'

'Who did it to you?' she asks, coming into the room and sitting on a red and black mock leather pouffe.

'I don't know, love.' He smiles as best he can. 'Somebody I didn't see.'

'Oh.'

They sit in the room together in absolute silence. The child looks hard at Liam's injuries, occasionally pursing her lips when she sees another bruise or cut on Liam's body.

He asks her, 'Shouldn't you be in bed?'

'I suppose so,' she replies with a backward glance to the door. 'But I couldn't sleep without Mummy.'

'She's just in the kitchen getting me a cup of tea,' he reassures her.

'I'm seven,' she volunteers.

'Like school?'

'Oh, aye. I love school,' she confidently replies with a dip and a nod of her head, which has the same copper hair as her mother.

'Well, that's good. If only my wee boy liked school as much.'

'He doesn't?'

'No.'

'Oh,' she commiserates.

Her mother returns from the kitchen with a tea tray and a glass of water.

'What are you doin' up?'

'Can't sleep.'

'Never mind "can't sleep"! You go back to your bed.' She waits for the girl to get up from the pouffe and head for the door before setting the tray of tea things down on a glass coffee table near to the gas fire in the hearth. 'Are Kenny and Rachel asleep?'

'Yes,' replies her daughter.

40

'Did Mrs Gibbon come in to see you?'

'Four times.'

'That's good. Now away to bed. I'll come up in a wee while.' The child disappears from the room and they listen as she slowly, unwillingly climbs the stairs.

'I don't like leavin' them, but Rachel's nearly eleven an' very grown up, you know.'

'Ach, you have t' get out once in a while.'

'Aye,' she replies without believing it. 'The neighbours are very good; they're in if they hear anythin'.' She hands Liam the glass of water and opens a small bottle to shake out a couple of Paracetamol. 'Here you are, they'll not do you much good, you know.'

'As long as they kill the headache.'

'Better clean up them cuts a bit. Like your tea now?'

'Like a man needs water in a desert.'

'Right,' she replies. She turns to the tray and pours out a mug of strong tea. 'Sugar?'

'Three, I'm afraid.'

'Aye, you have t' watch yourself. Though you're not carryin' any weight.'

'It comes off, you know.'

'Aye, but it's really the heart you have to watch.'

'So they say. Though if you listened to what they tell you not to eat you'd be dead from starvation.'

'Well, I fry nothin' in this house. Don't have a fryin' pan.'

'Wish I could say the same,' he laughs.

'Wait 'til it cools a bit,' she warns as she hands him the mug of tea.

'I can hear from your accent that you've lived across the water.'

'Aye. I lived in London.'

'Whereabouts?'

'Hammersmith. Me an' m' friend went over t' work in the Charing Cross hospital. You?'

'Camden.'

'Ach, Camden. Was up there a lot.'

'You came back.'

'More's the pity.'

'T' get married?'

41

'We married over there. Came back to live. Divorced now.'

'Oh. Sorry.'

'Sorry?'

'Well . . .'

She soaks a piece of cotton wool in some antiseptic and lifts up Liam's right arm to clean the abrasions which run down his forearm.'Looks as if you've hit a wall.' She throws the cotton wool into the basin and tears another piece from the roll.

'You've three young 'uns, have you?'

'Aye,' she replies, 'three. Kenny's the youngest.' She shifts her attentions to his face. His jaw and forehead are badly bruised with one or two tears in the skin.

'I'm not tryin' t' be funny, but you don't look old enough t' have three kids.'

She laughs. 'Well, there you are then. I've three an' they're all upstairs if you want t' count 'em.' She brushes back his longish black hair to have a look at a cut on the temple close to his hair line. 'What about you?'

'I've a boy an' a girl,' he replies.

'Your wife'll be wonderin' where you are.' He laughs. 'What's the matter?' He continues to laugh and she realises why he is laughing. His wife has left him. 'You, too?' she asks.

'Ach, you know . . .' is all that Liam will say on the subject, for the moment.

'Aye, I know,' she softly sighs. Carefully she cleans away some dirt and pieces of cinder from the cut on his temple. He can feel her fingers gently moving across his skin.

She goes about her work with an efficiency that perhaps was learned in an hospital emergency department. She is close to him, he can smell a mixture of perspiration and perfume coming from her opened blouse; her clothes seem to have been hurriedly thrown on, as if she hasn't checked her appearance in a mirror. He tries not to, but his gaze fixes upon her breasts which seem just a bit too large for the lace-fringed brassiere; he notices a hint of moisture which glistens on her chest. Ordering himself to look elsewhere with a silent curse, his eyes settle upon some bookshelves to the right of the hearth.

'You've a few books,' he says, trying to break a silence that has gone on for too long. She doesn't answer him, so concentrated upon the job in hand is she. He notices some files stuffed with what he takes to be notes on the bottom shelf; then he spots a familiar logo on a book resting by a notebook on an armchair which faces the television set across the room. 'Doin' a bit of studyin'?' he asks, hoping she'll answer. She doesn't immediately; instead she picks up some more cotton wool and antiseptic to clean a cut on his chin. Has he upset her? Has she noticed his fixed stare? He starts to feel he should make his excuses and leave before anything is said.

'I'm studyin' with the Open University, you know,' she says without apparent umbrage.

'What 're you studyin'?'

'Sociology.'

'Ach, yes . . . sociology,' he lets her know he's familiar with the subject. 'Takes a bit of brains, eh.'

'It's hard doin' it when you've three kids, but I'm almost finished now.'

'How long's it taken you?'

'Only four years,' she answers with a laugh. 'Not bad, eh? I've a brain as well.' She reaches down and buttons up her blouse and Liam feels put down as he averts his eyes. He looks at the bookshelves to see if he can see a book he recognises.

'I've thought about doin' a degree with the Open University m'self.' He cannot help lying; all his life he has found it easy to lie when he feels he is being belittled, or put in an awkward, pride-endangering situation.

'What were you thinkin' of doin'?'

'Ah, history,' he says, seeing a history book on a shelf.

'I've always loved history m'self,' she replies, seeing Liam looking at the history book. She decides he's very good-looking, but harmless.

'What particular age are you interested in?'

'Oh, Irish history, you know,' he replies, feeling himself on quite sturdy ground.

'Who needs t' read it when it's all bein' made in front of your very eyes?' she asks, juggling a pair of scissors, pieces of sticking plaster, gauze and bandage.

43

'I'll do the best I can, but you should be in hospital. This cut on your temple might need a stitch.'

'You're doin' a grand job,' encourages Liam. 'I don't want t' go all the way to hospital for a few wee cuts an' hurt ribs.'

'Are you frightened of the RUC?' asks Ann accusingly.

'Why should I be scared of them? I've done nothin'! I walked out m' front door t' see what was goin' on in m' own street an' the next thing I know I'm lyin' in a stinkin' entry near half murdered!'

'Well, I'm sorry for you,' says Ann. She cuts a piece of gauze and looks into his face. 'The RUC would let your kids know where you are.'

'Ach, I'm okay,' he protests.

'You need your head looked at. You need it scanned.'

'I've a job t' go to in th' mornin'.'

'Forget your work,' she says firmly.

'If I don't show up in the mornin' I needn't come back. The boss knows I need him a lot more than he needs me.'

'Your health should come first,' she says, becoming rather imperious. 'Though it's up to yourself. I'm not responsible for you, or your health.' Yet she clearly does feel responsible for him now that he has, in a way, put himself in her care.

'I'm okay. Never felt better.' He laughs and then ceases to laugh as he feels his ribs begin to hurt. He's not going to hospital to be poked at.

'You're doin' a grand job,' he tells her.

'Aye,' she replies. 'You're not the first an' I suppose you won't be the last the way things are.'

In the silence he can hear each click and snip of the scissors as she shapes the material into suitable dressings. She is so concentrated on the job that Liam starts to feel invisible. Notwithstanding the pain, strength seeps back into his muscles. The tea has done him a power of good, he tells himself. Once he has thanked her and said goodbye he'll be home in just a few minutes. It can't be far away. The thought of asking Ann exactly where he is passes through his mind, but he decides against it; he doesn't want to be completely helpless, completely at her mercy. He makes a

44

note in his head to look at the door number so that he can send her round a bunch of flowers, or a box of chocolates. Should he ask her out? Where would he take her? Where could he afford to take her? Nowhere much. The idea dies in his mind. It's no time for romantic fantasy. Men are being shot for going out with women from the other side. Men are being shot for walking down the wrong street. For saying the wrong thing. It's mad, but it's as real as a bullet in the back.

'You're doin' a grand job: thanks a million.'

'You're welcome. We're not all bonkers.'

She releases a little laugh and then silence overwhelms them; they become patient and nurse again. Liam looks to his left and through a slit in the curtains he can see the face of the moon.

'You all right?' asks Ann, following his gaze.

'It's a lovely evenin'.'

'It is that,' mutters Ann before returning to her work. She places a piece of gauze and cotton wool over a cut and presses down a strip of sticking plaster. They listen as the silence is broken by a pair of bare feet thumping across the floor above their heads.

'Kenny,' says Ann, 'always gets up in the middle of the night to go for a pee. Drinks too much orangeade, that's all. This will have to do you. I'm leavin' the wee cuts open t' th' air. There's nothin' I can do about the ribs. I don't think they're damaged. Best not to bind 'em up. You must go an' get a few x-rays done. Have you a doctor?'

'Ach, aye.'

'Well, see him t'morrow mornin'.'

'I will that,' says Liam, knowing that he won't.

'You're bein' stupid in not goin' up t' Dundonald.'

'I'd rather keep m' job. I've a big delivery t' take down to Tandragee in the mornin'.'

'What is it you do?'

'I work for a wee buildin' suppliers, you know? In th' office takin' orders, doin' th' bills an' invoices, you know?'

'Aye,' says Ann. She sits on the pouffe to sip her tea.

'I've a good head for sums, you know? Nothin' else, mind, but I can count.'

'Well, you're a better man than me,' says Ann. 'I have trouble with m' shoppin'.'

'Ach, it's a wee knack I have. Th' boss likes me t' go down with the stuff t' check nobody pinches it. Some of them fellas on the sites would steal the shirt off your back. Not a bad wee job, but I get paid a pittance. Though you can't pick an' choose in this town.'

'Aye,' says Ann. 'Why'd you come back?'

'Now you're askin',' says Liam. How can he answer her? It unsettles him to see that she is looking directly into his face, waiting for a reply as if she is interested and not just talking. Can he tell her that it had a lot to do with spite, revenge, anger and humiliation? No.

'Ach, I missed th' oul place,' is what he replies with a certain smiling plausibility.

'Pull th' other one, there's bells on it.' She throws her head back and releases an enormous laugh that has Liam amazed. They stare at each other for a few seconds until Liam looks away, back out to the moon.

'Ach, I got fed up with it. Started drinkin', you know? No good. No good at all. Wanted t' come home where I knew a few people, you know? She likes it over there. Hates this country, but pretends otherwise like the rest of 'em over there.'

'So she's still in London?'

'Aye, but I don't know where.'

'Where's she from?'

'Derry.'

'Meet her over there?'

'Aye, I did. In a pub. You?'

'He lived a few doors away from us on My Lady's Road. I had to go an' marry him. Hadn't a brain in m' head; but he looked good in his uniform.'

'Soldier?'

'Aye.' Ann releases another laugh in Liam's direction. He cannot decide if she is still looking at his injuries or at him as a man. He begins to feel naked and eases his shirt towards him with his right hand. He can feel her eyes on him, without having to look up. If only she'd say something, or give him a signal to leave. Could she be thinking of asking him to stay?

'I suppose you better put your shirt on,' says Ann in a tone of voice that is open-ended and requires a subtle answer that is beyond Liam.

'Aye, I better be on m' way,' he replies, setting the mug down and picking up his shirt, which he now sees is ripped and stained with blood. He leans forward to slip in his arm, but he has to give up.

'Here, let me give you a hand.' She takes hold of his arm and puts the shirt sleeve over it.

'Ta,' says Liam.

'Listen, are you sure you won't go up to Dundonald?'

'Sure.'

He slips in his other arm by himself.

'I doubt if you'll be fit for work.'

'I'm sure I'll be just dandy after a few hours in my own warm bed, Missus.'

She laughs and casts her most appealing smile in Liam's direction. He'd be a good laugh, a good lover, she tells herself; unlike the one she'd left half-an-hour ago.

'Have you far to go?'

'Not far at all.'

'It's a pity I don't have a wee car.'

'Ach, don't trouble yourself any more.'

No trouble at all, her smile says.

'It's a lovely night t' have a walk on,' he says with as much finality as he can muster, and stands to stuff his shirt back into his trousers. To his embarrassment Ann takes a hand to do up his zip and his belt. She gives a smile that lets him know that she has seen it all a million times.

'The sooner I get goin', the sooner I'll get home.'

'Well, look after yourself.'

'I will that.'

Strength has returned to his legs. He is sinewy, tough; he can take the punishment. He puts out a hand and pats her arm as he passes her. She can smell his cheap aftershave as she takes hold of his arm and guides him out into the hall.

'Safe home.'

'Thanks for the tea.'

She feels guilty for not having done more for him. Perhaps she should go across and wake Mr Smith and ask him to drive the injured man home. Or telephone for a taxi? But no taxi would come at this time of night.

'Shall I see if I can get you a taxi?'

'Ach, you're all right.'

She admits to herself that he is a handsome man, in a very Irish way. He stops at the door.

'My jacket.'

'Ach, aye!' She fetches his torn brown jacket and helps him slip it on.

'I'd forget m' head if it weren't screwed on.'

He's a charmer, she tells herself as she watches his dimples deepen on his cheeks.

'Now you know where you are?'

'Aye.'

She tells him the name of the street and he nods.

'Don't worry. I'll be home before you're in your own bed. I feel grand.'

He notices that she hasn't bothered to shut the front door. They're a friendly people, he tells himself. He reaches for the latch and pulls the door wide open. He looks up and is surprised to see that the door is missing its number.

'Oh?'

'What?'

'No number?'

'Dropped off.'

'Oh.'

'Why do you want to know my number?'

'So as I can send ye a bunch of flowers.'

'Ach, don't bother.'

'No bother.'

They again exchange laughs and they feel comfortable as if they have known each other for a considerable while.

'It's fifty-five.'

'What's your favourite flowers?'

'Roses.'

'Red?'

'Yellow.'

'Right.'

He steps out into the warm evening air.

'Don't forget: doctor in the mornin'.'

'Right.'

'I'm tellin' you!'

'Okay.'

They grin at each other before Liam turns away from the neat, comfortable, little house and walks off on up the street. At his back he hears the soft click of the door closing. He is alone again. Never mind, he will soon be home.

FIFTEEN

IT'S THE OWL in the cypress tree that's keeping him awake,
James tells himself. Raising his right eyelid he peers into
the luminous face of the bedside clock. It is just after one
o'clock. He closes his eye and thinks pleasant thoughts.
Quiet, blossom-filled, sunlit country lanes come into view.
He rides a bicycle, without effort, as if he were as light as
the breeze cooling his face. By his side, blonde unruly hair
flowing in the breeze, his wife rides along, smiling and
talking animatedly about their future. Thirty years gone,
he reminds himself. How happy they had been. Back at
the start of it all. Back when they knew too little. Now
he knows too much and he feels cheated, unsatisfied and
betrayed. To end his political career in such a place, doing
such a job. He should have resigned and allowed himself
to be kicked upstairs. Bitterness sweeps through his heart
and his mind, overwhelming the warmth. The owl hoots
again and he realises that he isn't tired at all.

Reaching into the darkness he flicks on a light. He'll do
a bit more reading. As he brings himself up from the bed a
shudder vibrates through his naked body as if he has woken
from some terrible, clinging dream. He drains the whisky
tumbler of its contents, and mutters a curse. Dragging a
pillow from his wife's side of the bed he props himself up.
If only she hadn't gone to London, but he knows she detests
the place, even more than he, though her people are from
the province. She'll be gone more often now. She had tried
to stay with him, but they couldn't pretend that things were
the same since he accepted the demotion. He curses into
the deep hush of the large bedroom. Yet he cannot be angry
with her, just with himself. He had failed their contract.
He allows himself a self-pitying sigh before picking up
the thick paperback and opening it. Automatically he

clears his throat before starting to read; years of ploughing through dense collections of official papers have left him with the ability to read fast and accurately and he turns the pages quickly. A chuckle escapes into the bedroom, briefly obliterating the soft clicks of the bedside clock, as he reads about a particularly nasty character going to his death from off the roof of a Swiss ski-lift.

Should he, he asks himself, sneak into the large drawing-room and pilfer another measure of government Scotch? If he is caught will he have to resign? He allows himself his most childish chuckle and wonders if his drinking of government hospitality whisky is misappropriation; what is it when he has to pour it down the throats of a bunch of men he thinks should be in Her Majesty's internment camps or prisons?

Putting the novel down on the duvet he slips out of the bed, tumbler in hand. It is the most delicious stuff, he tells himself. As he comes to a long mirror he pauses before his reflection. He grins at his nakedness. A shortish man gone badly to seed. He holds in his distended and flabby stomach, but not enough to make a pretty picture. His hair is mostly grey, but a few black patches remain at the back of his head. All his life he has had to rely on the force of his personality to gain women's attentions. Opening the heavy door he steps into the corridor. The chill makes him shiver. Walking along it, the carpet pleasantly tingles his bare feet. Down a flight of stairs and along another corridor to a pair of large white doors and into the high-ceilinged drawing-room. He does not immediately switch on the chandelier, but enjoys his mild feeling of fear and danger in the darkened room. With only the light of the moon slipping through an uncurtained window at the end of the room he walks to the drinks cabinet. He flicks on a little lamp sitting by the cabinet before slipping his hand into the ice bucket – he likes the feel of the cool water, but he finds no ice for his whisky. No matter, he pours himself a generous measure.

Up in his bedroom again he switches on the wireless in time for the news round-up. He is pleased when he hears his own voice saying a few condemnatory words about that day's violence. He is amused by his own pompous, moralistic, tone of voice: a voice he keeps strictly for condemning violence: at times he allows it to become a parody of itself.

Back in his bed he makes himself extremely comfortable before picking up the book. Since his experience of the hardships of war he has done everything possible to ensure his comfort. He reads, sips his whisky and wonders if he, too, could make his living from writing such splendid nonsense.

He feels a stirring in his loins as a young lady reveals all before being taken by the hero. He flicks over the page and is pleased to read that the author has turned up the heat.

He checks the time. Perhaps he should give his wife a ring? She should be back from the function he knows she has attended. He decides against it; if she has something to say she'll do the ringing. He yawns and feels slightly sleepy, perhaps he should try to catch a little sleep? He turns another page.

SIXTEEN

KATHLEEN SITS ON the edge of the settee in absolute stillness, except for her right hand which twists a button on her coat round and round until it comes off in her hand. The coat her father had bought her. The coat she had so much wanted. So much needed. Now she stares at the button with a numbed indifference. She feels so isolated it physically hurts. From the kitchen an electric buzz breaks the silence of the house as the voice from the wireless says goodnight and God bless. God has not blessed her, she thinks.

She walks into the kitchen, flicks the wireless off and looks up at the clock, but its face is in shadow and she can't see the time. She reaches up and takes the clock from its hook, down into the moonlight pouring over the roofs of the houses into the kitchen. It is five past one. If only she had more strength, were not so sick at heart and so frightened. She replaces the clock and pushes her way through the plastic strip curtain and back into the living-room. She turns the catch and opens the door a little way. The street seems as peaceful as before. Why is she hesitating? Out she steps, her foot sinking slightly into the sand on which the pavement slabs once sat. Should she close the door? Has she the keys? She feels in her coat pocket and finds the small bunch of keys which she grips tightly before letting the door click shut. As soon as it is closed she feels the need to open it again to prove to herself that she can escape into the house if need be; but she fights to control her panic. For what seems to her like minutes she is unwilling to turn round and face the street, but eventually, letting her hand fall, and with her head down, she turns. She receives the almost physical impression of being watched, but she sees no signs of life in the houses or the church and its buildings.

On the grass surrounding the church she can see a thousand reflections of the moon in the shattered glass lying all around. The smoke drifting from the smouldering car rolls through the church's railings, across the grass and up the church's walls into the night sky. Feeling more secure now that she has braved the night, she turns away from the main road, which had been the source of danger, to walk up the street, constantly turning her head. The first half dozen houses she passes show little sign of being occupied, but then she sees the glow of a light in a window. Should she knock on the door? No. She can't bring herself to. Better if she finds some of the men who have been out on the streets all evening. She carefully picks her way across the treacherous remains of the pavement. How far has she to go before she finds help?

'Oh, Mary, Mother of God,' she mutters into the night air.

As she walks farther down the broad streets the tension starts to ease as she leaves the main road behind. The houses are the same old houses, the windows and doors exactly as she knows them to be. She has left the broken glass and smashed pavement slabs behind her and the street seems quite normal.

'Kathleen!'

She turns her head sharply to see a face she knows, but to which she can't put a name.

'Did I scare ye, Kathleen?'

'Course you scared me, you stupid eejit!'

'Sorry,' he says. He steps towards her and Kathleen sees that it is Michael.

'Michael, have you seen my dad?'

'No.'

'Well, he went out this evenin' and he hasn't come back.'

'Is he maybe havin' a drink somewhere?'

'No!'

'I haven't seen him, Kathleen,' says Michael, softly.

They stand in the hushed street bathed in the soft light of the moon.

'Was he out fightin'?' Michael asks.

'He just went out to see what was happenin', Michael.'

54

'I haven't seen him, sorry.' He tries hard to think of something useful to say. 'Look, Kathleen, come into Mrs Burke's house. There's a lot of fellas sittin' in there. Maybe somebody's seen him?' He waits for her answer. He has always liked Kathleen. Perhaps because she has never really belonged, with her slight English accent and her lack of a mother.

'Will you go in an' ask for me?'

'Okay,' he gladly replies. He turns on his heels and walks back to the Burkes' house. From it comes the sound of a familiar song sung by a woman Kathleen knows to be Mrs Burke; her voice is dry, broken and straining to put emotion into the traditional words. Kathleen waits, waits as she has waited for many hours. She has grown increasingly sure that mere waiting will not bring her father back.

Michael reappears quickly from the darkness of the house's hallway.

'Nobody's seen him, Kathleen,' says Michael, concern sounding soft in his voice. 'Wouldn't he be over in Alec's?'

'He didn't say he was goin' to Uncle Alec's.'

'Aye, but he might've dandered over there anyway.'

'He wouldn't've gone anywhere without tellin' me.' She turns away and looks down to where the street joins with several others. She feels sick; her hands grasp her stomach.

'Ye all right, Kathleen? Come in an' have a cup of tea.'

'No.' She looks into his face. 'I want m' da.'

Without waiting for a response she walks off down the street. Michael wonders if he should follow her. He'd been at the front door of Mrs Burke's house to catch some fresh air when he'd seen her coming. Now he slightly regrets calling out to her. It has taken him away from the songs, drink, baked potatoes and the tales of heroism and cowardice of the night's defence of the area. Yet he knows he must follow her, help her, see what more he can do. In a few seconds he is walking beside Kathleen. She seems so set in her purpose; her stride is fast and aimed. He waits until they come to a halt at a corner before he says anything more.

'Some fight, Kathleen. If we'd let the bastards in they'd've burnt us out. Burnt us out.' He stops talking and follows

55

her gaze down a small traverse street that connects the long streets either side of the church. She's searching every corner, every doorway. 'Has your uncle got a telephone?'

'He hasn't an inside bathroom, Michael.'

'Ach, neither have we, but we've got a telephone.'

'So you keep on tellin' everybody.'

'Ach, what's wrong with that?'

Michael runs his hand through his curly mass of black hair and shifts his weight from one leg to the other as he thinks of something else to say. He doesn't get the time: Kathleen decides to walk away down the street to the entrance of an alleyway. Down the alleyway she can make out the side of the church and part of a building. The alleyway is in moonshadowed gloom, but no matter how nervous it makes her feel she will have to go in and make sure he isn't lying among the uncollected rubbish.

'Father Connor was out smashin' up flag stones with the rest of the men: you should've seen him go, Kathleen! If they'd got in they'd've burnt us out for sure!'

'Michael, will ye give over?' She listens for any sound from the gloom, but none comes. Michael shifts his weight from his left foot to his right. He more than ever wishes he'd stayed in Mrs Burke's. It strikes Kathleen that everything seems to be made of cardboard, the walls, the pavement, the smashed gas lamps, the one parked car: everything is unreal.

With her hand over her mouth to fend off the stench she slowly enters the alleyway and walks towards the back of the church. She does not look back to see if Michael is following her; she knows he is not.

'Where're you goin', Kathleen? He won't be down there, now will he? Why don't you go over to Standfield Street?'

'He's not at m' uncle's!' cries Kathleen. She steps round a dustbin and feels her shoe sink into something soft. She shakes whatever it is off her shoe before going on.

'I'll wait for you.'

'If you want.' On down the gloomy alleyway she goes, her heart only a little more at peace with itself. Soon she can see the large back gate to the church.

'Watch yourself!' Michael shouts after her.

She can clearly see that the back gate is partially open,

as if someone has just walked through. Would he have gone in? She thinks not. Never has she known her father to go near a church, or to say anything good about it. Yet he had attended her confirmation and had always mildly insisted that she took her brother to church occasionally. Her eyes are better used to the light now and she sees that the alleyway is perfectly harmless, the same as always, except for the overturned dustbins.

She walks back towards Michael, who is crossing and recrossing the end of the alleyway with his head firmly down. He stops, hearing Kathleen kick a dustbin and curse her luck. She pushes the dustbin out of her way and walks on towards the end of the alleyway. She knows what she must do, but the idea of doing it causes her to tremble.

SEVENTEEN

TOMMY STANDS AT the open door looking out to the street which is awash with the light of the moon. The street is calmly at peace and the music from the club drifts out over the wasteland to provide a lullaby for those still lying awake in their beds. Tommy hums the tune softly and thinks about Kenny. He would do anything for Kenny. Do anything for his people. The best in the world, he tells himself. He is elated, buoyed-up by the events of the night and by the attention he has received. His lazy gaze strays over the night sky, past the moon and around the crush of stars until his eye is arrested by a meteor scraping across the sky. For its brief burn he forgets Kenny and thinks about the girl Gloria, before making a wish.

'It's a lovely night.'

He feels a weight upon his shoulder.

'It is that,' he says, turning to face Kenny.

'Brought you a bit of protection.'

Kenny, with a smile as wide as his face, holds the butt of a revolver towards Tommy. He takes hold of it apprehensively. Kenny laughs.

'Know how to use it, don't you?'

'Aye,' replies Tommy, remembering the detailed back-room blackboard lessons he has received.

'Stick it in your pocket.'

'Right, Kenny.' Now Tommy feels even more elated. Trusted. He feels the weight of the snub-nosed .45 before slipping it into the pocket of his black nylon bomber jacket.

'Now keep an eye on passin' cars, Tommy. If they open up with a machine-gun, duck.' Kenny lets out another laugh which makes Tommy almost believe he would enjoy being shot at, so long as Kenny was by his side. He has heard from other men that Kenny has been shot at in far-off places he can only vaguely imagine. 'Search the men when they come in. No headbangers.'

'No headbangers, Kenny,' says Tommy.

'Good man.'

Kenny pats him on the shoulder before disappearing through the doors into the noise of the hall leaving Tommy to catch the swinging door. He can see Gloria sitting by her friend. Her legs are drawn up and her hand cupped over her mouth as she responds to her friend's joke. If she leaves should he ask to escort her home? He feels sick at the thought of being rejected.

He lets the door close as he hears a car passing the club. It pulls up near to the club and a man's head comes through the driver's window.

'Open?'

'We're open.'

''Til when?'

'As long as you want to drink. It's all for a good cause.'

'In that case we better come in.'

His head retracts as the car zooms off to find a parking space. A couple of women scramble from the back of the car, fix their dresses and walk down the middle of the street to the hall.

'How much to get in?' asks the taller of the two.

'Nothin',' Tommy replies.

'Want to search us?' asks the tall woman's much smaller and plumper friend.

'No,' says Tommy feeling the colour coming to his face.

'Sure?' asks the tall woman, draping an arm over Tommy's shoulder. 'I may have a bomb in m' bra.'

'Not in *your* bra, Frances,' says her friend.

'Okay, so you'd get a couple of atom bombs in yours.'

They fall into each other's arms and laugh loudly. Frances squeezes her friend and lands a kiss on her cheek.

'I'm Catholic – hope you don't mind.'

'Don't listen to her, fella. She's Protestant all the way through. Even has a pair of Union Jack knickers on.'

'Don't you tell him that.'

'Lift your skirt up and show him.'

Frances attempts to lift her friend's skirt, but she shies away in a fit of laughter.

'What's the matter?' asks the driver of the car. He stands in the street holding another man by the arm.

'Sorry, you two can't come in 'less youse 're on leashes,' says the plump woman.

'Margaret, get in there before they have all the drink drunk!'

'Hold your horses! We're bein' searched, Bill, so we are!'

'My horses need somethin' t' drink and so does Frank here.'

'Frank's had enough,' says Margaret.

'He'll have a drink if he wants t' have a drink!'

Bill pushes his friend forward so that he can bring him into the small entrance hall. He lets him sag into a chair by the door.

'He's okay. My mate Frank's okay.'

'He's drunk!' cries Margaret.

'No he's not,' replies Bill as he slaps Frank's cheeks. 'He's only a wee bit tired.'

'I'm sick of him,' protests Margaret. 'He can't hold his drink.'

'He's only a wee fella. He gets filled up easy.'

'I'm goin' in for a drink,' says Frances, walking straight into the hall without waiting to see if Margaret will follow.

'Are you okay?'

'Wha'?' replies Frank with a general wave of his hand as if he's dismissing the whole world.

'Margaret, give's a hand with your oul man. Help me get a grip.'

'All right, but you keep your hands off.' She goes to her husband. 'Come on, you eejit.'

She helps him to his feet and they go through the doors arm in arm. Tommy hesitates, then decides to let him through without the obligatory search, but he puts his hand up to stop the other man.

'Have to give you a search, mister.'

'Dig out, mucker,' replies Bill. He raises his arms almost automatically. 'Shouldn't you be at home in bed, lad?'

'No.'

'Are you old enough to stay out past twelve?'

'Aye.'

'You don't look it.'

'Well, there you are. What do you want? A birth cer-
tificate?'

'I'm only bein' friendly.'

'That's good.'

Tommy looks straight into the man's face.

'Only tryin' t' be friendly.'

'Aye, so you said.'

'Okay.'

Bill nods and smiles a goodbye before pushing his way
into the hall. Tommy catches the swinging door and
searches the hall for Gloria. She's putting on her coat,
preparing to leave. What should he do? He feels a slight
hollowness in his stomach. He lets the door go and picks
up his beer from the table. Perhaps if he drinks some more
he will have the courage to ask her? He sees off half his
pint of stout.

He hears the doors swing open and turns immediately
to see Betty standing with a bottle held out towards him.

'Brought you a drink, Tommy.'

He does not take it from her. She drops her arm to her
side. She scans his face, trying to understand why she has
been rejected.

'Don't you want it?'

'Oh. Aye. Thanks.'

She hands him the bottle.

'I won a whole seven pounds on the one-armed bandit.'

'Did ye?'

'Aye. I did.'

'Betty, will ye do's a favour an' go an' get Joe t' come
out here?'

He looks into her face, waiting for her reply. Betty looks
past Tommy and out the open door to the street.

'You goin' to walk Gloria home?' asks Betty, displaying
her envy by biting her lower lip. Nobody offers to walk
her home unless they expect something in return, and
usually she agrees to the deal. She looks again at Tommy,
knowing he thinks little of her, but she is more than

61

willing to please him. 'I'll get him,' she says after a few seconds.

She goes back through the doors and Tommy turns away to pick up his glass and second gift bottle of stout. He forces the bitter, gassy stout down. He cannot hold his drink very well and already feels quite drunk, but warmly so. How should he behave towards her? Insistent, demanding, threatening? No. He'll do as she says, not try to take advantage, not behave as he has seen others behave.

Gloria comes through the door laughing at a joke. She stops before Tommy and unleashes her brightest smile.

'Hello, Tommy. On the door?'

'Aye.'

'Thanks a million for savin' me from yer man's clutches.'

'Ach . . .'

'Vera says you're m' white knight.'

'Ach . . .'

'You on the door the rest of the night?'

'Ach . . .' He stares into her face, utterly lost.

'Well, goodnight.'

'Gloria . . .'

'Yes?'

She stops and half turns to face him; her smile has left her face, and her serious expression throws Tommy into confusion: will she angrily refuse him if he asks? Has he any more right to ask because he helped her out?

'Yes?' she repeats.

'Leave you home?'

'But you're on the door.'

They both turn when Joe comes crashing through the doors.

'This'll cost you a couple 'f pints, Tommy.'

'Thanks. Won't be long.'

The girl is already out on the street by the time Tommy turns away from his friend. As he hurries after her he feels the weight of the revolver slapping against his hip. He puts his hand in his jacket to steady it before it falls out. What if she notices it? What will she think? Will she be impressed? He hopes she might be. He feels thrilled, excited. Holding the gun down in his pocket he hurries along the street to catch up on the girl.

Gloria halts and waits for him to join her.

'I love dancin', don't you? If it weren't for th' dancin' I wouldn't go near that oul place.'

'Ach, it's all right for a drink when the bars are shut. And besides it's doin' a grand job raisin' money.'

'Money for what?'

He doesn't answer, but instead looks down a street to check it's free of traffic before crossing. She accepts his silence. Better not to ask too many questions.

'You still at the bakery?'

'Aye. It's drivin' me mad, so it is.'

'I worked there last summer. Dead borin'.'

'You're tellin' me.'

'What are you doin'?'

'Fillin' the delivery lorries, you know?'

'Aye.'

They both turn a corner without a second's thought, they know the maze so well, each wall against which they kicked or threw a ball.

'You still at the wee college?'

'Ach, aye.'

'What 're you doin'?'

'Secretarial skills.'

They hear the clicks of high heels hurrying along a street towards them.

'Evenin',' says the owner of the high heels as she turns a corner and passes them quickly by, the clicks slowly fading.

'I want t' work over town in an office,' Gloria tells him confidently. Tommy starts to feel unable to cope with her, she's too certain of things for him: he has only ever been in a state of confusion, guided by what others have said and done.

'Ach, you won't catch me trapped in any oul office, Gloria,' says Tommy, not believing what he says; he glances up at the huge Union Flag painted on a wall.

'Ach, Tommy!' exclaims the girl, 'I've heard every eejit without a brain in their heads say that. It's utter nonsense. What's wrong with an office?'

A lack of manhood? Tommy doesn't answer, but walks on, clearly seeing every familiar crack in the pavement or graffito daubed on the wall. A dog barks in the distance and another replies from nearby.

'You passed your exams, didn't you?'

'Aye,' admits Tommy as if ashamed of the fact.

'Is there anythin' wrong with passin' your exams?'

'Ach, no.'

'You ought t' wise-up, Tommy. There's no money t' be made workin' in the Yard. Or that bakery. There's nothin' at all around here, nothin'.'

Tommy looks up into her face. Could she be right?

'You want t' see th' house our Brenda and her David's bought out in Holywood! It's absolutely gorgeous! They work every hour God sends 'em.'

'I work hard too, you know.'

'Usin' what? Your hands. If you used your brains you'd be makin' money.' She speaks in a soft but firm tone that does not admit contradiction. 'There's nothin' for anybody in this slum.'

They walk along the streets of the slum, slowly, steadily, Tommy aware that they are reaching the girl's street. They come to a halt beneath an electric street light.

'Thanks for seein' me home, Tommy,' says Gloria.

'Ach,' says Tommy, 'you're okay.'

He has left her home, hasn't expected anythin' for it.

'Wasn't that fightin' awful this evenin'?'

'Aye,' says Tommy.

'How'd it start?'

'They started it.'

'Did they?'

'Aye. They started throwin' stones at some fellas comin' out of a bar.'

'Were you there?'

'For a wee while.'

'Do you like fightin'?' asks Gloria as if she is interviewing him for a job.

'Naaa . . .' says Tommy, aware that it is the only answer she will allow him. He had been frightened for most of the time, especially when the guns started firing. Yet it had released something within him: it had made him feel good afterwards. 'If they don't like Ulster why don't they pack their bags an' move where they belong?'

'There's a lovely wee Catholic girl at the college,' says Gloria, ignoring the shibboleth uttered by Tommy. 'She's dead nice, I really like her. She's so smart.'

'Is she?' asks Tommy accusatorially.

'Aye,' replies Gloria. She stares into his face, challenging him to say something more. 'Tommy, I have t' go in now. I'm already dead late.'

'Okay.'

His acceptance of her decision restores her confidence in him. He is different. Others would have tried to take advantage, tried to force themselves upon her. He is more intelligent than most, more thinking. She steps towards him and presses her lips over his. The decision has been made for him. He takes hold of her around the waist and returns the kiss.

He wants the embrace to continue, her softness, her warmth, to continue; yet he can feel her begin to pull away. Must she make the decisions? He tries to keep her in the embrace by increasing the pressure of the kiss, but immediately she increases her desire to break away.

'I've got t' go in or m' ma will kill me.'

'Okay. Goodnight.'

Again his diffidence provokes in her an affectionate response. Their second kiss lasts for a little longer, but still only serves to increase his thirst.

'Look, you won't go blatherin' about this all over the place, will you, Tommy?'

'Ach . . .'

'Promise.'

'Promise.'

She steps back from him and into the shadows of the alleyway and beckons for him to join her there. Their third kiss is long and open-mouthed. She drapes her right arm over his shoulder and wills him by her passionate response to do something more than merely kiss. Eventually Tommy screws up his courage to start his fingers on an upward movement to her brassiere strap, but when he reaches his goal he is totally confused by the mechanism of release. Pulling away from him a little and letting out an angry sigh she reaches up and lets her bra strap slip. Her breasts fall lightly from their restraint. Looking into his face she smiles.

'Don't bite,' she says softly.

'No,' he mumbles, stepping back towards her. He fumbles at the buttons of her blue shirt until it is open and her breasts have caught the sheen of the moonlight. He cups her right breast in his right hand and squeezes.

'Don't,' mutters Gloria, objecting softly to his inexperienced grope.

'Sorry,' mutters Tommy, who wonders how far he can now go. He feels yet more elated, yet more transported: his real life starts from tonight, he tells himself. His days at school, being bored and frustrated, have been a waste of time, only leading up to this day, this night.

EIGHTEEN

LIAM CRADLES THE heavy story book between his knees; he turns a page and reads the last few paragraphs to discover the fate of the boy lost in the wilderness of northern Canada. He grips the page in open-mouthed excitement, almost tearing the paper, until a snow-muffled rifle shot rings out and the bear drops dead at the boy's feet and he runs to embrace his father.

He lets the book fall from his hands, completely satisfied with the outcome. What a country Canada must be! He is nervously excited by the thought of seeing Canada some day.

Picking up the book from between his knees he lets it slip down on to the threadbare carpet before turning over to lie on his side. The house is silent; the world outside absolutely hushed except for the dull wail of a crane in the distance. Where has she gone? Where is his father? He feels annoyed that they should leave him alone. He feels angry that his father should go off. Liam isn't too concerned, he knows they'll come back soon and all will be explained.

Springing on to his knees he switches off the bedside light before poking his head through the curtains. The street is as it was before, utterly strange, transformed. He cannot believe that it will ever return to its normal, intimately familiar self. He cannot believe that people will again walk down it as they did every day and night of the week. He lets the curtains close and gets down from the bed. Switching on the bedside light again he looks under the bed and quickly finds his shoes. He casts off his pyjamas and pulls on a pair of trousers and shirt.

Down the stairs he tumbles, excitedly determined to seek out his father and sister. He takes his school blazer off the back of a chair by the front door and slips it on as he reaches up to open the latch. He is filled with a spirit of adventure and would quite happily face a grizzly bear if one happened to come round the corner. He feels anything can happen on a night like this. The door swings open and the street, in all its strangeness, lies before him.

NINETEEN

LIZZIE CASTS A watery smile at Ginger as she makes her way to the bar-hatch. She ignores Eddie and Eddie looks elsewhere.

'She doesn't look too pleased, Eddie,' Ginger says. 'What did you do to her, for dear sake?'

'What do you think I did to her?'

'I daren't think.' Ginger flicks off the ash from his cigarette and picks up his glass of beer. 'Whatever it was she doesn't look too satisfied.' He throws back his head and laughs extremely loudly: his small, wiry frame curls up as he abandons himself to his joke. 'Hey, did she look pleased when you took your breeches off?' he asks as he brings himself under control.

'She'd collapse laughin' if you took yours off.'

'Ach, she's a touch old for me, Eddie.'

'Well, I can tell you that she's learnt everythin' an' forgot nothin'.'

'Like an oul dog, you mean?'

'She'd chew you up an' blow you out in bubbles.'

'Are you collectin' pension books, or what?'

'You lookin' a dig in th' head?'

'Has she all her own teeth?'

'Give over,' protests Eddie, lamely. He has never been able to get the better of Ginger.

'You could get a nasty suck if she tried givin' you a love bite,' continues Ginger with the mock concern he so loves using.

'Will ye give over, Ginger?' Eddie wishes he'd kept his big mouth shut; he feels helpless in the face of Ginger's mockery. 'Do you want another drink or do you want another drink?' Standing up he towers over his friend. 'Well?'

69

'That's very kind of you, Eddie. I'll have a bottle of Harp, if that's all right by you.' He looks up at Eddie and smiles into his face.

'You'd be lucky t' get near her. She's got her own teeth an' a lot more besides,' says Eddie, not quite knowing what he is saying.

'No offence meant, Eddie. She's a handsome woman: I was pullin' your leg.'

'Aye: ye cynical wee gobshite.' Cursing him allows Eddie to turn away with the feeling of having retained his pride.

Ginger watches him go and makes sure he releases a loud enough laugh for Eddie to stop, turn, curse and go on his way. Ginger smiles at a nearby acquaintance.

'Can't take a joke.'

'Aye,' says the older man dismissively, 'who can?'

'Ach, me for one.'

Kenny slips down by Ginger's side and hits him on the shoulder to attract his attention.

'What were you an' our Eddie fightin' about?'

'Nothin'.'

'Nothin'?'

'Wouldn't like to say, you know?'

'Wouldn't you? Th' way you treat our Eddie is desperate,' mocks Kenny in a friendly, though somehow threatening tone of voice. He nods and smiles at an elderly man with a cap on his head, pipe in his mouth and walking stick in hand who passes their secluded table.

'How are you, Mr Ferguson?'

'I'm well, son, I'm well,' says the unwell Mr Ferguson.

Kenny allows himself a satisfied smile. He is known by all; men and women come to seek his advice, company and favour. He is famous: if not infamous. His infamy deriving from certain brutalities he had meted out to his men while forming the local defence association: if they were to defend their country, people and way of life there had to be discipline, and none of the beatings he had given would ever be forgotten. Once he had shown his fist he had relaxed, relying on memory to back up his words. Now Kenny liked to make sure the old folks had bread and milk in times of trouble and were reassured that no bombs or bullets would find their way into the area so long as he ruled. He knew he had won the battle for their hearts and minds.

'Ginger,' says Kenny firmly, looking him in the eye.

'Kenny,' replies Ginger, returning the look, 'what can I do for you?' He picks up his beer glass and sees off its contents.

Kenny edges a little closer. 'Where'd you put that gear?'

Ginger looks at Kenny without showing any desire to reply. 'What gear?'

'Don't what gear me, Ginger,' says Kenny with a slight threat in his voice. They both look around the immediate area: it seems safe enough.

'In the usual place.'

'All wrapped up?'

'All wrapped up.'

'Cleaned and oiled?'

'Better believe it.'

'Good man.'

'Course I'm a good man!'

'What did you hit?'

'Might have winged one.'

'Winged?'

'The bloody thing wasn't sighted right.'

'Don't give's that oul guff.'

'It wasn't sighted right, I tell ye, Kenny.'

'What did you set it at?'

'Two hundred.'

'And it did what?'

'Off t' th' left.'

Kenny thinks for a good while, raising his glass occasionally to take a sip of his beer.

'I got a couple of shots at a fella. Thought he was made of iron, or somethin'. It was shootin' all over th' place. I packed it in t' save th' ammo. Friggin' useless.'

'You need your eyes tested, Ginger.'

'No, I do not!' exclaims Ginger, indifferent to who hears him now. Was he being accused of cowardice, or failing to do his duty? Was that a threat in Kenny's voice or a genuine bit of banter? Sure he had been extremely nervous before he got himself into position, but once he'd set himself up his shakes had gone and he had aimed the old rifle as he had been taught by his small arms instructor seventeen or so years before. 'You take the fuckin' thing out an' see if you can hit anythin'!'

Kenny reaches out and pats Ginger's arm.

'Okay. Okay.'

'It's useless, Kenny. You ought t' get our money back.'

'Can't get our money back.'

'Well, we've been done.'

'I'll take it out on Sunday an' give it a go.'

'Okay.'

'Not accusin' you of anythin', Ginger.'

'Aye,' replies Ginger, lifting his glass to his lips to cover the anger he feels.

'Want a drink?'

'Eddie's bringin' me one,' replies Ginger with a laugh that is childlike and has always acted as a mask for his true feelings. He's older than Kenny. Why should Kenny dominate everything? Why should he give all the orders and treat everyone in the same way?

Eddie slowly approaches the table with bottles of beer and glasses of whisky slotted between his fingers. He can see that they are in the middle of a discussion they want no one else to hear. So in the middle of the busy floor near the bar he pauses discreetly, looking round the hall as if he's in search of a friend.

'Have you been turned to stone or what?' asks a woman's familiar voice.

'I'm lookin' for somebody,' returns Eddie.

'You're blockin' the way, you big eejit.'

'Go on ahead,' retorts Eddie, moving aside, blundering into a bunch of vacated chairs. As Lizzie goes past him without turning her head, 'See you later, Lizzie?' he suggests, seriously in fun. He glances over at Kenny and sees that he's drinking now and looking around. Now he can return. If there is one thing he knows Kenny dislikes more than loose talk in bars and clubs, it is your nose poked into business that has nothing to do with you. He weaves his way through the mass of empty chairs towards his table. The club is fully alive now. Almost everyone is either dancing, talking or laughing. He knows he will not see his bed before the light of day.

'Here you are, Ginger, ye wee bastard.'

'Hey, who's a bastard? I've the papers t' prove I'm legitimate.'

'Show them.'

'All Ginger's got to show is a dog licence,' opines Kenny. 'Have you brought me a drink?'

'Aye, I've bought ye a drink. Though you ought t' try buyin' your own drink once in a while.'

'Bloody cheek!'

'If Kenny bought the drink the BBC would be in here with their cameras t' record the event!' comments Ginger, running his fingers through his untidy, dirty hair.

'Right! I've had enough! I want the both of youse in yon back room givin' it a good scrub! It's a friggin' pig sty.'

'Pull the other one, there's bells on it!' says Ginger.

'Talk t' m' arse, m' head's sore,' says Eddie.

'I'll break both your legs if you don't do as you're told. I'm not jokin'!'

'I don't care if you're jokin' or not,' says Ginger, 'I'm not cleanin' that there room in the middle of the night.'

'Lazy bastards.'

'Get Jimmy, or somebody t' do it,' says Eddie, quietly, pacifically.

'Oh, no!' cries Kenny. 'None of this "let Jimmy" do it. We all lend a helpin' hand cleanin' the club.'

The men end their squabble by a silent agreement that it has become a useless argument. They sip their whisky and beer and gaze about the hall.

'How many oul rusty .303's will this crowd get us, Kenny?' asks Ginger.

'Look, if you can buy better you go out an' you buy better. If not, just keep your gob shut. Okay?'

Ginger fails to answer.

'There's nothin' decent on the market, Ginger,' says Eddie, siding with Kenny as always. He looks for some sign of gratitude from Kenny, but receives none. As always.

They sit in silence, sipping their drinks and listening to a sentimental ballad.

'Come on! Up and dance, all you lovers!' shouts the disc-jockey, waving his arms about.

'How much are we payin' that joker?' asks Eddie, with his glass clenched in his teeth.

'Thirty quid.'

'I'd do it for a fiver,' replies Eddie.

'You couldn't find the hole in the middle, Eddie,' says Ginger without a smile. He decides to shake off his gloom by standing and demanding from his comrades their orders for drink.

'Sit down,' orders Kenny, 'my round!'

'Eddie, slap my cheek. Am I dreamin'?' says Ginger.

'You'll be asleep if you don't shut your gob,' says Kenny cheerfully. 'Let's take a wee tour round the area. Is the car goin' well?'

'Like a dream.'

'Great. We'll take Tommy with us.'

'Tommy who?' Ginger asks.

'Your man who dealt with that headbanger.'

'If you say so,' says Eddie, not convinced.

'How old's the kid?'

'Sixteen, seventeen: old enough,' replies Kenny, firmly.

'Well, okay.'

'What's that long-haired git smokin'?' asks Kenny, looking in the disc-jockey's direction.

'Dope. He's been off his head all night,' says Eddie as indifferently as possible.

'God, what's this country comin' to? Eddie, away over there an' tell him it's illegal.'

'Sure I will.'

Kenny gives Eddie's head a playful push before heading to the bar. Eddie remains in his seat, sipping his whisky and gazing lazily around the hall with its gaudy red, white and blue slashes of colour. He pulls out an old worn tobacco tin and proceeds to roll himself a cigarette. Ginger looks up from his beer and pulls a face.

'Hear about the UDR man the filth killed last night?' asks Ginger almost casually.

'I did,' mutters Eddie.

They glance at each other and for a few seconds, as they

contort their faces to express their disgust, they are united in their hatred of their country's enemies.

'They waited in his house. Told his wife they were her oul man's friends. When he came in the door they blew his brains out all over his wife an' wean.'

In the silence that follows between the two men they share a vision of revenge, revenge that is unrelenting, cleansing, triumphant, absolute.

'They're vermin.'

'They ought t' be incinerated,' opines Ginger.

They sip their drinks in silence. Nothing more needs to be said. They have shown their loyalty to Ulster.

'A fella in the RUC who was at the house said they found bits of the guy's brain in the fish tank,' says Eddie.

Ginger gazes into Eddie's face in an attempt to see if he should take the story seriously. A smirk begins to develop on Eddie's face, humour never too far away.

'Well that's what yer man said to me,' says Eddie, defending his story.

'Wha'? The fish ate the poor bastard's brains?'

'Must've done.'

The black humour starts to have its effect upon the two men and they begin to chuckle and Ginger's mouth twists into a grin.

'Did they have the fish put down, do ye know?' asks Ginger.

'Ach, it's not funny,' says Eddie.

Ginger releases a loud laugh.

'You're sick in the head, Ginger,' says Eddie, unable to stifle a laugh himself.

TWENTY

LIAM SHOVES HIS bruised nose against the plate-glass window and takes a good hard look at the interior of the corner shop. Through a partially open door a triangle of yellow light cuts across the darkness to reveal a slab of cheese sitting on the wooden counter, a large kitchen knife gleaming by its side. Someone has been called away from his or her task, decides Liam. He lets his gaze stray over the lines of cans and packets, peat briquettes and bags of smokeless coal, over mops, buckets, brushes and dustpans; such a good shop, thinks Liam as he turns away. When he reads the name of the traverse street he vaguely recalls the name from many years back, then he is shocked when he realises just how far he still has to walk. Shaking his head in disbelief he hurries wearily down the little street until he comes to a halt, to search up and down for another street that will take him towards home; but there seems to be no break in the long row of identical houses.

Defeated and tired he sits on the kerb and emits a long, self-pitying sigh. Try as he might he cannot bring back the memory of the night's events. Kathleen's face slips into his mind's eye, red and tear-stained; the noise of running men, breaking glass and falling stones drifts in and out of his thoughts, but they come to a halt where there is only blackness. What had happened? He rests himself back on to the pavement and stretches out his tired legs into the empty, carless road. His legs are weak, insubstantial; he hits his right thigh and is reassured to feel the blow. His legs seem to hold a physical memory of having run hard and fast. He shuts his eyes and enjoys the splendid sense of isolation, the deep silence that seems to emanate from the moon hanging placidly above him. He feels no possibility of danger; what could happen to him on such a beautiful night? He remembers the pictures of the men driving across the craters of the moon he had seen on the colour television in the Washington Bar in the city centre. What wonders, he tells himself.

The street is deserted, without a single trace of life except for Liam enjoying a rest. His thoughts wander back twenty-five years or so, to when he had run about the very same streets in the company of his Protestant friends, scavenging for old car tyres, wood, old furniture or anything else that could be piled on the eleventh of July bonfire. His family had lived in a cul-de-sac. It was a mixed street that had seen little trouble. A cup of sugar or milk could be borrowed from any neighbour. On the eleventh of July the Catholics from the streets round and about watched the bonfire from their own little, separate vantage point. On the Twelfth he and his brother Alec, quiet, thoughtful Alec, were kept indoors 'til the fathers of their friends had shown their mastery of the streets. Occasionally, dragging Alec along, they went secretly, taking the back ways, to the main road and watched the bands pass. He liked the colour, the music; it meant nothing to him until years later. The parades were fun in those days. People smiled, laughed, cheered and waved at friends and relatives.

Now there was no fun to be had anywhere. No fun anywhere at all. The city was dying, going under, and Liam regretted it terribly.

He was a fool for coming back. What was there here for him or his children? Nothing. He curses his stubbornness and perversity. What had he expected? To slip back into the city as if he'd never left? But what had he in London? Nothing. He hadn't anything to leave except recriminations, bitterness, humiliation. London had made him feel lost, unimportant.

He pulls himself up and looks about the street, trying hard to recall his way through the maze. Left, he decides finally; away from the main road where danger passes. He crosses the street and starts to walk along the other side. He will press on through the streets, hoping to recognise something in a once intimately known area.

Twenty yards down the street he comes to a junction.

The name of the traverse street is not familiar, but he walks down it anyway. What choice does he have? The houses in the street are small, sunken. He stops after a few yards. Has he walked into a dead end? He decides to go on and soon sees the street turning off to his right. The slight dread of being trapped dissipates, only to be clamped back down again when he sees that he has indeed walked into a dead end.

Oh, will he ever get home? he exclaims silently to himself. Where the friggin' hell is he? He turns back the way he came and notices a small alleyway on the far side of the street. He searches the nearby houses and gardens for signs of danger before walking briskly into the gloom. In a matter of seconds he is out of the alleyway. He had hoped that the next street would take him off to the right, but it comes to an end at a small roundabout on which cars are parked. To his left the street goes up a small hill, probably rejoining the very street he had left. Nothing to be done.

The wail of a factory siren breaks into the clear, warm, air: night shift, Liam says to himself. He knows from the shipyard workers coming into the small bar by his own builders' yard that they are working every hour God sends them to fulfil a contract and finish an oil tanker. He had been overawed, stunned, by the sheer size of the shipyard when he had been taken on a tour of it, prior to a job interview. He could understand the pride the men had in the shipyard and its past. They believed they had built an industry where before there had been nothing but fields and bogs; they believed that having built that industry they should work in it, nobody else. Certainly not men like himself. The interview had been polite. They had not talked about religion or allegiance, but they had made it clear that they thought him a fool for even thinking of applying for a job in the yard. Yet Belfast was his home, the only one he felt comfortable in. The Republic to the south was a foreign country he had only put foot in on a couple of occasions. He could not feel loyal to the Republic because he had never lived there, yet he could not feel anything towards Northern Ireland except the bitterness of rejection.

What could he do about the way things were? Always had been? He wasn't going to wait for the start of a new world. He had to deal with the one he lived in, the city he lived in. After the interview he had gone out looking for a job day after day until he had finally walked into the Scrabo Street builders' yard and asked the owner to his face if he needed another worker. The rotund little man had said nothing while he sized Liam up, and when he did speak it was to ask him how much he expected to be paid. Liam had sighed and answered that he expected to be paid what the owner thought he was worth. The rotund little man had parted his thin little lips and smiled before mentioning a figure just a few pounds more than Liam was getting from the dole. He had smiled and said that he thought the figure was reasonable. When could he start? the rotund little man has asked. Right away, he had answered, to the rotund little man's satisfaction.

He knew where he stood with the owner. Though it was obvious that he had never hired a Catholic in the past, it was equally obvious that he thought more about making a profit than he thought about religion or nationalist affiliation. Liam thought the rotund little man's greed comic; his eyes were constantly darting about in search of the thieves he was sure surrounded him, waiting for their chance. Liam knew he had to work hard to prove himself. At first he unloaded containers and made ready customers' orders with three much younger men. Soon he knew almost everything there was to know and he was trusted by the boss. He would be put in charge of large orders, accompanying them to the sites. Then he was given the task of closing down the yard for the night and opening it up in the morning. As his responsibility for the general running of the yard increased, the open resentment, jealousy felt by his Protestant fellow-workers had increased. They were not pleased that a Fenian had taken one of 'their' jobs. While unloading a container, or as they drank their tea, comments would fly about his ears aimed at his co-religionists: how filthy, ignorant, indolent, treacherous the Taigs were. He'd heard it all a thousand times and mostly he let it wash over him. Occasionally he would defuse the aggression of the man he had supplanted in the boss's estimation by a carefully placed joke that got the others laughing; with no support the fella always backed down. Humour had always been his best means of defence. While he ran about with the Protestant gang of kids he used humour to moderate his relationships within the group, and when a joke failed he would fawn upon the leader to display his subservience.

He used similar means to get ahead in the building supply yard, and after a few months, after he'd learned everything there was to learn, he moved into the office, much to the anger of his former mates in the yard. The office was much more to his liking and he could easily outface the men; soon, once they knew he was there for good, they accepted his orders and they worked well together.

He comes to a junction and finds himself back in the seemingly endless street, which now turns slightly up-hill. The houses are more substantial than any he has seen all night. The doors and windows are broader, the brickwork about them is fancy and painted a brilliant glossy white. The doorsteps, heavy slabs, worn down by a million feet, are scrubbed clean, as are the milk bottles awaiting collection. He stops in the street to take a look at his watch: one twenty-five.

From a house a few yards in front of him light is thrown on to the pavement as a door is swung open. A shadow fills the light and a small, wiry woman with cropped dyed-blonde hair in her late thirties steps out into the night.

'Thanks for the tea, Mrs Parker.'

'Ach, you're all right, Brenda,' says the woman now filling the doorway. She is older than her neighbour, a blowzy woman with a voice that suggests she has been through everything life has to offer. On her feet are a pair of fur-lined bedroom slippers that are so worn they look as if she never takes them off. She wears a black skirt and a turtle-neck pullover. In her hand she holds a king-size cigarette. 'Away home, love. He'll be back when he's had enough to drink.'

'I hope so, Mrs Parker. He wasn't home at all last night,' says Brenda, in a thin voice nervously puffing on a cigarette.

'When he comes in stick his head down the toilet an' pull the chain. That lad of mine treats this house like a hotel. I'm goin' t' tell him to find somewhere else to live. It's about time he flew the nest.'

Liam decides he should walk on before they notice him standing close by. As he passes the two women he exchanges 'good evenings' with them, and the older woman comments upon the beauty of the night. As he reaches the top of the hill he hears front doors being shut and he is alone again in the street.

TWENTY-ONE

'WHERE ARE YOU goin'?'

'Where do you think I'm goin'?'

'Jesus knows.'

'I'm goin' t' th' police.'

'Is your head cut, Kathleen, or what?'

'M' head's not cut.'

'Then it's not screwed on right.'

'Will you go home?'

'No, I will not.'

They come to the corner. Across the street a few large railway sleepers have been lain. On the broad street a single-decker bus sits almost unscathed as if it has been badly parked.

'What d' you think the cops will do?' Michael asks her.

'They might know where he is!'

'If they know where he is, he's in their cells an' you can't do anythin' about it, Kathleen.'

'Well I'll see, won't I?'

'Up to yourself.'

'Aye,' sighs Kathleen.

They stand in silence. Michael's thumbs are firmly stuck in his torn and worn black trousers and his fingers pat his legs like a pair of penguin's flippers. His shoulders are hunched, his lower lip curled over his upper lip as he thinks hard.

'Well, do you want 's t' come with ye or not?'

'No!'

'You goin' down t' them fuckers by yourself?'

Kathleen turns away and folds her arms. She edges her head round the corner to look down the broad street to where four police landrovers form a barricade.

'Why don't you wait 'til I find Father Connor an' get him to go down?'

'Where is he?'

'Don't know.'

'Then I'll do it m'self.'

'If you wait ten minutes I'll go an' get him.'

'I'm not waitin' for him, Michael.'

'But he's been down twice already, Kathleen. Why don't you wait a wee while?'

'I'm not waitin' for him.'

'Look, Kathleen . . .'

'Wha'?'

'If I go down there now they'll knock the shite out of me.'

'Why?'

'Why d'ya think!'

'You tell me!'

'Because we've been chuckin' friggin' stones at 'em all night!'

'Well, you shouldn't've chucked stones at 'em.'

'I wish they'd've been made of lead, I can tell ye.'

'Why lead?'

'Bullets.'

'Bullets?'

She stares into his face, without expression, without seeming to understand. She mouths the word bullets and turns away again to look down to the police barricade.

'What use are bullets t' anybody, Michael?'

'Well, if we hadn't've had a few bullets t'night we'd've been burnt out of our homes, that's for sure.'

'How do you know?'

'I know all right. I know. A fat lot of good the fuckin' RUC were to us. They sat on their arses all night doin' nothin'. Cheerin' the Protestant fuckers on, an all.'

His anger makes Kathleen shiver and a tingle of fear strokes her back. She turns round sharply to see if he is still the same eejit she has always known him to be, but she sees that he is not. His face is altered, his yellowed teeth are bared, his mouth drawn up; his face lacks all colour and shines white in the light of the moon. She steps away from him and out round the corner into the broad street.

'I'll wait here, if you want,' he calls after her. 'If I went down there I'd come back black an' blue.'

'Okay,' mutters Kathleen over her shoulder as she steps nervously but determinedly towards the police barricade and the police barracks that lie behind it. In her rush to be away from Michael she steps on a lump of rock and her ankle twists badly. No matter, she tries to ignore the pain and goes on down the street. Her head is fixed, her eyes trained upon the police barricade, looking for signs of life, but she can see none. Surely they would not leave them unguarded? She stops. She looks about the street: at the underside of a toppled-over lorry, at the curtained windows and lifeless houses, at the glistening glass debris. In the black shadows of the improvised barricade she sees the red glow of a cigarette, which fills her with a little hope as well as a little more fear, and she walks on towards the barricade. As she comes within a few yards of the landrovers she sees a piece of the barricade detach itself.

'Hello, love, what's th' matter?' says a voice that is as warm and reassuring as the voice on the wireless.

'M' da's not home,' says Kathleen.

'Right. What's his name, love?' asks the black figure that seems to be made of shadows.

'Kelly.'

'What street?'

She tells him the name of the street.

'Come with me. We'll see if we can find him for you. Ben, look after the shop.'

'Right,' says a voice in the shadows.

Kathleen feels an arm go over her shoulders and she starts to feel less frightened. Even starts to feel safe again. She looks up and into the face that is peering down at her, smiling.

'What time did your da go off at?'

'Half-nine. He was just goin' out t' see what was goin' on.'

'T' see what was goin' on?'

'Aye,' replies Kathleen, firmly, pleadingly.

'Okay.'

She can feel tears start to seep out from her eyes against her will. She releases a sob.

'Ach, you're all right. I'm sure your da's okay.'

He takes her up some steps and into the vestibule of the barracks. It is stark, cold and unwelcoming. Kathleen immediately shrinks away from the barren room and steps back, but is guided to a wooden bench by the police officer. She can see his face now, moustached, serious, rough and pock-marked. She can see his peaked cap, rifle and pistol now.

'Cup of tea?'

She shakes her head.

'Wha's your father's first name?' asks the policeman, deciding that what she wants is her da.

'Liam.'

'Never heard of him; I suppose that's good news anyway. Where's your mother?'

'England.'

'Where in England?'

'London.'

'What is she doin' in London?'

'She lives there.'

'Oh,' says the policeman, 'I see.'

There is a silence between the pair and it is only broken when they hear the dull thuds of rubber soles hitting linoleum.

'Ere, who's that?'asks a fat little soldier.

'None of your bloody business.'

'Okay, mate. Okay.'

Kathleen takes her eyes away from the soldier and looks instead at a poster asking citizens to ring a telephone number with information.

'Away about your business,' the policeman tells the soldier.

'She's gorgeous, ain't she?'

'She's only a kid,' says the policeman with violence in his voice.

'Yeah, they all have t' start sometime, don't they?' The soldier's mates are coming up behind him. They emit cat-calls and whistles as they catch sight of Kathleen, who by now has her head firmly down.

'Give her one.'

'Give her two.'

'Good pair of tits.'

'Boat race not too bad, neither.'

They seem to scoop up their fat little mate and are gone from the vestibule as quickly as they came, in seconds.

'Animals. English scum.'

Kathleen glances up and receives a weak, sympathetic smile from the policeman as a reward.

'I'll settle them when they get back. If they get back. The gunman who shot that lot would be doin' humanity a favour, eh?' He lets free a laugh that is loud and gravelly. 'Now you stay where you are 'til I go an' see about your father. Do you hear me?'

'Aye.'

'What's your name?'

'Kathleen.'

'Well, you stay there, Kathleen.'

She has no intention of running away. She is so struck by the strangeness of her surroundings that she is disinclined to move or even to turn her head. The policeman disappears through a big brown door and she is left alone in the vestibule. Though not for long: the same brown door opens and another policeman appears, also smiling.

'Your father missin', love?'

'Aye,' replies Kathleen.

She knows they are being kind, but she longs to be away from the coldness of the barracks. She is certain that her father is not here and the policemen cannot find him for her: she must do it herself.

'When did you say your father left the house?'

'Half-nine.'

'Half-nine,' repeats the policeman, muttering to himself as he writes on a piece of scrap paper, squinting through half-moon spectacles.

'He just went out to see what was happenin'.'

'Oh, aye,' says the policeman, sceptically.

'Aye. He wasn't throwin' stones,' says Kathleen, defiantly.

'I'm sure he wasn't.'

'He just went out for a look, you know. They were fightin' all round the house. It was just awful.'

'Aye,' sympathises the policeman. 'Awful times.'

'I've no food or nothin'.'

'Shops'll open in th' mornin'.'

'Hope so.'

'Now have you any family round here?'

'Just m' uncle.'

'Oh, aye? Where's he live?'

'Stanfield Street.'

'Do you want me t' get him over?'

'No.'

'Why not?'

She does not answer.

'Why not?'

'I just don't.'

'Why's that?'

'Just don't.'

If the girl doesn't want her uncle, she doesn't want her uncle and there's nothing he can do about it. He isn't going to continue the conversation all night. Her father's away drinking somewhere, anyway.

'Well, up to yourself.'

The policeman removes his scholarly spectacles from his thin pointed nose and tucks them into his left breast pocket. He seems old, far too old to be up so late at night. A young policeman with two mugs of tea, their handles clamped in his right hand, pushes the brown door open and expertly lets one of the mugs drop on to the desk by the elderly policeman before coming round the desk towards Kathleen.

'Ta,' says the elderly policeman.

'Here you are,' says the young policeman.

Kathleen looks up, but doesn't reach out.

'Do you want it or not?'

'Okay.'

The tea is strong and sweet.

'Have you seen enough?' asks the elderly policeman.

'Naaaa . . .'

'Away back t' what you were doin'.'

'I was doin' nothin'.'

'Then away an' find somethin' t' do. Take your man in the cells a cup of tea.'

Kathleen's head jerks up from her mug.

'I'll take him a size nine boot, that's what I'll take him.'

Kathleen lets out a little squeal and stands up, spilling some of the tea to the floor and over the young policeman's trouser leg.

'Ach, look what you've done!'

'Now you're okay, love: your father isn't here. We're just seein' if he's anywhere else. You needn't worry. Sit back down.' The elderly policeman is at her side, taking her tea and helping her down on to her seat. She can smell whisky on his breath. It revolts her; it brings back memories that usually live in her dreams, beneath the everyday daydreams and thoughts. She sits absolutely still, eyes on the floor ahead of her. The elderly policeman places the mug of tea back in her hands.

'You all right, love?'

'She seen a ghost?'

'Away an' do what I told you.'

'All right.'

The young policeman turns away and disappears through the wooden door.

'Never you mind him. He's only a Protestant dunderhead. You sit there nice an' quiet. We'll find out where your da is. Okay, love?'

She stares into his face.

'He'll be home in time for Mass.' He pats her hand and winks, forming a conspiracy. 'Don't you be afeared. You're all right here.' He gives her hand a final pat before going back behind his desk.

Slowly Kathleen sips her tea, wondering which way she should go from the police barracks. Or if she should return to the house. What if he is sitting at home wondering where she has gone? Should have left a note, she decides, angry with herself. What of her brother? Will he be safe, alone? Surely he will be asleep by this time? The clock above the policeman's desk tells her that it is ten minutes to two o'clock. Never has she been awake so late. Except, perhaps, when crossing the sea from England, lying in the coffin-like bunk listening to the thump of the engines. Her mother's face flashes before her mind's eye, it is expressionless, hardened.

'We've had no reports about your father.'

The big policeman is back now, his rifle cradled in his arms. He is impatient, wanting to get back to his friends at the police cordon. He had welcomed the relief from boredom the girl had presented him with, but now he can do no more. Her father's in a shebeen drinking his money. What can he do? He looks into her large grey-green eyes and is struck by her fragility. She's been hurt before. The pain flits across her face, from the blinking of her eyes, the twitching of her mouth and lower lip to the clear conscious exercise of her will to gather herself together and stand.

'Thanks for helpin'.'

'Away home now. Your da will be back soon enough.' What more can he do? He puts an arm around her and embraces her briefly as he would do with his own daughter. 'As far as we know there's been only a few cuts and bruises t'night. That's all.'

'Thanks,' is all she can reply.

'Away home.'

'Aye.'

Out in the street she quickly walks back the way she came, seeing Michael resting at the corner.

'Well?' asks Michael, excitedly.

'Well what?'

'Did the peelers have him?'

'No.'

'What 're you goin' t' do now?'

'I'm goin' up here.'

'Why don't you go an' see if he's gone home?'

'I will in a wee while. Just as soon as I've looked up here.' She glances at Michael, openly challenging him to leave her, then goes on up the street without stopping.

'Look, I'm away back t' Mrs Burke's.'

'Please yourself,' shouts Kathleen as she heads for the opposite end of the broad street.

Michael watches her walk off up the street; he feels as if he has tried his best. What was he supposed to do? He turns away and heads back to Mrs Burke's. Back to the beer, talk and baked potatoes in the fire.

TWENTY-TWO

THE FORD'S ENGINE starts on Ginger's first attempt and he is thankful that it hasn't failed him. He presses his foot down a few times to impress Eddie.

'Good?'

'Great.'

'Done a ton on the way to Lurgan Thursday night.'

'Aye, goin' over a cliff.'

'Straight up. No problem.'

'I believe you. Thousands would call you a liar.'

'A hundred and five, no problem.'

'Aye,' says Eddie, looking out the car window at nothing in particular.

Ginger puts the car into gear and drives slowly back to the club, ready for patrol.

'Away an' see where he is,' he suggests.

'Why me?'

'Because you're not drivin' th' friggin' car, are you?'

'Have you lost the ability to walk, or somethin'?'

'Eddie, will you just go an' see where the hell Kenny is?'

'Ach, all right,' says Eddie, satisfied that he has put up a good fight. He is aware of their endless battle for superiority. He's not going to lose out. Yet he does not really mind anything, so long as he is with his friends: anything so long as he has someone to banter with. Someone to drink with and discuss football, racing and the desperate state of the country.

He feels a cold hatred for the enemies of his country. He wishes them gone, obliterated. Ulster's enemies seem to be all about them and in among them. Treachery is failing to stand quickly enough for the national anthem, a lack of vehemence in wishing Ulster's foes in their graves, or a thousand other things.

As Eddie turns to slam the car door shut he sees Tommy coming down the street.

'Where have you been?'

Tommy comes to a halt before Eddie, but pointedly does not hurry to answer his question.

'You deaf?'

'No. I'm not deaf.'

'Weren't you supposed to be on the door?'

'Joe stood in for me.'

'You were on the door: not Joe.'

Eddie is fully aware that he is attempting to lessen his own failure of security by upbraiding the younger man.

'Joe's on duty t'night. He can guard the door as well as anybody,' says Tommy, turning away to enter the entrance hall where Joe at the table is in the middle of an arm-wrestling match with Geoff. Joe takes the time from his physical concentration to grin at Tommy.

'You're houlin' on, you bastard,' cries Geoff.

'M' hand's nowhere near th' friggin' table!'

'Look! Look! It's on the friggin' table!'

'Ach, you need your eyes tested.'

The struggle, intense, vital, reaches its climax and the lives of the two young men seem to depend upon the outcome.

Joe, squat, barrel-chested, wins, whoops with joy and begins a dance of triumph around the little hall. His joy vanishes as he sees Geoff scoop up one of the five-pound notes.

'Hey, put that down, you fucker. You lost fair an' square.'

'You cheated. The bet's off.'

Joe flies at his opponent and catches hold of his throat. Geoff wilts under the ferocious attack. He spreads his arms wide, not resisting the bulldog that has him by the throat.

'Geoff, he beat you fair and square!' shouts Tommy just as Eddie comes behind him into the entrance hall. 'Give him the bloody money.'

'What's this?' Eddie demands.

'A fight, what do you think it is?' says Joe, increasing the grip he has around Geoff's thin neck.

'None of that in this club.'

'No problem,' replies Joe, allowing his victim to escape.

'Here you are,' says Geoff, slapping the five-pound note into Joe's hand.

'Anytime, Geoff.'

Geoff bursts out through the door to escape his shame.

'He could have kept his money if he'd asked nicely.'

'Buck eejit,' is all that Eddie will say about the matter. He pushes the doors into the hall open with an overly dramatic sweep and skins his knuckles badly on the hardwood. He winces, but quickly covers up his pain as a girl approaches.

'All right, Eddie?' asks Betty.

'Aye,' mumbles Eddie.

She passes on. He scans the hall for Kenny, but cannot find him.

'Seen Kenny?' he asks a fella sitting by himself near to the dance floor.

'Naaaa . . .' mutters the fella, drunkenly slipping from his chair slightly before pulling himself up. 'Kenny who?'

'Never mind.' Eddie walks towards the bar, dodging the couples as they shuffle to a romantic ballad. He pushes off a couple who crash into him.

'Sorry, mucker,' says the man, his hand firmly groping at the woman's breast. 'Haven't got m' mind on the dancin', you know.'

'Aye, I know,' says Eddie, without a smile.

'Hey! Keep your hands off her!' screams a woman slouched in a chair; she reaches over and gives a man's head lying on the table a push. 'Hey, away an' defend her honour, you useless pig.'

Eddie reaches Jimmy at the bar-hatch. 'Where's Kenny?'

'Back room.'

'Right.'

He pushes the door to the room open and sees the back end of Kenny sticking up in the air.

'Get out!'

'Kenny, are you comin' or what?'

Kenny straightens up. He wrings a filthy cloth and it foams pure white soap suds which drip into a metal bucket.

'In a couple of minutes.'

'Okay.'

'Eddie'

'Wha'?'

'You couldn't get your hands on a couple of oul arm-chairs and settee, could you?'

'I'll ask around.'

'Make this dump a bit more like home, eh?'

'Aye. I'll try t' get somethin' decent.'

'We want somewhere the men can have a wee rest and a cup of tea.'

'Aye.'

'I'll be out in a few minutes.'

'Right, Kenny.'

He remains looking into Kenny's face, wondering if he is being serious.

'Away you go,' says Kenny, the sharpness returning to his voice. Eddie closes the door and walks slowly back down the passage-way.

At the bar-hatch he reaches over and takes a bottle of beer from a crate and opens it with his own opener.

'Put it on m' slate, Jimmy,' says Eddie, drinking from the bottle. The hall is still packed, no one seems to want to go. 'How much have we taken?'

'Near five hundred,' replies Jimmy. Jimmy is exhausted. He sits on an upturned beer crate unwilling to move another muscle. His little moustache is wet with sweat and his bald head covered in little droplets. He takes his handkerchief from his pocket and wipes his face and head.

'Where's Alan?'

'He went home at eleven. Last time I do this by myself.'

'Ach, Jimmy, you should have asked me to give you a hand.'

'Ach,' is all he says, knowing that he has liked handling the club by himself, proving that he is the best barman without a doubt. 'We've done well, Eddie. We've pulled in a few spondulicks t'night.'

'Aye, we have that, Jimmy. You've done a brave job. They were round this bar like it was the end of the world.'

'Aye.'

'We'll put the money to good use, Jimmy.'

'That's all I want t' hear.'

'Away home. Get somebody t' take over.'

'Ach, I'll stay another wee while, Eddie.'

'Up t' yourself.'

'Aye,' says Jimmy, with a sigh.

Eddie finishes off his bottle of beer and emits a loud burp as he drops the empty bottle back into the crate.

'Must you?' asks Lizzie, who stands by his side with a bank note in her hand.

'It's healthy,' replies Eddie with another, smaller burp.

'It's bloody rude!'

'Is it indeed!'

'What d'ye want?' asks Jimmy.

'What I had th' last time,' replies Lizzie.

'Your oul man ask where you were?'

'You jokin'. He didn't notice I'd gone.'

They stare into each other's faces for a matter of seconds before Eddie allows himself a sly grin.

'Your oul man goin' t' work t'morrow mornin'?'

'If I can get him up. If somebody didn't bake th' bread we'd all starve.'

'Too true, Lizzie,' says Eddie. 'I'll be round for a cup of tea in th' mornin'.'

'Don't bother. I'll be out.' She knows she will be in.

Eddie merely smiles before heading back to the car.

TWENTY-THREE

YOUNG LIAM DIGS his clawed fingers into the damp sand and pulls out a fistful, enjoying the cold mess as it scrunches through his wiggling fingers. The fear he had felt whilst looking down from his bedroom window has changed to a tingling excitement as he looks over the transformed street. Looking up from the pavement he catches his breath as he sees that the night sky over the city is as filled with stars as the night sky described in his book of adventure stories. He smiles as he sees the moon, tranquil, benign, just to the right of the church steeple.

Turning his back on the moon and the moon's reflection lying on glass scattered across the street, he walks away from the safety of his home. He feels no fear at being out so late at night; nor does he see danger hidden in the shadows. He kicks a stone across the road, ignoring Kathleen's voice sounding in his inner ear telling him to look after his good shoes. He is free of her. Putting on a burst of speed he runs to the corner where a small, peaceful street crosses his own. A car lies in the middle of the street, its doors open and its bonnet up, as if it has suddenly died and its owners have deserted it. The car seems utterly out of place in this quietest of all the neighbouring streets. He crosses to the other pavement and walks slowly past the stranded car before stepping back out on to the road to take a closer look. He has been in a car once in his life, when his father took him and Kathleen on a long winding drive through the countryside to Bangor for a day by the cold sea. He had hated being forced by his father to swim in the water and he had cried.

The car's windscreen is smashed and the front seats are covered in lozenges of glass, glass that does not cut him when he picks up a few pieces and scatters them in the road. To his amusement the glass goes bobbing along the road. Grabbing another handful he throws it up into the air and is delighted when the glass bounces off the car's roof. What does it matter if someone hears him? Into the car he climbs, discovering a brick stuck between the driver and the passenger seats: why should anyone want to smash the window of a car? Cars are precious, scarce: they aren't for burning and smashing, or for leaving in the middle of the street. The ignition key is still in the lock, and without a second thought Liam twists the key first one way and then the other. The windscreen wipers clatter uselessly in the empty frame, scattering pieces of glass into Liam's face. Fumbling, his eyes tightly shut, he twists off the ignition.

Eyes still shut he backs out of the car: a piece of glass has hit his eye. He runs a finger across it and gazes at the nearby houses through his other eye to see if anyone is coming to investigate the noise. He turns away and walks to the broad street that runs parallel with the road on which the church sits.

The broad street connects with a nearby avenue which in turn joins the main road to form three of the borders to the area. Liam looks down the street and for the first time he shivers with unease. Across the bottom of the street there seems to be a black wall. What is it? Some form of barricade. He does not wait to find out. He turns on his heels and runs up the street towards the avenue.

Should he shout out for Kathleen. Should he call out for his da?

'Kathleen!'

He stops dead, so surprised is he by the loudness of his own voice. He waits for a reply, but nothing breaks the deep hush of the night. He walks on down the street, now more careful, now more aware of danger.

From some distance off he hears the roar of an engine. An engine that whines out into the night, complaining about its misuse. As the roar approaches young Liam pushes his way into a little garden, closing the wooden gate behind him. He crouches behind the low wall and waits for the sound of the engine to pass the junction, but it does not. Raising his head enough to peer over the wall he sees an armoured vehicle slowly come to a halt before the barricade slung across the broad street where it joins with the avenue. The armoured car is lightless and still. It seems to stand before the barricade and ruminate, its steel body half in shadow and half in moonlight.

Is it coming after me? Liam asks himself. He waits, breathing hard, sure that he is too far away to be heard, waiting to run as fast as he can back down the road to his own safe street. The armoured vehicle backs away from the flimsy barricade. He can see the wheels of the vehicle turn and then stop. Has it changed its mind? Yes. A throaty roar and the vehicle climbs the barricade as if it were made of cardboard. Liam stands up and as quickly ducks back down again as the metal pig creeps down the middle of the street towards his hiding place. Moving on all fours young Liam shifts himself over to the wall facing the street, before lowering himself in among the flowers and shrubs of the well-kept garden. He makes himself as small, as silent as possible. Should he make a run for it? He holds his breath until it hurts. The tension of waiting for the monster to pass numbs his brain until all his thoughts are concentrated upon an earwig as it crawls across the back of his moon-silvered hand. It seems to take forever to find its way across, it pauses below the knuckle of his middle finger as if it has decided on a new direction before it slowly, carefully moves on across his hand. He loathes all insects and desperately wants to brush it away, but even that might attract the armoured car's attention.

As the vehicle approaches, its metal doors are flung open and a cascade of harsh, angry, bitter abuse breaks into the warm night air. Liam takes his chance and brushes off the earwig before lifting himself up to watch the armoured car pass the garden with three laughing soldiers hanging precariously from the back. A fat, squat soldier is pushed by one of his comrades on to the road and the armoured car speeds off with the fat little soldier waddling behind like a piglet following its mother. Liam watches as the vehicle stops as if to allow the piglet to climb back on board, but then speeds off again.

'You lousy bastards!' screams the soldier. His cry is

answered with whoops of laughter, half-smothered by the thick steel casing.

Liam opens the wooden gate to the street and gazes down to the black wall at the bottom. He hears an engine start and red lights come on and the wall divides to admit the dark bulk of the armoured car. The fat little soldier has given up the chase and is walking casually down the right-hand pavement, his rifle swinging like a walking stick. Liam turns away and runs quickly up to the straggling barricade.

'Kathleen!' he shouts out. If he can't find his sister or his father how is he to get back into the house? Will he have to wander the streets all night?

'Kathleen!'

Silence. Emptiness.

'Kathleen!'

Nothing.

Liam steps into the broad avenue, his gaze wanders over the old baths' house and the adjacent street and he wonders if there are any people left in the world.

TWENTY-FOUR

KENNY LETS THE filthy cloth slip back into the bucket of black water. If you want a job done, do it yourself. He lights a cigarette before picking up his leather jacket and flicking open the door with his foot.

The club has started to empty, a few people still dance in the middle of the floor, but most sit around the tables quietly drinking and talking. As Kenny passes most men acknowledge his passing and he either smiles or nods, depending on how he feels about each individual. He knows exactly who warrants a smile and who does not. He kicks open the door to the toilets and is assailed by a stench that is a mixture of sour urine, stale beer and vomit. He quickly washes his hands, holding his breath, and gets out into the fresh air of the street, past Joe and some others in the entrance hall.

'Joe!' he calls.

'Wha'?'

'Away an' clean them friggin' toilets!'

'Are you jokin', or what?'

'No, I'm not jokin'! Away an' clean them fuckin' toilets or I'll use your coat to clean them m'self!'

He turns back into the entrance hall and gives Joe one of his most malevolent looks. It does not work on Joe.

'If you want th' friggin' toilets done, away an' ask oul Mrs McFarlane to clean 'em!'

'I'm not askin' you t' clean 'em! I'm fuckin' well tellin' you t' clean 'em! Now away an' do as you're told or I'll tear your head off an' use it as an ashtray!'

'Aye, an' I love you, too,' mutters Joe, glaring defiantly.

'Well?'

'Well what?' asks Joe, not moving a muscle.

In the silence between Kenny and Joe, Eddie goes on

99

smoking his cigarette and Tommy looks into his beer. They all wait to see what Kenny will do. When the blow comes Tommy looks away, divided in loyalty and emotion. Joe falls back against the wooden wall and stays where he has been put, but his fists clench and unclench.

'If you read the standing orders of the club you'll find that the duty watch is responsible for cleaning the club,' says Kenny, turning from the argument of force to the force of argument. 'That means gettin' down on your hands and knees and cleanin' it. Now go an' get the gear from the storeroom. If they're not clean you'll be in trouble. Come on, youse two,' he says coldly to Eddie and Tommy.

Eddie stamps on his cigarette and nods to Tommy to follow him. They leave Joe turning away and smashing his fist into the swinging doors.

'Discipline,' mutters Kenny as he sinks into the passenger seat next to Ginger. Discipline was going to run the club as it was going to save the country.

'He was goin' t' hit ye back there,' laughs Eddie.

'He was too, the wee bastard.'

'You'll have your hands full if he tore after ye.'

'Aye,' chuckles Kenny, 'thank Christ he didn't.'

Eddie and Tommy are in the back of the car. Tommy makes sure his revolver isn't falling from his pocket and wonders if Kenny really meant for him to come along on patrol. Is he really one of them? One of the special few? Why has Kenny picked him? Because he dealt with that troublemaker? Is that all? Is that really why? He folds his arms and looks out the window at the club's entrance. When Geoff tumbles out of the club with a girl and sees the company he is in, part of the inner circle, Tommy is elated by Geoff's astonished look.

'Did you leave wee Gloria home all right, Tommy?'

'Aye, I did, Kenny.'

The others chuckle and Tommy wonders if they are laughing at him.

'Did you get a goodnight kiss?'

Tommy says nothing.

'Well? Did you get a goodnight kiss or not?' asks Eddie.

'Leave the man alone. If he doesn't want to talk about his

women he doesn't want to talk about his women,' suggests Ginger.

'Did she let you kiss her?' asks Kenny with a warm laugh that almost makes Tommy break his promise not to blather.

'Leave the lad alone,' says Ginger. 'Still waters run deep.'

'Well if he's sayin' nothin' somethin' must've happened,' says Kenny. 'Right! Where 're we goin'?'

'Where d'ya want t' go?' asks Ginger, starting the engine.

'Ach, anywhere.'

'Anywhere? Anywhere it is.' Ginger slips into gear and twists the steering-wheel.

'Slow tour of the area.'

'Right!' Ginger doesn't mind if they drive for a few hours with no particular place to go. It's all the same to him. It's all a bit of excitement. An escape from the usual boredom of his life; an escape from working in the bowels of the oil tanker welding walk-ways in the holds. An escape from a nagging, never-satisfied wife and her constant demands for money. Money, and ways to get it, constantly occupy his thoughts. He dreams of holding five, ten, twenty thousand pounds in his hands; he dreams of ways of spending it, a car, a house, a garage business mending cars.

'Turn up here, Ginger.'

'Left?'

'Right.'

He steers smoothly round the corner and the headlights flash across the paint-daubed walls and into the darkest corners of an alleyway.

'Is your wireless workin'?'

'Na. It's not, Kenny.'

'Pity, could use a bit of quiet music after that racket.'

Ginger swings the car round another corner, he knows the maze so well.

'Take it easy, no rush: we've got all night.'

'Aye,' sighs Eddie.

'All night,' mutters Ginger to himself; he rests back into the comfortable seat. 'We'll have t' siphon off some petrol from somewhere.'

'No problem.'

'No problem,' agrees Eddie.

'You all right, Tommy?'

'Aye. I'm fine, Kenny.'

'Just makin' sure everythin's AOK, you know?'

'Aye,' replies Tommy, not knowing.

'How old's that wee girl?'

'Ach, she's seventeen.'

'Sweet seventeen, eh?'

'Aye.'

'Eddie, see how many love bites he's got on him.'

'Come here, then.'

Eddie attempts to pull Tommy's collar down, but Tommy escapes.

'Saw one at least, Kenny.'

'Just one, eh?'

They laugh easily before turning their heads to look out the open windows of the car as it slowly creeps along the silent street.

'Hey, where could we get ourselves somethin' t' eat? I'm starved so I am.' Kenny turns to look at Eddie who is sunk into the back of the car. He sits up.

'Well, there's that hamburger place down by the bridge.'

'Will that be open t'night?' questions Ginger.

'It stays open late most nights.'

'When there's been trouble?'

'Ach, what trouble was there t'night?'

'Well we can't go out of the area.'

'Why's that?' asks Kenny.

'Because we're up t' our teeth with gear, Kenny!' exclaims Ginger with annoyed disgust.

'So what?'

'So what if we get hauled over by the RUC or Army outside the barricade?'

'They'll steal our hamburgers.'

'They'll stick's in th' Kesh an' throw away th' keys!' Ginger's voice breaks and he looks to Kenny, begging for him to have some sense. Kenny smiles.

'Scared?'

'I've a family t' look after.'

'Who hasn't?' asks Kenny.

They observe each other for some seconds, each reconsidering their opinion of the other. To Kenny, Ginger seems to have lost some of his mad indifference. To Ginger, Kenny seems to have gained a pointless need to risk their freedom, as if he were looking for a brick wall to drive into. Sure he had done a lot of mad things in the last couple of years as their world seemed to break apart, toss and spin, but now things were quietening down. They had been lucky when others had not.

'What are you carrying?'

'A lifetime's worth of trouble.'

'What?'

'That 9mm.'

'You've had it rebored, haven't you?'

'Aye, but couldn't get a new pin.'

'Ach, what are you worried about?'

'What do you want me to do?' Ginger asks, flustered that Tommy should be listening to their conversation: another tacit rule of the game broken by Kenny.

'Up to get a cheeseburger.'

'Cheeseburger it is.'

'Come on, Ginger. They'll stop nobody t'night.'

'How do you know, Eddie?'

Eddie remains silent. He doesn't like it either, but what can he tell Kenny?

Ginger puts his foot down and the car races off down a street heading for the main road and a late-night meal. Is this going to be it? Is this what had made him feel so uneasy earlier on in the evening? He can feel his right eye muscle start to twitch and his skin grow cold. Why isn't he strong enough to tell Kenny to catch himself on? Of all the stupid things to do! He curses himself and then curses out loud.

'What's the matter?'

'Kenny, this is fuckin' stupid.'

'I want a cheeseburger. Th' trouble with you, Ginger, is that you're too smart. You think too much.'

'Well somebody has to.'

'You could be right. But I still want m' cheeseburger all the same.'

'You're gettin' your cheeseburger.'

'Good man.'

'Mad man.'

They fall silent and look at the road ahead as Ginger takes his anger out on the engine. He ignores the traffic lights and all the white lines on the road.

'Okay, Ginger,' mutters Kenny quietly so that Eddie cannot hear him, 'take it easy.'

'What's the matter?'

'Ginger, for God sake get a grip!' shouts Eddie, leaning forward to push Ginger's shoulder. 'We want t' eat a hamburger, not end up in one.'

Kenny laughs and squeezes the door handle. The car powers along the long, broad road until it passes under a railway bridge and Ginger takes his foot off the accelerator and changes down. He pulls the car into the kerb behind three or four other cars and a green landrover. A soldier crouches in the doorway of a car spares shop, his rifle pointed towards the roofs across the street. He turns his head as the car pulls in and looks long and hard at Ginger.

'Ah, fuck,' sighs Ginger.

'Ach, have some guts, Ginger. What do youse all want?'

'Out of here.'

'Cheeseburger and chips.'

'Same for me,' says Tommy.

Kenny opens the car door and smiles at the soldier.

'Mornin'.'

'Morning,' returns the yawning soldier.

'Nice night t' be on duty, eh?'

'Sure it is, mate.'

'Done nine years of it myself.'

'Yeah?'

'Aye.'

'What regiment?'

Kenny tells him the regiment and where he was stationed. The soldier seems impressed.

'Sorry I ever left.'

'Yeah?'

'Aye,' says Kenny with a sigh.

Kenny waves a goodbye and heads for the welcoming lights of the hamburger bar. Inside a soldier is searching for his money to pay for his order while another gazes out on to the dangerous city streets with a bored expression. Kenny nods towards two fellas he knows from the club and waits for the serving girl to get round to him. He can feel the weight of his pistol stuck in his jeans, but he tells himself it will be better if he pays for the food.

His laugh attracts the attentions of those waiting to be served.

'Just laughin' at m' own joke, you know?' he says to the soldier as the man heads out to the landrover with his mates' meal.

TWENTY-FIVE

'DAMN!' EXCLAIMS LIAM to himself.

He looks about: he has five choices. He immediately excludes two of them, obvious dead-ends; a third looks promising until he turns a corner and sees that it, too, comes to an end in a little roundabout; the fourth choice is to retrace his steps, the thought of which he cannot bear; the fifth is to set off down a long street and hope it leads him nearer to home. He rests against a gable wall. Has he been walking in the wrong direction, he asks himself? Yes. Pain has returned to his ribs and legs. The memory of running, of being hunted and chased, comes into his mind with jagged sharpness; but not the memory of who had done the hunting. Fear returns, tightening his muscles and quickening his heart.

He remembers stepping out from his house on to the pavement and immediately being swept along by the crowd as they ran away from danger. Danger they had perceived as if they were connected by a thousand electric wires into a single mind. He had run too, until it hurt to run. He stopped when others stopped. He turned when others turned. He watched as flames burst into the night sky for a second or two before dissolving. He watched as windows were smashed and flames ran up the walls of the houses. He did not run to counter-attack. Instead he sat on the kerb and looked on as the crowd ran towards the flames to put out the fires.

He turns down the long street, now walking slowly: what does it matter if it is three o'clock, four o'clock or five o'clock before he reaches home? What does it matter if he doesn't go to work in the morning? He is exhausted, hungry, profoundly weary of having to survive day after day with little to show for all the effort and all the worry.

His life is finished, he tells himself half seriously; only Kathleen and Liam keep him going on. Keep him fighting for work and a decent wage.

He rests against a lamp post and swears to himself that he will take his kids and himself back to England. Back to a decent life. Away from the hatred and hysteria. What has it to do with him? Would his life improve if tomorrow they lived in a united country? No. Would he be any better off? Definitely not. No use waiting on others to improve his lot. No use waiting for the first day of a new age.

What wouldn't he give for a sit down and a pint of stout? What wouldn't he give to be wrapped in blankets and dreaming of Ann, the nurse. He can still smell her scent on his clothes. Still remember the curve of her breasts and the warmth of her body as she had bent over to attend to his wounds.

Where had she come from? He seriously starts to think she may have been a part of a dream. He closes his eyes and leans his head back against the lamp post. He can see her face more clearly now, she is smiling at him, her hands on her hips and her legs slightly apart. She begins to unbutton her shirt and remove her brassiere.

He shakes himself out of the daydream. Ask her out, but don't fantasise, he tells himself. He peers down at his legs when he feels something nudge against them. A black cat looks him in the eye.

'Sorry, pussy, am I in the way?'

The cat miaows and rubs the side of its face against Liam's right leg.

'Oh, what a beauty you are, pussy cat. Are you out havin' a good time, boy?' He tickles the cat under its chin and on top of its head. It purrs in response and starts to lick his fingers. 'You don't know how I can get home, do you boy? No, I don't suppose you do.'

He straightens himself up and leaves the cat to its lamp post. The street turns leftwards and goes down a bit of a hill. The houses are identical in almost every respect, except for the occasional occupier who has painted the window and door surrounds a colour other than white. Union Flags hang from flag-poles fastened to the brick work just above the doors; many of the flags are worn and tattered, dirty and old. He comes to a junction, a small street leads down to a warehouse-like building, some garages and a couple of tattered shops. The street offers him no hope whatsoever and he sighs a deep sigh before trudging on.

Liam comes to the end of the street and at last sees a familiar name high on a gable wall. He will be home soon. He has made it difficult for himself by avoiding main roads, but now he hasn't far to go. He passes the street name and walks out on to the main road: he's not five hundred yards from safety. He turns right and passes a bar. His foot kicks something lying on the pavement and when he looks down he sees his own unshaven mug and a perfect image of the moon above his right shoulder. He smiles to himself. He picks up the unbroken mirror and sets it against the white tiled wall of the bar. He thinks it a miracle that anything could remain intact on such a night. He walks on, relaxing as he sees well-known shops; little danger now. He has two choices, either to walk on down towards the river before turning right to his street, or to turn into the tree-lined avenue before entering his area. The thought of walking down the avenue doesn't please him, it is too open, leaving him exposed; walking towards the river provides him with many shop doorways to hide in, but means he'll have to walk past the police barracks.

He halts before the gutted remains of what used to be an off-licence. Smashed bottles of whisky and beer lie over the pavement and a heavy stench of alcohol rises into his nostrils. He peers into the dark interior of the shop and understands why no one has bothered to board it up; the place has been cleaned out. A few bottles of beer lie on the floor. Why not? he decides before stepping into the off-licence and picking up a bottle of beer and banging off its top against a shelf. It's not what he usually drinks, but it quenches his thirst and cleans out his mouth.

He finishes off the bottle with three large gulps. It's done him some good. He thinks about the pints he'll have after work on Saturday afternoon: four pints, that's all. He'll make it an even half dozen this week. Every pound he can afford goes into the bank and stays there, no matter what. He runs the figures over in his head, and is pleased with the total. He drops the bottle to the floor and picks up another two which he fits into his jacket pockets. Why let them go to waste? Nobody will miss them.

He stands by the window frame, looking up and down the road, making sure he will not be seen emerging. It would be stupid to be arrested for looting after all that he has been through. He steps out on to the street and immediately halts.

What is that?

From somewhere down the road he can hear an engine race. Back into the off-licence he goes. Putting both his hands on the bottles of beer he makes ready to throw them to the floor, just in case. The racing engine quickly bears down on his hiding place. He crouches. He waits. Is it slowing down?

No.

The car races past. Back out into the night he goes, sure that he will soon be at home enjoying the only gain he's had out of the night's events. He leaves his right hand on the bottle of beer; if something happens it is his only weapon.

TWENTY-SIX

THE HELICOPTER SEARCHLIGHT casts its false daylight upon the sprawling roads and streets of the city, momentarily poking its intense glare into the moon shadows and on to roofs, houses, factories and shops, overpowering the gentle moonlight before flitting elsewhere. It never seems to find what it is looking for, but it goes on looking into the corners of the urban spread without seeming to have pattern or purpose.

'God awful city,' mutters James into his whisky tumbler. From where he stands the beam of light seems eerily disembodied; he cannot hear the rotor blades that keep so many men, women and children awake. Catching a draught from the old casement window he pulls his dressing-gown tight around his tubby frame. He knows he is quite drunk, and when he is drunk he cannot help but think of what might have been. Thoughts of failure and purposelessness invade his mind and he curses himself for not having pushed himself harder, taken more chances politically: even if he had suffered humiliating defeat at least he would have tried and so been able to live with himself. He reaches for the decanter, it is almost empty.

Looking across the city he can see the helicopter turn off to the right and merge with a thousand other lights as it switches off its searchlight and becomes another part of the amorphous Christmas tree. He takes a sip of whisky and lets it slop back in his mouth.

'God awful fucking city.'

For a few seconds he thinks about the tens of thousands of people lying in their warm comfortable beds, most of them, he thinks, losers like himself. He thinks about those locked within their ghettos who have always lost in the quasi-state and mythologised their loss. Now they were taking their revenge, but revenge is avenged, action has a reaction – ad infinitum. He yawns. He thinks about those who had always considered themselves to be the winners, but who were destined to lose in the end. He could sympathise with both sides. A clash of nationalities, both incipient; little to do with religion, he knows. He yawns and covers his mouth. Better to have the island united, but in blood? Never. No matter what lines are drawn on a map. A pointless, grubby little war that disgraces absolutely everyone. He should pack it in and go home to write his memoirs. He laughs, the thought of chopping down a small forest to trouble the world with his minor role in its affairs is not appealing.

He turns away from the window to sit himself down. The small room is absolutely still, hushed. He surveys the home decor and thinks about the pleasant evenings he has had with his wife in the room, watching the television. They could quite often forget the outside world. Forget that the violence on the TV news was happening just down the road. His son had sat in the armchair opposite and commiserated effusively with him. He had protested, with little conviction, that the job wasn't at all as bad as everyone thought it was. He wasn't in the graveyard yet. The job was a challenge, he protested . . . one he wished had been offered to some other poor bugger. An interminable mess. Impossible to untie? Perhaps it would be best to cut and run. He sips his whisky and notices that the time is almost two-thirty. He tells himself that he should be in bed preparing his body and mind for a morning before the cameras as a world-weary politician fed up with the barbarism of the natives. He will talk sententiously about the battle going on between the civilised rule of law and atavistic violence, about those who seek to change the order of things by an inexcusable waste of human life. He will inform those watching that if a majority of the populace wishes to change the constitution of the province all they have to do is vote for it. He knows how to talk to a camera, how to speak, pause and look. He always imagines himself to be speaking directly to the most obtuse of his constituents. He is readily aware that he was only offered the job because of his ability to appear before the camera and look like a reasonable man talking commonsense. He rather enjoys being somewhat famous, a weakness he accepts.

Violence, he knows, is quite an acceptable fact of life in the province. Violence, he knows, is politics by another name. Violence, he knows, will continue and continue, no matter what he or his colleagues say: heaven and history know that his own country has used it often. Crimes committed in youth, forbidden to others in old age. The thought produces a chuckle.

Time, James tells himself, is the only solution. Time and an end to the awful banality of murder. He picks up the decanter and refreshes his glass for the last time: no more. He raises the tumbler to his lips and sees the whisky off. He enjoys the bite as it sinks into his stomach. He's turning into an old soak, he decides. So what? Does it matter? Slightly better than being hit by a bus or waiting to die in bed of cancer, famous last words composed.

He chuckles again as he twists the door open. Out he goes into the hushed corridor. What silence. What solitude. He allows himself to feel slightly, self-pityingly sad at being alone.

Pack it all in, he tells himself.

TWENTY-SEVEN

KATHLEEN COMES TO a halt as the little row of houses comes to a halt. A large open space begins. Like an animal nervous of stepping into the open, she pauses by the last window of the last house. Up and down the street cars are parked and she watches as a car drives off from outside a wooden hall built into the far corner of the derelict land.

It is a new world to her, strange and confusing. She turns and looks down the street: how does she find her way back to the avenue? Does she go on? Does she go into the wooden hall? The buzz of people talking and laughing inside sounds warm and friendly to her; yet she is not where she belongs. Not at all where she belongs. She dismisses from her mind the idea that her father could be in the hall. Never in a million years would he go near such a place, in such an area.

From out of the hall come a man and a woman, walking slightly apart. The woman, who is taller than her companion, leads the way with confidence. The trailing man is dressed in a three-piece suit, white shirt and brightly striped tie, his hair is swept back and held with grease; he moves slowly over what used to be the pavement, but when he has stumbled a couple of times he takes the easier route of the roadway. The woman stops before Kathleen, swaying slightly.

'Wha's th' matter, love?'

Kathleen stares into her face.

'Are you waitin' on your daddy?'

Kathleen can smell the drink on her breath and the strong sweet scent of her perfume.

'Aye,' mumbles Kathleen with nothing else to say.

'What's his name?'

She does not, cannot, reply.

'Wha's th' matter, Lizzie?' asks the man, coming to a swaying halt behind her. 'Who's th' wee girl?'

'Ach, shut up, I'm tryin' t' find that out, amn't I.'

'Give's th' key an' I'll open the door,' slurs the man with his hand upturned at a ninety-degree angle; he sways from his waist up. He lifts his other hand to make sure his tie is straight.

'Wha's your father's name, love?'

'Dave Inglis,' says Kathleen, pulling the only name she can think of out of the back of her mind.

'Dave Inglis?' the man repeats. 'Isn't he on the radio?'

'No.'

'Well there's an Inglis on the radio.'

'Ach, shut up. Here's th' key. Away in an' sleep it off.' Lizzie slaps the door key into his hand and turns away from him with as much contempt as she can display in a single movement.

'Ach, you look after her, Lizzie.'

He saunters off unsteadily.

'I've heard the name, but I don't think I saw him in the club. You want me t' go an' get him?'

'No. You're all right.'

'Are you sure now?'

'Aye.'

'He shouldn't leave you out here at this time of night.'

'Ach, I'm okay,' says Kathleen, standing.

'Where do you live, love?'

'Over there.'

'Over where?'

'There,' repeats Kathleen with a wave down the street.

'What street?' asks Lizzie. The girl's definitely not from round here, she decides.

'I have t' go.'

'What street?'

Kathleen stares into the woman's face, trying her hardest to remember the name of a street she has passed.

'Have you just come from across the water?' asks Lizzie.

'Aye,' replies Kathleen, hoping her answer will get rid of the kind woman.

'Well, you go in there an' pull your father out by the scruff of his neck.'

114

'He said he'd be out in a wee while.'

'They're all the same, so they are. There's not one of them worth a fart.' Lizzie smiles her warmest smile for the pretty young girl with the English accent. 'I'll come out in five minutes to see if you're okay,' says Lizzie as she follows her husband to their house just down the road.

'Ach, you're okay,' says Kathleen, softly.

'What sort of father would leave you standin' in th' street at this time of night?' asks Lizzie as she turns back to face Kathleen. If only she had had a daughter like her, she thinks.

'Ach, I'm all right, Missus.'

'Nonsense!' exclaims Lizzie good-humouredly. She turns away from Kathleen and walks on down to her door.

Kathleen squeezes between two parked cars and starts towards the wooden hall, walking down the middle of the road. She halts just before the entrance and listens to the noise of talk, music and laughter coming from within. They must be enjoying themselves, she decides. She steps towards the doors.

'What can I do you for?' asks a fella sitting on the floor near to the entrance doors.

'I'm lookin' for m' da.'

'What's his name?' asks Joe.

'Dave.'

'Dave what?'

'Smith.'

'Dave Smith?'

'Aye,' confirms Kathleen, hoping that it sounds okay.

'Never heard of him. Do you want t' go in an' take a look?'

'Can I?'

'No problem,' confirms the man before putting the glass of beer to his swollen lips. He moves his feet to allow the girl to enter. 'You wouldn't do's a favour, would you?'

He reaches into his jacket pocket and fishes out a crumpled five-pound note which he dangles before Kathleen. She hesitates, should she turn and run? The bird in her stomach has begun to flutter again and she can taste a sickness in her mouth. Does he know who she is? Where she comes from? Was he one of the fellas who tried their best to destroy her street?

'Wha'?' says Kathleen, softly.

'Bring's a couple 'f bottles of Harp lager, will ye?'

She does not respond, does not reach out to take the money. She remains still, ready to turn and flee.

'Wha's th' matter?' asks Joe. He keeps the five-pound note dangling before her, but does not bother to look at her: he wants a drink, he wants to be drunk. 'Will you not do's a favour?' he asks again, pleading; how can he walk to the bar, past all those who he knows will look at his battered face and laugh. 'You can buy yourself a drink if you want.'

'Well okay,' mutters Kathleen; at least it will give her a reason to enter the hall.

'Hey?'

Kathleen turns back to face him, sure that he has discovered that she does not belong. Is it her clothes? The way she talks? Her face and hair? She looks into his face and then past him out to the street.

'Wha's m' face look like?'

What does he mean?

'Is it cut? Do I have a shiner?'

He pushes his face up at Kathleen. She bends down slightly to look at his features.

'Your lip's cut.'

'Bad?'

'Na, not bad at all.'

'Have I a black eye?'

'No.'

'You sure?'

'Positive.'

'Ach,' mutters Joe, 'he didn't hit me too hard.'

'Who?' asks Kathleen, softly.

'Ach, your man,' is all that Joe can be bothered to answer. 'Where're you from?'

'Over there.'

'Over where?'

'Over there.'

Joe shakes his head and decides it doesn't matter. He's never had any luck with girls. He wishes he was taller, but he is never going to be.

'Bring's them beers, will ye? I'm dyin' of thirst here.'

'All right,' says Kathleen, deciding she is safe with this particular Protestant.

She pushes open the doors and immediately sees a red and white flag hanging on the opposite wall. The tables near to the door are mostly empty except for a girl who sits by herself and smiles at Kathleen as she comes through the doors.

'Hello.'

'Hello,' returns Kathleen.

She lets the door close behind her and searches the hall slowly and carefully. She knows at least one set of eyes are staring at her, but she feels strangely indifferent. She has steeled herself to do what she has to do.

'Who're you lookin' for?' asks the girl sitting alone.

'I'm lookin' for a friend.'

'What's their name?'

'Dave,' says Kathleen; she glances at the girl as she walks a little way into the hall. She can feel more eyes fixing upon her.

'Dave who?'

Kathleen turns to face the voice. The girl's eyes are shining bright.

'Dave Rogers?' asks the girl. Her voice is excitedly strained. 'Or Dave Kennedy?' She comes very close to Kathleen and raises a finger to point into a dark corner of the hall. 'Dave Kennedy is over there.'

'It's not Dave Kennedy.'

'Then who is it?' the girl asks.

'Dave Smith,' says Kathleen, sharply. She walks further into the hall, but the girl continues to follow her. None of the faces sitting at the tables or dancing around the floor is the face she wants to see. She hardly expected him to be here, but he just might have been.

'Dave Smith? What street's he from?'

'He's not from around here.'

'Where's he from?'

'England.'

'England?' says the girl with mild surprise. She stops dead to watch the stranger walk hesitantly to the bar-hatch looking from table to table as she goes.

117

England? Does that explain why she looks out of place? Betty is determined to ask her more questions.

'What can I get ye?' the barman asks Kathleen.

'Can I have two bottles of Harp lager for the fella on the door, please?'

'Sure ye can,' replies Jimmy with a knowing grin.

'Can't Joe come an' get his own drink,' comments a middle-aged man propping up the bar at Kathleen's elbow. 'Doesn't wee Joe wants us to see his big black eye?' The man's laugh splutters into life, it sounds harsh, but is warm and good-natured.

'He doesn't have a black eye,' says Kathleen.

'Oh, doesn't he?' says the man with a deeper laugh that makes Kathleen feel safe to be by his side. 'Well if he doesn't get that toilet cleaned he'll get a lot more than a black when Kenny comes back. Won't he, Jimmy?'

'You're tellin' me,' says Jimmy, dropping the bottles of lager on the counter and taking the banknote from Kathleen's hand.

Betty comes to stand between Kathleen and the middle-aged man. She stares closely at Kathleen, without seeming to care if Kathleen notices her glare or not. Kathleen feels threatened by her presence, as if at any moment the girl at her back is going to raise her voice and denounce her. Then what? She waits with increasing impatience and annoyance as the barman fumbles in his cash box for some change. Is he deliberately being so slow? Are the men and women at her back closing in on her? She feels Betty's eyes gnaw into her neck and she begins to regret ever having come near the hall. Her gaze strays over the bar, over its flags, pictures and drawings; over the whiskey, dark rum, vodka and gin.

Kathleen glances over her shoulder and sees that Betty has taken a seat at her back. Briefly she catches her eye before turning back to the bar as the middle-aged man speaks.

'You Joe's wee girl?'

'No, I'm not,' says Kathleen sharply. 'He just asked me to get him the beer.'

'Well you're a good lookin' wee girl. He could do a lot worse for himself.'

Kathleen smiles weakly and starts to roll up a beer mat as her nerves tighten.

'Ach, Jimmy, where's the wee girl's change?' asks the man.

'Just hold your horses. I've no change left, Sammy.'

'Give the wee girl back her money an' put it on my slate,' says Sammy.

Jimmy returns to Kathleen and gives her the note.

'Tell that bloody eejit to do as he's told!' says Jimmy.

'Or he'll have plastic kneecaps by the mornin',' says the middle-aged man with a booming laugh.

'Or a plastic brain,' says Jimmy.

'Ach, you're an awful hard man, Jimmy.'

Kathleen turns away from the bar with the two bottles of beer in her right hand and the five-pound note in her left. She knows, without looking, that Betty has stood to follow her through the hall. As she reaches the dance floor a record she loves starts to play and a tall man with a small woman comes twirling towards her out of control.

'Sorry, love,' says the little woman as they push Kathleen into a chair.

'That's all right.'

'Watch where you're goin'!'

'I can't do two things at once,' protests the man as he slides his hand on to her bum.

'Hands off!' protests the woman, 'concentrate on th' dancin'!'

Kathleen avoids the other dancing couples and makes it back to the entrance hall. She puts the bottles down by Joe's glass and starts to step over Joe to reach the freedom of the street.

'Have you no change for me?'

Kathleen stops and turns.

'Ach, sorry: I forgot.' She hands him the five-pound note. 'A man at th' bar bought you them.'

'Did he indeed. What's his name?'

'Sammy.'

'Ach, he's a decent man. Where're you goin'?'

'Home,' says Kathleen, not having anything else she can say.

'Aren't you goin' to' stay an' have a wee dance?'

'Can't,' says Kathleen.

'Wha's th' matter?' asks Joe seeing the girl's face twitch almost as if she's been slapped.

'I have t' go.'

They both turn as the doors to the hall swing open and Betty stumbles through them.

'She's a Fenian.'

Joe looks into Kathleen's face and immediately sees that Betty is right. He stands and places an arm across the doorway to the street. Kathleen remains rooted to the spot as if she were an animal caught in the lights of an oncoming car.

'What are you doin' here?' asks Joe, not at all unfriendly.

Kathleen glances up, not answering.

'She's probably left a bomb in the club, Joe.'

'Ach, she had nothin' with her.'

'Well maybe she's got friends waitin' outside?'

'No!' cries Kathleen. She feels desperately trapped; desperately afraid. Pleading to be allowed to leave she stares into Joe's eyes. 'I was lookin' for my dad.'

'What would your da be doin' in here?'

'I was just makin' sure.'

'If your da came in here he wouldn't get out again,' says Joe in a neutral, matter-of-fact sort of way.

Kathleen can feel her hands and legs start to tremble.

'What are you goin' t' do with her, Joe?'

Joe eyes Kathleen and Kathleen studies the beer-stained floor.

The silence, absence of a decision, is unbearable for her and she can feel the tears start to form in her eyes. She will do anything he tells her to do. She will not struggle.

'Joe, what 're you goin' t' do?'

'Ach, will ye shut your mouth, Betty?' says Joe with a soft disgust. 'Don't you know where your da is?'

'No, I don't,' says Kathleen.

'She's lyin',' says Betty with a huff. 'She's in here spyin' for the IRA.'

'Why do you think he'd come in here? Is he a drinkin' man?'

'He doesn't drink that much,' says Kathleen.

'Then why would he come in here? After there's been trouble an' all?'

'I don't know.' She finally dares to raise her head. The once friendly face is now impassive. 'I was just lookin' for him. I don't know where he is.'

'Well your da would have to be a moron t' come danderin' in here for a pint of double!'

She drops her head and studies the floor again as he takes a little step towards her. She steps back and flinches, cowering. Can she push past him and make it out to the street?

'I've been lookin' for him all night,' says Kathleen, finally managing a lie.

'You English?'

'We lived there.'

'Not anymore you don't!'

'Aye, I know!' cries Kathleen, dearly wishing that she did live there again. England had meant lying awake listening to shouts, screams and banging doors: but had not meant the electric hatred she can feel now, tingling her skin as she waits for the young man to decide her fate. He folds his arms and examines her thoughtfully. Kathleen can almost sense his indecision as she bows her head and waits, waits as she seems to have been waiting all night; waits as she seems to have spent much of her life.

'Put her in the back room 'til Kenny gets back, Joe.'

Joe looks up at the mention of Kenny's name.

'Away an' get yourself a drink, Betty,' says Joe, holding out the five-pound note. She hesitates, but eventually comes timidly forward to take the proffered money. Once the money is in her pocket she turns swiftly to Kathleen and brings her opened hand sharply down upon her head. Kathleen shrinks away and cries out in pain and disgust as she feels the girl's spittle land on her cheek.

'Dirty Fenian bitch!' exclaims Betty, exhilarated that she has found someone she can spit on. She turns and pushes her way through the doors.

'You'll get more of that if you don't go back t' where you belong,' says Joe in a hard, but not threatening tone. He takes his handkerchief from his jacket pocket and wipes the spittle from off Kathleen's face and hand. 'She's not all there, you know?' Joe touches his forehead and smiles.

121

'Can I go?'

'Sure you can go.'

She steps towards the door with a look over her shoulder to make sure he is really letting her regain her freedom.

'Take care.'

'I will,' says Kathleen.

She steps out and hurries back down the street as quick as she can without actually breaking into a run.

Joe stands at the entrance door watching her go, knowing his generosity may not be appreciated by Kenny, Ginger and Eddie when they return from their patrol. Why should her da come back to this place? Joe asks himself. He thumbs the money in his pocket and wonders if it is enough to take him to England.

TWENTY-EIGHT

YOUNG LIAM DUCKS into a shop doorway to crouch low and wait for the speeding car to scream by. A small kitten looks out at him from the shop and it paws the glass in salute; Liam smiles and returns the salute by tapping his fingertips lightly on the window. The car passes his hiding place. He stands to watch it take a corner and scream off into silence.

Out on the road a set of traffic lights go through their colour changes with no one except Liam there to witness it. A dog waiting by a Belisha beacon looks carefully before ambling across the empty road to raise a lazy leg at one of its territorial markers. In the night sky, near the place where the road crosses the river, a set of red lights flash urgently as a helicopter drifts over the city.

As Liam walks down the broad main road he feels himself to be wrapped in warm bedclothes. To check that he is not in fact still asleep he kicks an object lying on the pavement and runs to catch it before it goes spinning into the gutter. He is sad to see that he has scratched, but not broken, the plastic sphere of a souvenir snow storm. Holding it up to the light of a street lamp he gives the sphere a flick and watches the snow fall over the little figures standing in a family group. Bringing it closer to his face he studies the family. They all seem well wrapped up to survive the blizzards going on in their world. A little boy, half the size of his sister, holds the ropes to a sleigh. Liam sticks it in his pocket and continues on his way, not knowing what he is doing, except that he feels if he walks about for long enough he will find his father or his sister somewhere.

His eyes dart from doorway to doorway, attempting to see into the shadows, hoping that he can detect danger before it leaps out at him. He wishes he had a rifle like the boy in the Canadian story; he wishes he had the boy's courage; yet he is enjoying the feeling of excitement, as if he were really in his own adventure story.

He comes to a halt before a shop that has lost its windows and has had bare boards stuck across its wounds. The glass from the smashed windows has been brushed into a heap by the entrance to the shop. Liam stands on his tiptoes to look over a sign in the untouched glass door and sees the shelves filled with bric-a-brac, old clothes, old books and old records. Then he notices a square of orange gas flame and a pair of hands illuminated by the fire; the pair of hands take him to a pair of arms, and then to the ashen face of an old man with gaping mouth and wide open eyes.

He does not stop running until he has reached a bar which sits at the confluence of two major roads. He stops by a piece of smooth granite that looks as if it might have been a milestone many years ago, but now serves as a boundary marker to the bar's property; turning to look back he sees the old man emerge from his shattered shop.

'Take yourselves off! Haven't yez done enough damage?' The old man shakes his head and turns away from the street and the hooligans he imagines wait for him.

Sitting on the smooth granite stone young Liam looks all about him. The bar is small, grey, anonymous; its windows, high up on the wall, are boarded with wood taken from tea-chests. He catches sight of a chest-of-drawers sitting in the road to his left. The chest-of-drawers shines white in the light of the moon. It looks as if it has been placed in the road as a practical joke. Slowly he walks over to the chest-of-drawers, eyes on the hedges which front the houses opposite. Will someone leap from a hedge and attack him? He steps into the road, he can't go back until he has seen if the drawers are filled with clothes. He hesitates with his right hand held out to the gold-coloured plastic handle; will something terrible happen if he pulls open the drawer? A nervous excitement makes him pull out the drawer with a single, noisy jerk. An empty beer bottle rolls to and fro in the drawer. He runs fast up the road, his laughter strained by the effort of running. He turns round to look down the small hill to the white laminated chest-of-drawers sitting in the middle of the road. He smiles and goes on up the hill; he almost dances along the pavement. His usual moroseness has lifted, replaced by delighted excitement; to be out so late under the moon and the stars. He turns to face the moon; it looks so close, is it about to crash into the earth? He laughs and remembers the men walking, driving across the moon!

Normally he is a quiet, placid boy, but now he feels like shouting, giggling, running. Normally he never runs, not in the street, nor in the tiny school playground. His school friends accept that he does not want to join in their banter and games; they put it down to the fact that he has no ma. Usually he likes to sit in the library at lunchtime and read a big book or scan the atlas. Or sit and watch the others play while he eats his sandwiches. He likes watching. Likes seeing how others behave. He had watched his mother pack her little light blue suitcase and walk out the front door of their flat without a backward glance. He rarely thinks about his mother now. He can hardly remember her. He doesn't mind. He doesn't mind being ragged for not having a mother.

He stops by a post box as he sees a man walking towards him. The man is too far away for the boy to see his face, but he is immediately convinced that it is his father. He starts to run; he starts to shout. The man halts at the corner of a junction and waits for the boy to approach.

'What can I do for you?' asks the man.

The joy that had begun to rise up within him dies away. Young Liam mutters an apology and turns away.

'What are you doin' up at this time, son?'

'I'm lookin' for m' da,' replies Liam, turning to face the man again.

'You're lookin' for your da?'

'Aye.'

The man laughs and Liam turns away again.

'Hold on, son. You shouldn't be out walkin' the streets at this time. Do you have any idea what time it is?'

Liam shakes his head and wishes he had not been so quick to run after the man.

The man is short and thin, but he carries a large beer gut.

His upper lip is covered by a well manicured moustache. He pushes his sandwich box farther up under his arm and allows his pale grey eyes to drift off to gaze down the avenue towards his place of work.

'Where's your da gone?'

'I don't know.'

'Where d'ye live?'

Liam tells him the name of the street.

'What are ye doin' up here?' asks the man, surprise sounding in his voice on hearing the name of Liam's street. He straightens himself up and runs his fingers through his cropped brown hair and studies the little Catholic boy for a while longer. What's he going to do with him? Surely he can't pass by on the other side of the street. He knows he should take him down to the police, but the knowledge that the police station is a long way away saps his will to do the right thing. 'You shouldn't be out at this time of night, son. It's not safe for anybody. Away home an' wait for your da t' get back.'

'Okay. I will, mister,' says Liam, knowing he won't.

'You better,' says the man, shaking a finger in Liam's face as if he were a boy learning his catechism under his instruction. 'Your father will give ye a good hidin' if you're not in your bed where you belong.'

'My da doesn't beat me,' replies Liam defiantly, proudly.

'Well he ought to!' says the man. 'He should tan your hide for not doin' what you're told!'

The violence of his words, but the harmlessness of his appearance causes Liam some confusion, but finally he decides that it is safe to turn away from the man. Liam goes prancing on up the road, sure that nothing can hurt him.

'Ach, where are ye goin', wee boy!' cries the man.

'I'm lookin' for m' da an m' sister, mister!' shouts Liam with a laugh.

The man slowly turns away and starts to walk down the avenue. What else can he do? Grab him by the neck and drag him down to where he belongs? He looks up as a car passes on a road that cuts across the top of the avenue. They let their children run wild, he tells himself. They have so many they can afford to lose one or two and not miss them, he muses. He quickens his pace, he's late for his shift.

Liam runs on, enjoying his new surroundings, making sure he sees everything.

TWENTY-NINE

GINGER, WITH A mischievous smirk spread across his gob, sneaks a look in his rear-view mirror to check that big, thick Eddie is set up just nicely. Tommy lies in a corner dozing away, but Eddie is upright, his large fleshy eyes closed and his mouth wide open as if he were catching flies; his heavy body does not resist the twists and turns of the car. He could sleep on the edge of a razor, thinks Ginger, as he swings the car to the left before turning hard right.

Eddie wakes with a furious curse as his head goes thumping against the door. He immediately knows that it has been no accident. He lashes out with his boot and hits the back of Ginger's seat. Ginger, with the image of Eddie's startled face still in his mind's eye, releases a bottled-up chuckle and slams on the brakes as he sees Eddie rise to seek revenge. Eddie is precipitated forward before being flung back as the engine stalls.

'Ye nasty wee shite!' screams Eddie. His fists flail wildly and ineffectually on Ginger's back as Ginger ducks beneath the steering wheel. Ginger's chuckle increases to a guffaw as Eddie's fingers slam into the steering wheel and he releases a pained cry.

'Hey!' shouts Kenny from the passenger seat. 'Don't youse two ever stop actin' the goat?'

'Wait 'til I get m' hands on ye, Ginger! I'll tear your bollocks off an' stuff 'em down your throat!'

'Will ye really, Eddie? Make sure you put salt an' pepper on 'em!' cries Ginger.

'You're as funny as a . . .' Eddie decides not to go on, it only encourages the evil wee ginger-haired bastard.

'Funny as what?' asks Ginger, coming up from his shelter and retaking his seat. 'Funny as a sore hand?'

'Funny as a kick in the teeth.'

Eddie reaches over and slaps Ginger across the head. Ginger accepts the blow; it was worth it at twice the price.

'Now stop the coddin', youse two. I'm tryin' t' eat m' chips here, you know.'

'My chips, you mean.'

'Did you want 'em?'

'I might've done,' says Ginger in a good-humoured voice. He laughs loudly and turns to see if Eddie is still rubbing his hurt head; Eddie is still rubbing his hurt head. 'If you can't take a joke, you shouldn't've joined.'

'I'll joke you, you wee bastard.'

'Aye, ye wee bastard: we'll joke you. We'll debag ye an' hang ye upside-down in th' back room!'

'Eat your chips an' shut up,' says Ginger.

Ginger twists the ignition key to try and get the stalled car going again. With his left hand pulling out the choke and his right hand twisting the key he is absolutely sure it will start the first time. It does, and Ginger smiles confidently at Kenny.

'Do you think you're at Brand's Hatch, or what?'

'What's the matter?' Ginger slips the car into first gear and eases it back to the left of the road.

'Your crazy drivin's th' matter!'

'Wha's th' matter with m' drivin'?' asks Ginger, giving Kenny a challenging look. 'Am I driving too fast?' asks Ginger with high-pitched mock incredulity.

'We're here to let th' people know they can sleep safe in their beds: not to wake 'em up!'

'Ach, I wouldn't want t' wake 'em up.'

'I hope so,' says Kenny, with a warning in his voice.

'I'll sing 'em a lullaby, if you want me to, Kenny,' says Ginger, aware of the warning, but choosing to ignore it.

'No, you're all right, Ginger. I wouldn't inflict that voice of yours on a herd of sheep.'

'Flock of sheep,' corrects Eddie, quietly.

'Flock of fuckin' sheep, then!' Kenny takes his anger out on the chip paper. He rolls it into a tight ball and chucks it out the window. Ginger slams on the brakes again. The car comes to a halt in the middle of the main road. The jolt wakes Tommy from his dreamy doze and he sits up.

'Why have you stopped the car, Ginger?' asks Kenny in his most threatening tone, soft but dull. He drums his fingers on the dash board to underline that this isn't at all needed.

'Keep Belfast Tidy,' says Ginger. 'Don't litter.'

'Wha'?' asks Kenny.

'Keep Belfast Tidy,' repeats Ginger, looking Kenny in the eye and expecting the punch to come any second. Ach well, so what, he decides, you only live once. He can see, in the half-light cast by the moon, Kenny's face flinch slightly as he makes up his mind.

'Ach, Kenny,' says Ginger in the tone he keeps for his most intimate exchanges of wit, 'don't you think the rebels have put enough rubbish on to our streets without us makin' it worse?'

'They're puttin' dead bodies on the streets, Ginger.'

'And a lot of rubble and litter, too, Kenny.'

'Really?' says Kenny.

'Maybe you should go an' pick it up if you're so concerned about litter?'

'They left a bomb in a litter bin once,' Eddie mutters. 'An' didn't the binmen come round and empty it int' their lorry? It made an awful mess when it went off in Great Victoria Street.'

Kenny and Ginger turn in unison to look at Eddie. Eddie glances away over the shop fronts. What has he said? Eddie decides he should keep his mouth shut. Part of him wants Ginger humiliated, but another part of him hates any real disturbance in their always edgy relationships.

'Eddie, is that right?' asks Ginger.

'Aye,' replies Eddie, not taking his eyes off a blackened square gap in the shop fronts where he knows an off-licence once stood. 'Kenny, are you pickin' up the chip paper or what?' He turns back from the street to look into Kenny's face. Kenny is smiling.

'Ach, all right,' says Kenny.

'Wait 'til I find a cloth an' you can clean the car while you're at it.' Ginger blunts the edgy nervousness of his voice in a laugh. 'Kenny, there's a bin over there.'

'Aye, I see where the bin is.'

Kenny clicks open the door and steps out into the clean

night air. His gaze immediately strays to the moon and he shivers as if someone has walked over his grave; for a second he wants to grab hold of the door handle and climb back into the safety of the car and the company of his comrades. The moment of fear passes and he walks into the centre of the road to pick up the discarded chip paper, fully aware that his legend will increase in the telling and retelling of the tale. He turns as he hears the soft click of the car door behind him.

'Kenny, I thought I saw somethin' over there,' says Eddie as he gets from the car.

'What somethin'?'

'Somebody in yon shop.'

Eddie comes towards Kenny with his eyes firmly fixed on the black void of the looted off-licence. In the silence of the night they can hear each other inhale and exhale the dry, warm air; in the silence of the night they can hear a crane wail in the shipyard; in the silence of the night they can hear the distant roar of an armoured vehicle.

'Well we better go an' take a look,' murmurs Kenny.

He flicks the chip paper into the litter bin and draws out his revolver. It's always better to be safe than sorry, he tells himself. You never know what you might meet on a dark night.

'You never know what you might meet on a dark night.'

'Aye,' replies Eddie. He too draws his revolver.

The stench of squandered alcohol fills their nostrils as they step gingerly over broken glass, smashed crates and drained bottles outside the gutted shop. Kenny sticks out an arm to bring Eddie to a halt by the twisted remains of the shop's steel shutters that had clearly proved useless in the face of a thirsty mob. Kenny peers into the gloom, hoping his eyes will grow accustomed to the lack of light.

'Want me t' go in, Kenny?'

'Are ye daft?'

'Wha'?'

'Stay where you are.' Doesn't Eddie know if he walked in front of the off-licence he'd be silhouetted against the moonlit street? A dead man if there's a gun lurking in the dark. From the interior comes the sound of a rubber soled

131

shoe scraping glass over the linoleum-covered floor. He squeezes the trigger of his revolver and the cylinder turns past the chamber he keeps empty for safety reasons.

'Who's in there?'

Again he hears the shoe scrape glass across the floor.

Fuck it, he says to himself.

'I'll go in,' Eddie says.

'Eddie, will you shut up?'

Kenny steps over the sill and into the gloom. He waves his hand ordering Eddie to remain where he is. The broken glass crunches impossibly loud under his feet and a bottle goes spinning across the floor. He comes to a halt near to the wooden counter he knows is there and crouches as low as his pride will let him. In the absolute stillness of early morning he listens intently to the short, hard breathing coming from somewhere in the blackness. He feels about him with his fingertips until they send an empty bottle spinning round. He picks the bottle up and sends it clattering across the floor; the bottle comes to a halt with a dull thud as it hits some wood.

'Whoever you are, you better get on your feet or I'll blow your fuckin' brains out.'

The breathing stops and there is absolute silence in the blackness until Kenny allows himself to exhale, in exasperation. He gets to his feet and goes crashing into the counter, which he kicks and curses; feeling along the top of the counter he finds the access door which he kicks open. Immediately he hears feet move within reach of his arms and sees a white face appear above the counter. He catches hold of a pair of child's legs and hauls the rest of the body out as it attempts to escape.

Out in the street he holds young Liam's face up to the moonlight and gives him a good shake. Liam's face is deathly white and staring; the boy's body trembles and squirms as he attempts to break free from Kenny's grip. He gives the boy another good shake to make him cease his struggle, but the boy continues; he gives him a harder shake and the boy seems to quieten down.

'What were you doin' in there?' asks Kenny, looking into Liam's glaring eyes, into the face he somehow finds familiar. Kenny waits patiently for an answer. 'Has the cat got your tongue?' Kenny bends down a little until his face is just above the boy's. 'Well?'

'I was just lookin', mister.'

'Just lookin'?'

'Aye.'

'For what?'

'Anythin'.'

'Anythin'?'

'Aye,' mutters Liam. How he wishes he'd remained in his bed reading his book. 'I wasn't doin' nothin' wrong, mister. Honest. I was just lookin'.'

'What the friggin' hell are you doin' up at this time of night?' asks Kenny. He allows the boy to ease away from his grasp. The boy doesn't answer for a second or two.

'I just came out for a look around.'

'T' see what ye could steal, eh?'

'I've stole nothin'.'

'Haven't ye?'

'No.'

'He's a left-footer, that's for sure,' opines Eddie solemnly. Eddie can tell a left-footer a million miles away; he can smell them.

'Ach, don't worry kid, we're not goin' t' hurt ye.' Kenny smiles at the boy who is as white as a sheet and trembling. 'You should be home in your bed. Have you any idea what time it is?'

'No,' says Liam.

'Well it's away past your bedtime.'

Liam looks up.

'Is it?' asks Liam.

'What'll we do with him?'

'Let's take him home an' shove him in the oven.'

'He could be up here spyin'.'

'Eddie, away an' get yourself a brain.'

Kenny points the little Catholic boy in the direction of his home and gives him a gentle push.

'Away home. If I were your da I'd scalp your arse for bein' out so late.'

Liam does not turn to acknowledge the advice, but runs off down the road in search of a place to relieve himself. He decides he's had enough adventure for one night.

'I know what I'd've done with the wee shite,' says Eddie.

'Aye, I know; but it's against the law.'

'What's that suppose to mean?' says Eddie, turning away from his commander with an expression of innocence on his face.

'It means we don't hurt kids.'

'Do they care who they blow t' pieces?'

'It doesn't mean we copy them,' says Kenny with annoyance, beginning to think their argument daft.

Kenny surveys the looted off-licence and the remains of its contents scattered about the pavement and road. An adjacent greengrocer's windows have been smashed and apples and oranges lie about the pavement undamaged, as if spilled from an overfilled harvest basket. He walks to the fruit and kicks the scattered oranges and apples towards the shop. What a waste, he mutters to himself.

'What a waste,' he says to Eddie. 'The poor blacks in Africa could make use of them.'

'Aye,' agrees Eddie.

'What a friggin' waste. Destructive bastards.'

'Aye,' agrees Eddie.

Kenny bends down and picks up an orange.

'Watch th' glass, Kenny,' says Eddie, looking concerned.

'Aye,' says Kenny, dropping the orange. 'Who owns the off-licence?'

'Big Davie McIntyre,' answers Eddie confidently, his obvious admiration for the owner of the off-licence sounding clear in his voice.

'Big Davie? Ach, that's right. Does he contribute to the cause?'

'Everytime we ask.'

'How much?'

'Five quid.'

'He's a good man.'

'He is that, Kenny.'

'Keep your ear open for the names of the cunts who smashed up his wee shop. I want the fuckers' legs broke.'

'Right, Kenny.'

'Good man.'

They turn back towards the car. Kenny releases his anger on an orange which splits open against the car sitting in the middle of the road, as if it owned the road and everything on it. Ginger sticks his head out the window and waves an arm.

'Hey!' shouts Ginger, 'watch the paintwork!'

'I'll paintwork him,' mutters Kenny. He stops some ten yards away from the car, and turns to look into the face of the moon. Its mountains and plains look so clear, so near.

'Hey, d'ye think if we had a wee telescope we could see the spacemen danderin' about the moon?'

Eddie stops by Kenny's shoulder and looks up at the moon as if he were trying his best to spot the moon men.

'Aye, maybe you could, Kenny.'

'Ach, don't be daft.'

'No; maybe you could an' all.'

'Did ye see your man drive his wee car about a crater?'

'Ach, I did,' murmurs Eddie, enjoying the moment when he and Kenny seem to be sharing the same thought.

'Ach, it makes you wonder.'

'Wonder what?'

'Makes you wonder if there's more t' this world than friggin' Belfast!'

'Ach,' is all that Eddie will say about the matter.

They walk in silence back to the car. Ginger starts the engine and they drive off down the broad road in no particular hurry to go anywhere. Ginger is happy to prowl along the streets.

Eddie rests himself in the back of the car next to Tommy and asks himself if, for him, there is indeed more to the world than the tight little streets of Belfast? After a few moments' thought he answers himself in the negative. He does not want to live anywhere else, go anywhere else. Ulster is his country, his home and he'll die for it. It's good enough for him. His one trip across the water had been a disaster. He could not understand what the English were saying to him because of a particularly impenetrable accent; he had lived and worked in Newcastle, where he had family. His work mates had insisted upon calling him 'Paddy' and he had had to punch a few faces before he got the message across. Their voices had grated upon his ears, so much so that he often had to put his fingers to his ears to shut out the whine. The beer had given him diarrhoea and splitting headaches. He found the English a colourless, dull, boring people, happy to sit in a pub all night looking at the walls. He had almost got down on his hands and knees to kiss the ground when he'd arrived back at Larne.

'Are you two fallin' asleep back there?'

'Wha'?' Eddie opens an eye to find himself looking into Kenny's smiling face. 'Aye. I'm tired.'

'Dopey and Dozy,' mocks Ginger.

'Tommy, are you havin' a wet dream about wee Gloria McCann?'

'Wha'?' says the waking Tommy.

'You havin' a wet dream?'

'Wha'?'

'He's havin' some sort of dream anyway!'

'Ach, leave the fella alone! He doesn't know what a wet dream is!' says Ginger. 'Do you, kid?' Ginger swings around a corner and slows the prowling car right down to fit it into a tight little street lined on both sides by cars. He has to concentrate on his driving.

'Well,' continues Kenny, 'if he's keepin' his gob shut somethin' must've happen while he was leaving her home.'

'Leave the lad alone,' says Eddie, dully, 'I'm beginnin' t' think you're jealous.'

''Course I'm jealous.'

'Kenny's a married man,' jokes Ginger.

'Watch your lip,' returns Kenny; he reaches over and punches Ginger on the shoulder.

Tommy sits back in the warm car as silence is re-established. A fresh breeze blows over his face and he feels immensely satisfied with himself. The car comes to a halt at the end of the street. Its headlights blaze across the adjoining street and a patch of wasteland where a house once stood. Ginger takes a hand off the steering wheel and gives his scrotum a scratch before emitting a huge yawn. He doesn't cover his mouth.

'Where now?' he asks into the hush of the car and the stillness of the peaceful night. He feels lazy, bored, if things go on like this he'd rather be in his bed, he decides. He watches a tabby cat cross in front of the car, pausing briefly to look directly into the headlights, before slipping in under a nearby parked car.

'Where now?' asks Ginger again.

'Wherever you like,' replies Kenny.

'Well you're the boss,' says Ginger, challenging him to show his leadership.

'Take a dekko down the avenue.'

'I'll take ye down t' hell if ye want.'

'Just down t' the avenue.'

'Avenue, it is.'

Ginger twists the steering wheel to his left and heads slowly down the narrow street. The excitement Ginger had felt at first when his workaday world was torn apart by extraordinary events has worn off until he feels an endless boredom only briefly relieved by spurts of excitement. Like a drug addict he now needs great doses of excitement to gain the same sensation he had felt at the beginning of the trouble. The sensation of living your life close to death. He is aware that he has committed many heinous acts; but his conscience has been numbed by their frequency. At the beginning he salved his conscience with the thought that he was doing what he was doing for the sake of his country; now he no longer thinks such thoughts: it has become a way of life to which he is inured. Besides, he knows everything his own side did is matched in meanness, cruelty, cowardliness by the other side. He isn't proud of his actions, but it has to be done. The other side has always lain in wait for a chance to destroy, obliterate his country and its people, and when you're fighting for your country you don't stick to rules. He knows what it is like to furtively wash another man's blood from your clothes, from your hands, from your face, from your hair. Now he feels a constant numbness behind his laugh, behind his smile, behind his talk: nothing matters very much anymore. Nothing can ever be the same again.

He brings the car to a halt at the junction to the avenue. To the left a baths house and swimming pool tower over the surrounding streets and houses.

'Turn the friggin' lights off,' mutters Kenny as he covers his eyes to cut out the dazzle coming from a shop window across the avenue. Ginger flicks off the lights, allowing his own reflection to appear on the opposite window, lit from beneath by the dashboard lights; his face is hollow, like a cadaver.

'Where now?' asks Ginger.

'Why don't we stay here a wee while?' says Eddie into the warm interior of the car; he eases back in his seat and makes himself comfortable as if he expects to stay the night.

'Aye, why don't we do just that,' says Kenny, softly.

'Okay,' agrees Ginger.

Tommy says nothing, but relaxes in his seat and closes his eyes. In his mind's eye he can see Gloria's breasts shine in the bright light of the moon. He can still remember the touch of her skin, as soft as a child's. He can still smell her perfume, her warm moisture. He can still hear her words of encouragement, guidance and censure. He can still hear her soft moans and softer words, he can still hear his own even softer words.

The car settles down, like a bedroom late at night. Eddie begins to snore and Ginger fidgets in his seat, attempting to find a more comfortable position. Tommy can hear his own breathing and the soft, banshee-like wail of a distant crane. Something causes Tommy to open his right eye just as a figure walks slowly down the avenue.

'Who's that?' asks Tommy, sitting up and leaning forward to see more clearly.

'Wha'?' says Kenny, reluctantly pushing himself up in his seat. 'What's th' matter?'

'Over yonder,' says Tommy into the murmurs and annoyed muttering as Ginger and Eddie shift themselves.

'Oh, aye,' Kenny softly sighs. 'Let's go an' see who he is.'

'What?' asks Eddie.

'Action,' says Ginger, twisting the ignition key.

'What's up?'

'Ach, will you wipe th' sleep out of your eyes?'

'What is it?' Eddie asks again.

'Look for yourself!' exclaims Ginger. Ginger lets the car crawl into the middle of the road and turns it to the right. He is good at letting the engine turn over just above its stalling speed. He lets the car creep along behind the figure.

'What shall we do, Kenny?' asks Eddie.

'Let's take a look. Nothin' better t' do.'

'Aye,' agrees Ginger.

'Aye,' agrees Tommy.

Liam stops and turns around as he hears the car brake and the car's doors click open in the still night air. He knows he should run, but he seems as transfixed to the spot as one of the nearby trees.

THIRTY

THE WOMAN'S TEETH are a brilliant white, framed by the deepest red lips; her skin is brown and flawless, it flows down to the curves of her oversized breasts, which are barely covered by an animal hide. The hide ends across her upper thighs, the rest of her legs being bent and slightly parted; they are long and without a blemish. Her face reacts with ambivalence to a man in a loin cloth standing over her with a spear in his hand. In the background amongst the palm trees weird creatures from the remote past roam about.

Young Liam steps away from the poster and swears that he will go to see the film. Then he notices its rating and realises that he'll not be allowed in. Disappointed, he turns away from the shabby cinema and heads on up the main road. After a few steps he comes to a halt. Should he go on? He has come this way only once before, upstairs in a red bus. His father had taken him and Kathleen for a walk in the hills. He is weary, he is wary; he wants to turn back, but is afraid of meeting the men again. He glances down a side street and wonders if he should make his way home through the warren of streets he knows to lie off the main road.

The moon is covered by a drifting cloud and Liam feels a chill as a cold wind blows. He turns on his heels and looks down the road. It is deserted. He starts to retrace his steps, but he is brought to a halt by the sound of a car in the distance. Quickly he runs to the cinema and down a side street. He presses himself into a doorway and waits for the car to pass, but the car does not come his way; he listens to the car fade in the distance. He comes out of the doorway and decides it's best if he stays off the road. Into an alleyway he goes. It stretches along the back of the main

140

road's shops for as far as Liam can see in the half-light of
the moon. Filled with a light-headed indifference he runs
down the alleyway, avoiding piles of empty boxes, bins and
milk crates.

Maybe he won't go home, he muses, as he comes out
of the alleyway at the point where two usually-busy roads
join before heading towards the centre of town. On the
other side of the road there is a postal sorting office and a
bar; just down from the bar the avenue begins, leading to
the road on which the church stands. If he runs down the
avenue he will be home in ten minutes. He scans the roads
and nearby streets looking for his sister or his father but he
is alone. Or almost alone. A mangy-looking mongrel dog
with bandy back legs comes towards him, its head down
in submission. The dog begins to whimper as Liam kneels
to stroke its back and head; the dog licks Liam's hand and
then his face, overjoyed at the attention.

'Good boy. Good boy.'

He pushes the dog away, but it will not go.

'Go on.' Liam gives the dog another, firmer push and
it goes.

Liam crosses the road and walks past the bar. Perhaps
Kathleen is sitting at home waiting on his return? Perhaps
his father is lying in his bed, sound asleep. He knows his
father will be angry with him, but his anger never lasts
for very long. He turns into the avenue and immediately
feels frightened. He hesitates, his eyes scanning the many
shadows cast by the trees. He has never liked walking
along the avenue, maybe because it is so wide, so open;
maybe because it forms the border between Protestant
and Catholic, the baths house half-way down the avenue
usually being the point of conflict. He tells himself not to
be so scared and walks on, glancing from side to side as
he goes.

THIRTY-ONE

GLAD TO SEE the avenue again Kathleen allows herself a sigh of relief before stepping out into the open danger of the road to gain the other side.

She is a couple of dozen yards away from the road on which the church stands, but instead of turning to her right and thus regaining her home via the main road she turns left and heads to the barricaded street from whence she came.

'Kathleen! Kathleen!'

Liam comes running down the avenue towards her.

'What 're you doin' out, wee boy? Didn't I tell you to stay home?'

'I came out lookin' for m' da!'

'Did you see him?'

'Na! Did you?'

'No.'

'Ach . . .'

Young Liam's head droops and the hope that had begun to grow in his heart dissolves.

'Where is he, our Kathleen?'

'Probably at home wonderin' where we've got to.'

'Where have you been?'

'All over.'

'What shall we do?'

'What we should've done in th' first place.'

'What's that?'

'Stayed home,' says Kathleen. She turns her brother round the way she wants him and pushes him up the avenue. She has had enough of being abroad so late at night; the novelty has worn off and she feels tired and hungry. She is sure that her father has found his own way home.

'Kathleen, will you take me to the pictures?'

'What pictures?'

'Up there. There's a picture I want t' see.'

'I'm not taking you to any pictures up there.'

She pushes him again, but this time he resists and turns to face her.

'Why not?'

'It's too dangerous.'

'Why?'

'Ach, none of your nonsense, Liam! You know why! We don't belong up there when there's trouble.'

'It's a really great film. It's got all sorts of monsters in it.'

'Well you can't see it.'

Liam kicks a stone to vent his anger.

'Don't kick stones! If you ruin them shoes you'll not get another pair in a hurry.'

'Aye,' sighs Liam, aiming at another stone: he kicks it and it goes smashing into the side of a car. Kathleen's hand is quick to rebuke him.

'What did I tell you?'

'You tell me nothin'!' exclaims Liam, almost spitting out his words into Kathleen's anaemic face. He turns away from her with a finality and passion that tells her he will not accept her slaps so easily in the future. He runs up the avenue towards the barricaded street.

Wearily she follows him. Her feet are heavy and her stomach empty. She wants only to have something to eat and to climb into bed and find her father in his room in the morning. She had begged him not to leave the house, but he had protested that she was worrying unnecessarily. She says a silent prayer, knowing that none of her prayers has been answered in the past. Looking up the avenue she sees that Liam has reached the street and is talking to someone hidden by a wall. She quickens her pace, perhaps it is her father. She breaks into a run and for a few seconds her spirits rise.

THIRTY-TWO

THE HEEL OF the big man's shoe is stuck in his wind-pipe, making it difficult for him to breathe. Liam can smell stale beer and dirt from the shoe and it reminds him of the alleyway where he had lain. He realises it would have been best for him to stay where he had found himself until morning. A sharp feeling of anger grabs his heart and he curses himself for not running from the prowling car. He can only tell himself that had he run he might have been shot in the back; now at least he has a chance to talk his way out of trouble. He has always been able to talk his way out of trouble, or into trouble.

Well, he tells himself, if you're a dead man, you're a dead man. Giving himself up to fate eases some of the nagging fear. He opens his eyes and immediately sees, in the gloom of the car with its occasional flashes from streetlights, that the shoe jammed into his neck has a hole in its sole. Beyond the sole with a hole he can see the beginning of a leg and its white sock, beyond that he can see the trouser leg, the back of the passenger seat and the car's roof lining. As the car is driven through the streets Liam catches sight of the moon which now seems cold, distant.

'Slow down: you on your way to a fire?' says a voice from the front of the car. Liam isn't sure if he likes the silence they had shared broken; perhaps it is the beginning of the human contact that will lead to his hearing the last words he will ever hear.

'No names,' says the voice in the front of the car.

'Does it matter?' asks a voice in the back of the car.

'Aye, it does,' says the voice in the front of the car.

Liam does not want to know their names, or see their faces again. He attempts to recall a prayer and some words

144

flit through his mind; he calls for God to intercede in this, the hour of his death.

He feels the car slow down and pull over to the side of the road. His breath catches in his throat. A car door opens and the shoe is lifted from his neck.

'Get the cunt out,' says the voice in the front of the car as another door clicks open.

Hands take hold of him and he is lifted out of the car. He keeps his eyes shut tight and his head bowed. The noise of a wooden door being kicked open sounds dully hollow. The house smells musty, neglected, filthy. His feet drag along bare boards until he feels himself shoved into a chair. The blackness before his eyes is tinged with blood red when a light switch is clicked on nearby.

'Open your fuckin' eyes!' screams one of his captors, whose voice Liam recognises as that of the man in the back and probably owner of the worn shoe.

'I'd rather not,' says Liam.

'Open your fuckin' eyes!' the same voice repeats.

Liam is propelled forward by a kick applied to the back of his chair. Falling to his knees he opens his eyes and sees a wallpapered wall. The wallpaper is off-white, with bright red roses; Liam recognises it as one he had had in his own bedroom when very young. The floorboards are a sandy colour, and here and there, tacked in against the skirting, pieces of old linoleum remain. He allows himself to expel all the air in his lungs; no need to pretend to his captors that he is not utterly petrified. He keeps his head down. Kathleen's smiling face comes into his mind's eye to tell him all will be well. He reaches out a hand to feel behind him.

'Stay where you are, Pat.' Liam recognises the older-sounding voice from the front of the car. 'What's your name?'

'Kelly.'

'Kelly what?'

'Liam Kelly.'

For a second or two there is a profound silence in the room and Liam can hear the slight movements of his captors' feet as they shift their weight on the bare boards. He knows there are three or four men in the room and the fact that only two of them have spoken makes him nervous. What can he do to make the others speak?

'You got a family?' asks the man from the front of the car, who Liam now realises must be the leader.

'Is it a full football team that you have?' asks the man with the hole in his sole.

'Ach,' says Liam thickly, managing to keep his voice from breaking up. 'It's a rugby team.'

'One a year, is it?' asks a voice he has not heard before. It is a thin, energetic, nervous voice; something in its tone causes Liam to fear it the most.

'I've two weans: a boy an' a girl.'

'Two? What happened? Did ye tie a knot in it? Or have it chopped off?' asks the nervous voice.

'I had the operation, you know? If it's all right by youse I'd like t' get home to see them.'

'Would you indeed?' asks the man in charge.

'Aye, I would. They'll be wonderin' where I've got to.'

Liam can feel a presence very close to the back of his head. His body instinctively tightens as it prepares for the blow. When the blow comes he makes no display of bravery; he falls to the filthy floor and emits a sharp, loud cry of pain.

'Did it hurt?' asks the leader.

'Aye.' He is aware that he must play up the pain his captors cause. He pulls himself up to the chair.

'You can scream all ye want: nobody'll hear ye. You want more?'

'I've had enough.'

'You sure?' asks the leader.

'Aye.'

The second blow hits him in the kidneys and causes him such pain that for a few seconds his world fades into blackness. As if he were in the midst of a falling-dream, he falls back to the floor.

When he lifts his head from the dusty boards he is picked up and put back into his chair. Warm blood trickles down his nose and into his mouth. He keeps his eyes tightly shut.

'Lovely punch, Eddie,' says the thin, nervous voice.

'What did I tell yez?'

'Don't worry, mister,' Liam says. 'I heard nothin'.'

146

'Why? Are you deaf or somethin'?'

'I just want to get home. I've nothin' t' do with what's goin' on over here. I live across the water: in London. I'm only here for a wee holiday, you know?'

'Aye, I know. I believe you, Mr Kelly.'

'Thousands would call you a lyin' wee cunt!' the man with the hole in his shoe tells him.

In the silence that begins to stretch to breaking point, Liam can sense the thoughts of the leader; he knows his life is being weighed, he knows the eyes of the other men are trained on their boss and that the silence is deferential. Better to keep his mouth shut now and wait either for the next painful blow or question. He knows he will have to answer many questions if he is to stand a chance of being freed. Yet he does not think he has done badly so far.

'Where'd you get your cuts?'

Liam's breath once more catches in his throat.

'Ach, I got int' a fight, you know?'

A board squeaks as someone moves up behind him. A slap tosses his head sideways.

'What fight?' asks the leader.

'Ach, comin' home from th' bar, you know?'

'What bar?'

'Crawfordsburn Hotel.'

'Crawfordsburn?'

'Aye. One of the few places you can get a drink without havin' t' look under your seat t' see if there's a bomb.'

'Who's leavin' the bombs under the seats, Pat?'

'A load of madmen who want t' be strung up.'

'Is that right?' asks the leader's voice a few inches from Liam's right ear.

'That's right,' says Liam, 'they don't deserve to breathe the same air as decent people.'

'Don't they?' says the voice at his right ear.

'No.'

In the silence he can sense the eyes engaging behind his back as his captors seek each other's silent opinion.

'They don't care who they kill or maim,' continues Liam, 'do they?'

By involving them in an argument he can turn their attention away from himself. His brain races with things to say, and things not to say. He must prove that he is not the man they want; not the kind of man they want to murder. He opens his eyes and sees the lower half of one of his captors. He shuts his eyes and wishes it would end.

'What fight did ye get int'?'

'Ach, with a couple of lads. I was with my brother-in-law an' m' sister. They started passin' comments about her, you know.'

'What comments?' asks the leader.

'Ach, well, you know,' replies Liam.

'No, I don't know.'

'She's a big girl.'

'She got a pair of headlamps?' asks the young man with a hole in his shoe.

'She's a bit heavy on top, you know. These fellas got a bit out of order, you know. I ended up bein' kicked. Though m' brother-in-law knows how t' handle himself.'

'Does he indeed?' asks the empty, nervy voice.

'Aye, he done twelve years in the Army, you know.'

'What army?' asks the man with a hole in his shoe.

'What army do you think?' asks Liam, allowing a little annoyance to sound in his voice to add authenticity to his lies. If he can only continue to make himself connect with his captors, show them that he is more like themselves, then they will not be so eager to hurt him.

He hears a metallic click by his right ear and his hopes of escape evaporate. Every muscle in his body immediately tightens in preparation for being attacked. If he gets it in the head then it will be mercifully instant. He feels the barrel of the hand gun being rubbed behind his ear.

'You know what that is, Pat?'

'It's not your dick, is it?'

A few strangled laughs reach Liam's ears and he is pleased with himself for a split second before he feels the heavy weight of the gun on the lower part of his skull. He does not wait to be pushed, but tilts his weight forward so that he lands on the floor. He is safer on the floor, he decides, but he knows his joke may end up costing him too much. The pain starts immediately and Liam emits the necessary loud cries and moans, also hoping that they will reach outside ears.

THIRTY-THREE

IT IS COLD now. Her prayers have not been answered. Michael is in the middle of the street hitting stones into the barricade with a piece of wood. Her brother wanders about, head down, kicking everything and anything that comes into view. Kathleen shivers and pulls her coat tight around her body. Soon, she knows, the sun will return. She sits on a kerb stone, her feet in the gutter. Her mind is blank, numbed: she no longer wants to think, needs to think. Her eye spots a large piece of glass from the bottom of a milk bottle. A thought, a terrible thought, flits through her mind.

'Ach, I don't know if it was him or not, Kathleen,' says Michael, stopping his game to look over to where she sits. 'It could've been anybody.'

'It was him: I know it was him.'

'How d'ye know?'

'I just know.' She does not bother to look up.

'They just pushed the fella int' the back of the car and went off down yon street.'

She does not want to hear! Her hands go over her ears and she buries her head down between her knees.

'It probably wasn't your da, Kathleen.'

'It was!'

Her cry causes Michael to turn away from her and reach down to pick up half a brick lying on the road. With all his might, all his hatred and every ounce of his passion he runs towards the baths on the other side of the avenue and lets the brick fly at a window. It hits a branch high up in a sycamore tree and clatters to the pavement by the railings. Besides, how can he possibly break through the thick wire mesh covering the large windows high up in the gable wall? He's wasting his strength, he tells himself.

He needs a gun if he's to do some real damage. How often had he swum in the pool beyond the thick, high walls? How often had he swum in the pool as early morning light streamed through? Swum early in the morning before the boys from the other side of the avenue came to claim back their territory. How many fist-fights had he had? Dozens. He was never afraid. Even when he got the worst of it. Who did they think they were?

He turns to see young Liam running towards him, he ducks just in time and a stone goes whistling above his head.

'Hey!'

'Don't throw stones!' cries Kathleen, but there is no force in her scolding. Her voice seems distant, withdrawn. Liam picks up another stone and lets it fly towards the baths: if Kathleen doesn't like it, that's too bad.

'You're wastin' your time, Liam: them windies have wire on 'em.'

'Need bigger stones,' is all that Liam replies. He turns away and kicks a beer-can against a crumpled dustbin, causing a clang to echo about the street. 'Could we burn it down, d'ye think?'

'Burn it down with what?' asks Michael.

'Burn it down with petrol bombs.'

'Where'd we get petrol at this time of night?'

'Never mind petrol bombs!' cries out Kathleen.

Liam sullenly kicks a stone towards the barricade and ignores his sister. The street is dominated by the red brick, sandstone and glass bulk of the Victorian bath house, making the houses on the opposite side of the street seem far too small to contain whole families within their walls. How he would love to see it burn. How he would love to see the Protestants burn with it.

'Liam, away an' see if our da's in the house.'

'Aye, Liam, I'll come with ye,' says Michael.

Liam doesn't reply, but instead stares at Kathleen with open eyes. Tears begin to flow, all attempts to hide them abandoned. They are tears of anger, hatred and frustration: they sting and burn. Can they ever be stopped? He sinks to his knees and buries his head between his arms, cutting out the world except for a few sparkling pieces of glass lying on the road. He wipes his eyes on the sleeves of his school blazer, but still they come.

'Away home,' says Kathleen, kneeling by his side, but not taking him in an embrace: she feels that he would not welcome her touch.

'Have the fuckers got him?' asks Liam.

'No,' replies Kathleen. What else can she say?

'They have, haven't they?'

'No. Maybe he's waitin' at home, wonderin' where we are? Will you go round and see for me?'

'Okay,' says Liam, brushing away the remaining tears. How he hates to cry in front of Kathleen. She's the one always doin' it. He stands and avoids looking at Michael.

'I'll see if I can find Father Connor,' Michael suggests.

'Okay,' says Kathleen, smiling weakly up at him. She still thinks Father Connor will do no good whatsoever. Liam's tears have stopped her own: now she must be strong and look after him.

'I'll wait here,' says Kathleen.

'Right,' answers Michael, softly, as if he does not want to intrude, to disturb a family matter. 'Won't be long. Have you got your key?'

'Oh, aye.'

She reaches into her pocket and hands him the door keys.

'Come on, Liam,' he says.

Kathleen watches them walk slowly down the street, Michael's left arm hanging lightly over Liam's shoulder. Liam, still clearing the tears from his eyes, walks along, seemingly happy to be in Michael's care. She retakes her seat on the kerb stone and reaches down for the round piece of glass. She shuts her eyes and is glad to be alone. She must stop her hands from shaking, she must. A sob breaks: she is unable to keep the tears away. Lifting the glass to her eyes she finds what she thinks is a good edge and drags it slowly across her left wrist; she draws no blood. Again she drags the edge of the glass across the blue veins of her wrist, but again she leaves only a white scratch. In the bluish-grey light of the pre-dawn she searches about the road for a better piece of glass but has to settle for the one she's got.

151

Using her thumb she feels out another edge and this time she is satisfied to see tiny beads of blood break her pale white skin. She licks the blood from the cut and watches as the beads seep back. From her sleeve she extracts her piece of crumpled toilet tissue and wipes the blood from her skin and then presses the tissue on to her wound. The muscles in her back relax and the tears dry up. She pops the glass into her pocket and feels better, knowing it is there.

THIRTY-FOUR

THE BIRD'S VIBRANT song can be heard loud and clear in
the murky room: the bird, perched on the other side of a
boarded-up window, sings joyfully, as if for the first time.
Tommy, standing in the centre of the room, cocks an ear
to listen. Through a few chinks in the boards that cover
the window he can see the faint, bluish-grey light of early
morning. He shivers. Never before has he stayed awake all
night. Never before has he caressed and kissed a girl for so
long, or so passionately. Never before has he heard a grown
man cry so pitifully.

'Give him it again,' says Ginger, kicking the man.

Eddie brings a short piece of two-by-two down upon
a pair of hands ineffectually protecting a bleeding head.
Kelly emits a blood-stifled cry and attempts to make himself
smaller. His moans do not deflect Eddie and Ginger from
their task of breaking his back. They pummel him with fist
and foot, Eddie occasionally using his makeshift club.

Tommy knows he must not cover his ears, but he dearly
wishes that the sounds would cease. He moves nearer the
window, hoping the bird-song will obliterate the cries of
their victim.

'That's enough,' says Kenny from the shadows at the side
of the room. He steps into the single pool of light from the
bulb overhead and looks down at Liam, as if finely judging
the damage his men have caused. 'Like a couple of pigs at
the feedin' trough.' He pushes Ginger out of his way and
glares at Eddie, Eddie's foot still being in the pig trough.
'D'yez hear what I'm sayin', or what?' Eddie steps away
from his cowering victim and enters the shadows around
the edges of the bare room before slipping a hand into his
pocket to give his erection a stroke.

'You all right, Pat?'

Kenny kneels beside Liam and shakes his shoulders. Liam groans and falls over on to his side. His face is streaked with blood, blood coming from his mouth and blood coming from his head to meet on his cheek. Opening an eye he looks into Kenny's face, without fear, without hatred.

'Wha' do you think?' says Liam, thickly.

'Aye,' returns Kenny, 'I'm sure it's a bit sore. You've taken it well. You're a strong wee fucker, aren't ye?'

'Not so strong.'

'If you co-operate with us, Pat, I might be able to keep yer man from hittin' ye.'

'Co-operate?'

'Names.'

'I don't know any names.'

'Don't ye?'

'I'm over here for family reasons. I don't know anything about it.'

'He wants more of the same.'

Eddie does not wait to be asked. His blows are hard, vicious, frantic. Ginger joins in on the attack with well-aimed kicks at Liam's ribs. He shows his enjoyment by emitting a sharp, breathy laugh. Ginger grabs hold of Eddie's arm to balance himself as one kick misses its target. When Kenny holds up a hand to halt the attack, the two men reluctantly break off.

'Are you two enjoyin' yourselves?' asks Kenny as they regain their breath.

'Aye,' says Ginger, with a childish grin.

'We are that,' says Eddie, panting, his hands on his knees.

Kenny turns his attention away to the back of the room. He steps towards Tommy, knowing he has a problem on his hands. The lad is white-faced, wide-eyed and trembling, but he cannot be excused from the room.

'You okay?' asks Kenny, patting Tommy's arm to reassure him. 'It's nasty, but it has t' be done.'

'Aye.'

Liam hears every word and his heads sinks; what will placate these men? His death? Liam looks into Kenny's face as Kenny crouches by his side. For a minute or so they stare into each other's eyes without speaking. It is as if he has already been obliterated. Kenny stares into his face as if he were not there. Liam knows that this man will do anything he has to do; nothing he can say or do will stop him. He begins to think of names and addresses. Why not invent a few? Does it matter?

'Well?' asks Kenny. The silence and stillness seems far too absolute for any words to break.

'There's Brendan O'Fee,' says Liam, carefully.

'Brendan O'Fee?'

'Aye.'

'Never heard of him.'

'There's talk of him bein' one of the boys.'

'One of the boys?'

'Aye.'

'You wouldn't be tellin' me lies, now would you?'

'He was organisin' things in th' area, you know? Well that's what I heard from m' brother.'

'Is that right?'

'They say he's a republican.'

'Aren't yez all republicans?' asks Eddie, standing in the light.

'Ach, most of it's talk.'

'Where's he live?'

Liam mentions a street. What does it matter? What are these men going to do that they haven't already done, or tried to do? Is he going to be responsible for everybody? He can understand them wanting to get back at the men leaving bombs in cars. Leaving bombs in crowded bars and restaurants. He knows a few names. He's listened to the talk.

'What number does this Brendan O'Fee live at?'

'Now how do I know a thing like that? I've no idea. Look, for Jesus sake, if you listened to every blatherskite in the area, every man jack of 'em would be captains in th' IRA!'

'You in the IRA yourself, Pat?' asks Ginger.

'No, I am not!'

'No?' asks Ginger, crouching low, just out of the light so that his face is not visible to Liam. Liam stares in the direction of the voice, indifferent now to whether he sees his captors' faces or not.

'Look, I live in London. Have done for the last ten years. I'm over t' see the folks, you know. My mother died last week, you know?'

'Aye, I know.'

'I want nothin' t' do with it, fella. I'm away back across th' water next Monday.'

'Is that right?'

'Aye.'

'Are you sure about that?'

'That's what I've got planned.'

'Ach, plans can go wrong, can't they?'

'Aye. They can.'

'Aye,' says Kenny in a soft, friendly tone.

'I've got nothin' t' do with them headbangers,' says Liam, aware that his voice has started to tremble. He sits himself up a little, giving vent to the pain he feels. Yet the pain is not quite as bad as he makes it sound. It is as if his brain has become so overloaded with pain it has anaesthetised his body.

Kenny, with a sudden jab, takes a grip of Liam's neck and shakes him violently; Liam is so surprised by the ferocity of the attack that he lies still and accepts it without uttering a sound. His quiet acceptance, his unwillingness to plead for quarter, have their effect upon Kenny and he ceases his attack. He stares, unblinkingly, into the face of the man he can have destroyed at the snap of his fingers. The face of the enemy. Yet from somewhere at the back of his mind he cannot fully convince himself that this man is the enemy. It is not just the hint of an English accent, or his bantering manner, but more a niggling familiarity with the man that makes him think that he should be buying him a drink rather than beating the living daylights out of him.

Well, Kenny tells himself, dirty jobs have to be done. He would far rather meet his country's foes out in the open where, he is utterly convinced, they would be beaten – no matter how many they happen to be. In his dreams he stands alone against a swarm of them. In his dreams Ulster is cleansed of all its disruptive, treacherous citizens.

The silence in the room is complete, except for the bird singing its song. Liam knows that he must be strong and continue to look his captor in the eye; that he must believe that they will not display more of the wickedness that has left so many dead or mutilated. What reason do they have to kill him? None. Except their hatred.

'Whereabouts in London do you live?' asks Kenny, dropping his right knee to the floor, causing Liam to flinch.

'Camden,' says Liam, waiting for the blow to fall.

'Where in Camden?'

'Up near Kentish Town, Castle Road.'

'What do you do?'

'Storeman.'

'Where?'

'Buildin' supplies.'

'Is that right?'

'It is indeed,' says Liam. 'Anytime you need roof insulation give's a ring.'

'A smart fucker, eh?' says Ginger from the shadows. 'He'll not crack his jokes if I kick his teeth in.'

'He's subtle, isn't he?' says Kenny.

'Aye, I'm subtle.'

'How long have you been in England?'

'Ach, near enough twenty years, off an' on.'

'Like it?'

'There's work.'

'No work here?'

'Ach, you know yourself.'

'I've never had problems gettin' a job.'

'Ach, well . . .'

'Why can't you get yourself a job this side of the water? Aren't we good enough for ye?'

'If you hear of a job let's know, will ye?'

'There's a job goin' up in Dundonald, I hear,' says Kenny, looking around at Eddie and then to Ginger. 'They need a worm catcher up there on th' hill.'

'Ach, I'm no good at catchin' worms.'

'Sure you are.'

'I don't think I am.'

'You dig with your left foot, don't ye?'

'Tell you the truth, I can't remember what foot I dig with.'

'Ach, you dig with the left. You're needed up on th' hill, in th' cemetery where you belong.'

157

'To tell you the truth, I was rather hoping to save the dig-
ging 'til I retired an' had m'self an allotment, you know?'

'Will you listen t' him! Doesn't he sound English?'

'Aye, he does,' says Eddie, laconically. He rhythmically
beats his piece of two-by-two on the floor. He knows
how to unsettle the nerves of those he is interrogating;
occasionally he will change the rhythm to unsettle them
further.

'I think he's puttin' it on,' says Ginger. 'Aren't you
puttin' it on?'

'I am not!'

'Aren't ye?' asks Kenny.

'As God's my judge.'

'God? You a religious man?'

'Cursin' religious. It's been a few years since I set foot
in a church.'

'Ach, we can change that,' says Ginger.

'No, thanks.'

'Names.'

'Names?'

'Aye, names!'

Kenny's fist goes into Liam's jaw with every ounce of
strength he can muster. Liam falls back with a terrified
cry and rolls himself up as much as he can to receive
the flood of blows from fists, feet and club. He is sure
his jaw is broken, he is sure his head is about to cave in,
he is sure his ribs are smashed to pieces, he is sure he's a
dead man.

'Have ye had enough?' asks Kenny.

'Aye,' cries Liam, allowing the tears to flow and the sobs
to obliterate the bird's song and to cause Eddie to stop
beating his piece of wood on the floorboards. He cries
easily, always had done; Mary despised him because of it,
she never could. His thoughts run through a collection of
names, some familiar, others inventions.

'Alec Riley.'

'Who's Alec Riley?'

'I've heard them say he's involved.'

'Heard who say?'

'The men.'

'What men?'

'The men in the street.'

'What street?'

'My street.'

'What street?'

Liam tells him the name of his street.

'What number?'

Liam tells him a lie.

'What number does this Alec Riley live at?'

'I think it's ninety-seven.'

'You think it's ninety-seven?'

'Aye.'

'Don't you fuckin' know?'

'I'm not sure. I think it's ninety-seven.'

In the silence that follows the bird stops singing and Eddie bangs a floorboard with the blood-stained piece of two-by-two. Kenny kneels before Liam. As if they have some sort of understanding they stare into each other's eyes until Liam decides that it is wise to look away. Look away from a face he somehow trusts. Somehow trusts to come to a fair decision. Across the room he sees that the door at the back is partially open, but that the fourth man stands by it. He would not have much of a chance. Better to stay where he is and try to talk his way out of it. The morning light has begun to seep into the room from the outside world and Liam cannot help but feel more hopeful.

'Ninety-seven?'

'Aye.'

'Have either of you two heard of Alec Riley?'

'There's a Sean Riley,' says Ginger, seemingly with some authority. 'He was picked up and questioned by the RUC last month.'

'Where's he live?'

'We don't know.'

'Alec Riley?'

Liam decides not to hesitate. What if he is being fooled into changing his mind? 'As far as I know his name's Alec.' Better to believe in your own lies than allow yourself to be tricked into believing theirs. He remains still, unwilling to move and cause his aching body more pain. Should he add anything more? He must not allow himself to be seen as too willing to offer information.

159

'What's he look like?' asks Ginger.

'Look like?'

'Aye, look like,' says Eddie.

'He's tall.'

'How tall?' asks Kenny angrily.

'A good four or five inches above me: near six foot.'

'Is that right?' asks Ginger.

'Aye, it is right,' returns Liam.

'What's he look like?' asks Kenny.

'T' tell you the truth, he looks a bit like yourself.'

'You're a funny man, aren't ye?'

'I'm tellin' you the truth. He's your height an' size, but with dark hair an' a bit of a beard.'

'I don't believe a word this pig's sayin',' says Eddie, attempting to give his opinion more authority by aiming a kick in Liam's direction.

'I'll decide that,' says Kenny, deciding the matter. 'Where'd you get the beer?'

'Beer?'

'Bottles of beer we found in your pockets.'

'Ach, lyin' in th' street.'

'Lyin' in th' street? Not from an off-licence?'

Liam is aware of why he is being asked about the beer. Looting a Protestant shop was a stupid thing for him to do. He looks directly into Kenny's face, unable to hide his hesitation, but hoping his hesitation will be taken as innocence.

'I found 'em lyin' in the street.'

'Just lyin' in th' street?'

'Aye,' says Liam, aware that more blows are coming his way. His head is down and his knees up to his chest by the time the first kick lands.

'You thieved 'em from the off-licence on your way down from the hospital, didn't ye!'

'I found them lyin' in the street after I got out of my brother-in-law's car!' says Liam, believing the lie himself.

'You're lyin'!' screams Kenny into Liam's face.

'I found them lyin' in the street. If you won't believe me then don't believe me!'

'You didn't walk down from the hospital?'

'No.'

'Then who fixed ye up?' exclaims Eddie, grabbing a fistful of Liam's hair and giving his head a shake to make sure he has heard him clearly. 'Put them fuckin' sticky plasters on your face!'

'Fixed up?' How can he betray Ann? Surely they would punish her for succouring him? 'M' sister's a nurse. She fixed me an' Dave up.'

'Lyin' cunt,' mutters Ginger, not without admiration.

'Liar!' screams Eddie with all the force of his lungs. He pushes Liam's head down and steps back into the shadows, where he feels safest. A little more light finds its way into the gloomy room, pouring through old nail and screw holes to shine on floorboards and decaying walls in narrow dusty beams. But the inmates are unaware of, or indifferent to, the start of a new day. All attention is fixed upon the pale, blood-streaked face looking up with a quietly defiant, even slightly mocking expression.

'Who's Dave?' asks Kenny.'

'My brother-in-law,' replies Liam, satisfied that Kenny has taken the bait.

'Oh, aye?' says Kenny with his voice fluttering with anger and irony. 'That's the brother-in-law who was twelve years in th' Army, is it?'

'Aye.'

'A Prod, I suppose.'

'Aye. But I've got nothin' against Protestants.'

'Somehow I didn't think you would,' says Kenny.

'I've nothin' against Taigs, as long as they're dead Taigs,' opines Eddie in his usual laconic manner. He thumps the wall with his piece of two-by-two and the old plaster crumbles away to fill a beam of morning light with a million motes.

'My sister's a nurse up in Dundonald. She an' her husband live up in Gilnahirk. His family's from Cultra.'

'Is that right?'

'Aye.'

'Thanks a million for tellin' 's,' says Kenny.

'He's a lyin' cunt,' says Eddie.

'Ring him up and ask him!'

His simple suggestion throws his captors into a moment's thought. Eddie looks over to Kenny, about to

161

ask for a coin to go out and use the telephone. This fella is talking too much, he tells himself. Kelly had started off as an easy target for his own inner twists of frustration and hate, now he is a man with a brother-in-law from Cultra.

'I couldn't give a fuck if your brother-in-law was Ian Paisley's cousin.'

'Look, I want to go home to my kids. They'll be wonderin' where I am. I've got nothin' t' do with the IRA. As far as I'm concerned they're a bunch of murderin' bastards. They're killin' their own people as much as anybody else. I just want t' go home. I've seen nothin' nor heard nothin'. What use am I to youse fellas? I want t' go home to my bed.'

'You're goin' nowhere,' replies Kenny; he turns away and sees that Ginger wants a word in his ear.

'Look, what's happenin'? Are we givin' yer man th' message or what?' asks Ginger in a whisper.

Liam cannot hear Ginger's actual words, but he understands well enough the import of the conversation. Soon, he tells himself, it will be one way or the other.

'Well?' asks Ginger after a dozen seconds in which time Kenny has stared at him without response. Ginger feels unnerved by the concentrated gaze of Kenny's light blue eyes; he begins to wish he hadn't opened his big gob. Ginger feels as if Kenny would quite happily release the Fenian and put a bullet in *his* brain instead. He is just about to do something he very rarely does to anyone, apologise, when he hears the door at his back open and the boards creak. Turning, he sees Tommy disappear through the door. It gives him the excuse to break away from Kenny and catch the door before it closes.

'Leave the lad alone,' says Kenny softly, but in his most authoritive, undeniable, piercing tone.

'Where's he gone?'

'Get a breath of fresh air.'

'Fresh air?'

'He needs it.'

'He hasn't gone off home t' his ma, has he?'

'Leave the lad alone.'

'Or maybe gone t' th' RUC?'

'Close the fuckin' door,' says Kenny in a dull tone that lets Ginger know the subject is closed. Kenny makes a gesture with his hand, ordering Ginger back to the job in hand.

Letting the door close, Ginger is filled with a bitter hatred that encompasses the Fenian lying on the filthy floor and Kenny giving the orders. He hates being told what to do. He hates not being able to do what he wants to do and say what he wants to say. If it was up to him he would put a bullet in the Fenian's head and go home to bed. They are all the same. None of them is worth a fuck. He releases his anger in a vicious kick towards Liam. When it goes wild and misses its target Eddie laughs.

'You keep your gob shut,' says Ginger.

'You goin' t' shut it for me?'

'That's enough, youse two.'

Kenny orders his squabbling comrades away from the captive. He knows he will either have to finish the interrogation quickly or order Eddie and Ginger to do what he knows they want to. How easy it is to control his fellow men. All his life he has found it quite natural to tell other people what they should or shouldn't do.

'You weren't at last night's trouble?'

Liam looks Kenny in the eye before he answers with a negative and shake of the head.

'Lyin' bastard,' says Eddie.

'He's callin' you a liar. Are you a liar?'

'No.'

'You sure, Liam?' says Kenny softly. He has used his captive's Christian name for the first time, but it seems to him as if he has been using it all night.

'Aye.'

'You got a kickin' because your sister's got a pair of tits?'

'Na.'

'Na?'

'I got a kickin' for th' same reason I'm gettin' a kickin' now.'

'Is that right?'

'Aye.'

'So you were lyin' t' us?'

'Aye.'

'Why'd you lie, Liam?'

'It started off because a young fella passed a comment about my sister. It ended up with me lyin' in the car park. Okay? They didn't want us drinkin' in their bar. Okay?'

'Okay. I'll believe you. Thousands wouldn't.'

'I don't,' says Ginger.

'Neither do I,' says Eddie.

'Do you know why you're here?'

'Because I'm a Catholic.'

'Oh, no.'

'Because I was walkin' down the street?'

'Oh, no.'

'I give up.'

'Because you can give us some info.'

'I'm an ordinary workin' man like yourselves.'

'Are you really?' asks Ginger.

'Aye.'

'We're ordinary workin' Protestants,' says Ginger, dismissing any grounds for common cause, 'an' you are an ordinary workin' Fenian cunt.'

'You know what we do to Fenians?' chips in Eddie. 'We cut their bollocks off an' stuff 'em down their gob.'

To reinforce his threat Eddie thumps the floor with his piece of two-by-two; yet Liam finds it hard to accept that the big, slow, dull man with a hole in his shoe is really going to castrate him. He seems to be playing a part: Liam can see how the big fella constantly looks to his comrades for assurance. He is also aware that few of the big fella's blows are half as bad, or half as hard to deliver, as he would like his comrades to think and for him to feel. After one particularly ineffectual blow Liam had reacted with a long scream of agony where a yelp of pain would have sufficed. They had caught each other's eye after Liam's demonstration of agony and in a fraction of a second come to an agreement: Liam would supply the appropriate noises to his blows. It is the thin fella, now nervously smoking a cigarette in a cupped hand, who gives Liam the greater concern, the greater pain. There is a casual badness in the way his eyes dart to and fro, in the way his thin, almost non-existent mouth slits into a smile.

'Look, I know nothin' about the bombin' an' the shootin'.

That's the God's honest truth. I know it might not matter to you one way or the other, but there you have it.'

'You're an IRA man, aren't ye?' says Ginger, crouching by the side of Liam. 'Sure you are. Sure you are. I can smell an IRA fucker ten miles away: the cunts stink: you stink: have you shit your underpants, or what?'

'You don't smell like a bunch of roses yourself,' says Liam into the face of his persecutor, challenging him to do his worst.

Ginger's worst is unrelenting. He grits his teeth and strains against his own exhaustion as he lashes at Liam with foot and fist. Finally, when his blows become feeble, he falls back. He turns, sees Kenny's smiling face.

'Who won?' asks Kenny.

'I'll kill the fucker,' is all that Ginger will say as he passes Kenny to sit on the floor by the wall. A beam of morning light falls upon his face as he wipes the sweat away with a soiled handkerchief: it's warm work compared to squeezing a trigger, he tells himself.

'I think you won,' says Kenny to Liam.

'I don't think I did,' replies Liam as he pulls himself up.

They stare into each other's face and Kenny is now sure he knows the face from somewhere.

'Where'd you live before you went across the water?'

'I lived with m' parents.'

'Aye, but where?'

Liam mentions a street and Kenny nods his head.

'What did you say your name was?'

'Kelly, Liam Kelly.'

'Aye,' says Kenny. Memories well up in his mind: memories of summer days spent running through a maze of streets, laughing, screaming, bantering. The thoughts start to turn his captive from a member of the enemy to a once intimately-known, even loved, friend that he had always liked more than he let on. Liam. Liam Kelly. He dismisses the thoughts from his mind. This is business, he tells himself.

'Do you know a fella called Patrick McNally?' asks Kenny.

'McNally?' He knows he must not hesitate this time. 'There's a whole bunch of McNallys,' says Liam.

'Which one's Patrick?'

'Is he the eldest?'

'You're tellin' me.'

'I think he's the eldest McNally.'

They both turn to see Ginger nod his head in agreement.

'What's he look like?' asks Ginger.

'Wee fat man.'

'How wee?' asks Ginger.

'He couldn't be more than five foot four.'

'Has he a job,' asks Kenny.

'Ach, I've no idea.'

'None?'

'Doesn't he work as a barman?' says Liam, feeling uncomfortably close to giving something important away.

'Aye,' says Ginger.

'What bar?' asks Kenny.

'I've no idea. How'd I know a thing like that?'

'Maybe you wouldn't. We know what bar he works in. Is he involved?'

'Involved?'

'One of the boys.' Kenny crouches before Liam, never taking his eyes from Liam's face. He stares openly, honestly, seemingly without hatred or emotion: as if all he wants from Liam is a straight answer to a straight question.

'Well I've seen him about the streets.'

'Oh, aye?'

'Aye.'

'Doin' what?' asks Kenny.

'Talkin'.'

'Talkin'?'

'Aye.'

'Talkin' about what?'

Liam does not reply. Has he got himself into trouble?

'Talkin' about what?' asks Kenny, allowing an edge of a threat to lead his question. 'Any talk about guns?'

'Aye.'

'Aye?' says Kenny with excitement. 'Has he got a couple of oul rifles?'

A laugh, the first genuine laugh heard in the room that night, breaks the silence and causes Kenny to turn his gaze away from Liam to Ginger.

'What do you find so funny, you wee cunt?'

'Nothin',' says Ginger, glancing over to his right at Eddie before backing slightly away.

'Keep your gob shut.'

Kenny turns his attention back to Liam.

'Has he talked to you?'

'Aye. He's talked to me. He'd talk to the back end of a bus.' Why should he care if they shoot Patrick McNally? Patrick McNally isn't worth ten minutes of pain. If they want to shoot Patrick McNally they're going to shoot Patrick McNally no matter what he says or doesn't say.

'Was it McNally who was out last night?'

'Out?' says Liam with genuine incomprehension.

'With the rifle.'

'I don't know anythin' about it.'

'Nothin'?' asks Kenny, looking straight into Liam's eyes, unblinkingly.

In the silence, the silence that Liam thinks he will meet in his grave, he lets his gaze wander from Kenny's face to the faces of Eddie and Ginger. All three are passive, blank, as they wait, wait for an answer and wait to carry out the sentence they had all passed upon Liam the second they knew his religion.

'All I know is that he's got a big gob an' is always goin' on about what happened sixty years ago. Him an' Pat Burke are a couple of gobshites.'

His interrogators show their interest in his words by shifting their weight towards their captive and grinding the dust and dirt into the dried-up wood.

'Pat Burke?' says Ginger, not bothering to hide his interest in Patrick Burke.

'Where's he live?' asks Eddie.

Liam answers with the correct address. Why should he be bothered what happens to Pat Burke? Pat Burke can look after himself. Pat Burke can go to hell.

'Are they the two leaders?' asks Kenny, in a flat tone that somehow smacks of finality.

'They're the two mouths,' says Liam, with a light, high-pitched tone of voice that attempts to express a lack of interest.

'Where do they meet?'

'How do I know?'

'Where do they meet?' repeats Kenny, allowing the threat to re-enter his voice, letting Liam know that he does not expect to have to ask the same question twice.

'I've no idea where they meet.'

Kenny's fist whips into Liam's face; Kenny's thumb-nail cuts the skin on the cheek bone and yet more of Liam's blood seeps out. He is exhausted. He no longer cares what happens to him. If only they would get it over with. He holds his face with his left hand and allows his tears to flow. If only it would end. If only it would end.

'They're always drinkin' in Paddy Brown's.'

'Aye,' says Kenny, already aware of where they drink. He is not after information, but confirmation: he does not want to kill the innocent, non-combatants. 'Who else drinks in Paddy Brown's wee bar?' He hasn't blind hatred for Liam and his kind. 'Are you in there a lot yourself?'

'I've been in there twice with m' brother.'

'Your brother involved?'

'No, he is not!'

'You sure?'

'Aye, I'm sure!' cries Liam.

'Okay,' says Kenny, finally allowing his captive to know that he is prepared to give as well as take. 'Who else drinks in Brown's bar?'

'For Jesus sake! Who doesn't drink in the place?' Using the end of his jacket he wipes his eyes and stares into a face he remembers from so long ago. He had always followed Kenny McIntyre. He had always done what he'd been told. He had always been glad of Kenny's company and his protection. He decides that Kenny McIntyre hasn't changed very much.

Liam starts to spill forth a list of names: names of people he knows or has known; a list of names that may buy his freedom, so he goes on and on until he can think of no more names to invent or reveal. What does it matter? They usually don't bother with names. They usually kill at random and read the name in the next morning's 'paper. Are they even bothering to write down the names? Or ask him to repeat a name? No.

'Okay. Okay.' Kenny waves for him to halt.

Liam falls silent and looks into Kenny's face, waiting for a decision, knowing what it will be. He expects nothing less than the cruelty others of his kind have received.

'Get the car,' says Kenny.

'About time, too,' says Ginger.

THIRTY-FIVE

THE SHAPES AND shadows that had caused Kathleen so much fear and unease as she walked the night streets are gone, obliterated by the cold honest light of the morning. The sun is still beneath the horizon, colouring a few clouds to the east of the city a deep orange. Soon it will rise and take the chill from the air; soon it will heat the streets for another long summer's day. She sits on the kerb stone, her skirt pulled tight about her legs and her chin resting upon her knees. She watches a small ginger cat as it paws the air and rolls over demanding to be tickled. Normally she adores cats, but now she has no feelings except ice-cold hatred for those who have taken her father.

The gathering noises of a new day start to eat into Kathleen's isolation to remind her that it will probably be the most miserable day in her life. She twists the piece of glass between her fingers in her coat pocket. Hadn't she seen her mother with bandaged wrists? Hadn't she heard her threats? Her warnings? She feels the sharp edge of the glass and knows that it will not be hard to face, like falling asleep.

Like falling asleep; she could fall asleep where she sits, her eyes are heavy and her body as light as a feather. In her mind's eye comes the image of her father; he is in a room filled with men and women listening intently as he sings a song. They nod their approval before joining in on the chorus. How everybody loved to hear him sing. She hums the tune to a song her father had sung to her and Liam on the ferry boat while they waited in the pouring rain for it to dock at Belfast. Not even his singing or his endless jokes could lift the feeling of dread that had descended on her as she looked over her new town from the open deck of the ship. He had become angry with her for not sharing his excitement. Belfast had seemed a miserable place. The next year in her uncle's house had been terrible and she had constantly fought with her father; but the following few years in their new house had been the best of her life. Not that anything very special happened; she liked the ordinariness of it. Her father had found work and she had found friends. She had also come to terms with looking after the house and her brother. She had quickly learnt to ignore the whispered comments in school about her lack of a mother. Not once had her mother written, or sent a birthday or Christmas card. She always told herself that she didn't mind. She believed her father when he said that it was her mother's fault and not her own.

She raises her head as she feels something warm brush against her thigh. She reaches down and scratches the cat's ear and neck. Picking it up, she squeezes it to her chest.

'Aren't you a lovely wee cat? Aren't you a lovely wee cat. Yes. Yes, you are.' She squeezes the cat tighter and it emits a squeal and jumps from her grasp. 'Ach, I'm sorry. I'm sorry.' She stands up to chase after the cat which looks out from the inside of an overturned bin, but freezes as she hears a car coming to a halt on the avenue. She instinctively starts to run, but then as she sees a bald head emerge from the back window of the car some thirty feet away she comes to a halt.

'Hey! Have ye no home t' go to, ye wee Fenian whore!' cries the little bald-headed man with a drunken slur. A woman's hand grabs hold of his shoulder and tries to pull him back into the car.

'Animals!' cries Kathleen, with all her hatred sounding shrilly in her voice.

'Away home, ye wee whore!'

'Animals!' She bends down and finds a piece of brick and quickly lets it fly towards the car. The brick hits the door frame and then glances off to strike the little bald-headed man on the side of his face. He winces and retracts his head. Kathleen feels overwhelming joy at the sight of victory and she immediately hunts for another missile. But then she looks up, as she hears the car door open. The bald-headed man is standing by the side of the car with his right hand held to his cheek.

'Fenian whore!' He starts towards Kathleen. 'Dirty Fenian whore!' His eyes are marble bright and sunk in a puffy, pockmarked, face. 'Dirty Fenian whore.'

'Fuck off!' screams Kathleen into the man's face as they stand within a few feet of each other. She holds up the piece of glass from her pocket, fully intending to slash it across the man's face if he comes any closer. He stands with his hand still to his cheek, now unsure what he should do to get his revenge.

'Frank, come back int' the car. Leave the wee girl alone. Come on.' A woman, short and plump, but with a pretty, delicate face, tugs her husband away and back towards the car.

'I'm bleedin',' says the man, hoping to excite his wife's maternal instinct.

'Ye deserved what ye got,' is all she gives him.

As the man and his wife climb back into the car Kathleen can hear uncontrollable laughter from its other two occupants.

She waits for them to drive off before turning away, turning away from her night's only triumph.

'You got him a smasher,' says Liam from the pavement by the barricade; he sounds disappointed to have missed his chance.

'Where have you been?'

'Lookin' for Father Connor.'

'An' did ye find him?'

'He was in his bed. Mrs Burke went an' got him up.'

'A fat lot 'f good he'll do's,' says Kathleen as she turns back to face the avenue. Face the avenue and wait.

'He wants t' see 's, Kathleen,' says Liam.

'Does he?'

'Aye.'

'Where's the keys?'

He fishes in his school blazer and hands her the keys to their home. He is aware that she hasn't asked him the most important question, and the fact that she hasn't doesn't really surprise him. Neither of them expected their father to be at home. They fall into a silence, a bottomless, hopeless silence.

'You took your time about it,' says Kathleen, with a dull anger that seems directed at the world rather than at her brother. Time would not be kind, time would bring pain. 'Where have you been, Liam?' she asks formally, her English accent sounding loud and clear.

'In Ma Burke's havin' a cup of tea,' answers Liam without a trace of contrition.

Another silence sweeps back in on them and they are left to stare into each other's eyes. Finally Liam speaks with a soft desperation.

'What 're we goin' t' do, Kathleen?'

'There's nothin' we can do,' she snaps.

'Nothin'?'

'Nothin'.'

Liam steps away from his sister, feeling an urge to pick up a stone and attack anything within range. As if she senses his violent emotion she lays a calming hand on his shoulder.

'I'll put you to bed for a start.'

'No, you won't!' cries Liam.

She makes a grab for him but he squirms free and runs out into the road. She realises that she has a fight on her hands, and even though she feels dead to the world it is a fight she feels she must win. For the sake of her brother.

'You have t' go to your bed, Liam.'

'I'm not goin' t' bed 'til m'da gets back!'

She makes a second grab for him and succeeds in taking a grip on his blazer. Liam quickly slips out of his blazer, leaving Kathleen holding it. She is furious and if he were in striking distance she would hit out.

He passes her, head down, and sits on the kerb. 'I'm not goin' t' bed!'

He places his head firmly in his hands and stares across the road to a house that has lost most of its windows. A black sooty stain streaks the brick above the lower windows.

'Just come round to the house with me.'

'Why?'

'Because . . .' she cannot think of a reason; if only she

173

had food to bribe him back to the house, but she hasn't. Defeated, she joins Liam on the kerb.

'I'm waitin' 'til he comes back.'

She cannot answer him. Her face twitches, and a rush of tears spills out, causing Liam to look away, unwilling to see his sister so diminished by emotion. Emotion he is fighting.

She buries her head in his school blazer and the muffled sobs resound in the deserted street.

'Just come home with me,' she says. 'You don't have to go to bed. Just come home while I get Father Connor over.'

'Okay,' says Liam, letting Kathleen know he is doing her a big favour; he doesn't *have* to do anything she tells him to from now on.

'Here's your blazer.' She holds the blazer out, knowing it is a little damp. 'Put it on, it's a bit cold now.'

He stands back on the pavement to slip on his jacket. He is tired, but so determined not to sleep. She comes forward to help him the way she always does as they rush to school; he sidles away and finishes putting on his own coat.

'Father Connor said he was goin' t' telephone the barracks.'

'Did ye tell him I'd already been round?'

'Michael told him. I didn't go int' his house.'

'What else did Michael tell him?'

'That them fuckers took him away in a car!'

She gazes down at the soft fresh face of her brother and sees on it the same expression as she had seen on Michael's. He has changed, in the few hours since they knew their father would not be coming back, he has changed. He looks down and sees a shoe lace that has become untied. He goes down on one knee to retie his lace. Kathleen looks up and down the street, searching out every corner. The police cordon of landrovers has gone from the bottom end of the street and a couple of policemen have started to remove some of the debris littering the road. The strong morning sunlight has touched the tops of the houses on the other side of the street.

'I wish I had a gun,' Liam mutters.

'A gun?'

'Aye!'

174

'Ach, don't talk nonsense, Liam.'

He jumps to his feet almost as if he were ready to strike out with his fists.

'They're dirty rotten fuckers!' His thin, immature voice is unable to carry the weight of his hatred and it breaks with a strangled watery sob.

'Aye,' says Kathleen. 'Aye.'

She puts an arm around her brother's shoulders and turns him towards their street. There is nothing either of them can do. Nothing anyone can do.

THIRTY-SIX

THE DOOR IS jammed and it takes Tommy quite an effort to push it open. After a few inches the door hits something. Sliding his hand through the gap he feels down until he comes to the obstacle, which he pushes out of the way. The small bedroom is brightly lit by the early morning sunlight pouring in through its single unbricked window. The window is covered in dirt and bird droppings, yet it remains intact. An iron bedstead is pushed into the far corner next to it. It seems as if the bed has just been stripped of its mattress and bedclothes; over the bottom end a piece of clothing is draped as if someone has just this moment left it there. Tommy crosses the few feet to the bed and picks up the piece of clothing and finds that it is the top of a pair of pyjamas coated in dust. He lets it fall to the bare floorboards.

Against the wall, at the head of the bed, a small cardboard box sits. In the box a stooped old man smiles out from a black and white photograph. Tommy picks up the photograph and sees that a very pretty young woman, with a smile of embarrassment, stands by the frail old man's side looking into the camera. Many years ago. Dropping the photograph on to the bed Tommy unzips his trousers ready to urinate. Something makes him stop. Is he about to piss in someone's room? He looks over his shoulder at the photograph. Then he notices the bright, unfaded wallpaper depicting daffodils wreathed in light pink roses surrounded by loops of violets. Against the wall next to the door a small table stands.

It is very plain and square. On the floor, next to the door, a broken chair is scattered. In the corner next to the table a rolled blind is leaning against the wall as if it has just been taken from the window and left. He re-zips his fly, deciding

176

that he will find another toilet. As he crosses to the door he glances out of the window, down to the yard and across to the row of bricked-up, deserted houses. He shivers at the sight. The yards are littered with bricks, bottles, cans, prams, mattresses and newspapers. It makes him feel sad, disturbed, cold. Out on the landing again, he turns to his left and goes into the front bedroom. The room is pitch black and the stench of urine and excreta is overpowering. He quickly relieves himself on the floor.

'Where are ye?' says a voice from below.

'Up here.'

Kenny waits at the bottom of the stairs, unsmiling, expressionless, haggard. Tommy pauses on the stairs and waits for him to speak, he expects harshness, even punishment; he expects a little of what the Fenian is being given. Will he have to watch them finish the Fenian off? Will he even have to do the job as his punishment? Will he have his nose rubbed in the Fenian's blood like a pup that has pissed on the carpet? He waits for Kenny to decide his fate. Waits and grows increasingly fearful. Waits and thinks about running for the door and the safety of his home. He waits for Kenny to speak, sure that he will more than likely get a bloody good kicking for being afeared.

'Christ,' Kenny says, 'I thought I was seein' a ghost! You're as white as a sheet! You all right, kid?'

'Aye.'

'You don't look it!'

Tommy reproaches himself for ever having thought Kenny would punish him for showing weakness. He isn't used to seeing men beaten near to death: not yet.

'Get in there an' help Eddie get your man int' th' fuckin' car.'

Kenny turns back into the room. Tommy hesitates for a few seconds, but goads himself to approach the door, knowing that he cannot possibly refuse Kenny's direct order.

'Out 'f the fuckin' way, ye stupid wee cunt!'

Before Tommy can step aside, Ginger has brushed past him and out of the door of the house. In the room he can see their captive lying on the floor with his head against Eddie's leg. He steps into the room and sees Kenny smoking a cigarette, his elbow resting on the mantlepiece. They do not speak, all is done with a look and a nod and Tommy takes a grip of the Fenian's arm.

The morning air has the smell of the sea in it, a gentle breeze blows in a handful of gulls from the lough; they screech above the five heads of Tommy, Eddie, Ginger, Kenny and Liam as they leave the tiny terraced house. Liam, accepting his fate, allows himself to be pushed down in the back of the car. He is too close to the abandonment of all hope to protest, fight, or cry out to the world for help. As he lays his head down on the filthy floor he thanks God for the chance to rest.

The small cul-de-sac, tight against a railway embankment, contains a dozen little houses. Except for a solitary house directly opposite the house of torture, the cul-de-sac is derelict, blinded by grey breeze blocks and colonised by grass and buddleia. The occupied house has its blinds down and white nylon curtains drawn across; the brown paint around its window frames is blistered, cracked, peeling. In the bedroom facing on to the cul-de-sac a frail, bird-like woman, almost as old as the house, lies in her bed listening intently to car doors open and close – just as she has had to listen to cries and screams all night long. Such suffering. Such cruelty. Have they no pity? She can do nothing, except pray, until her daughter comes to make breakfast and get her out of bed and into the armchair downstairs. Though by then it will be too late, too late.

Eddie slams the car door shut and jams his shoe into Liam's neck. He rests himself back in the seat and waits impatiently for Ginger to start the car.

'Did ye wind the elastic band?'

'Ach, don't you start.'

'Want a push?' asks Kenny.

The starter grinds.

'I've seen better motors takin' dead men up t' Dundonald for plantin'.'

'Shut it!' Ginger tries the starter again.

Eddie laughs his most sarcastic laugh. 'I'd like t' get home sometime this week if that's okay with you, Ginger.'

'What did I tell ye about names?' Kenny says.

'Ach, what's it matter?'

'Aye,' says Ginger, twisting the ignition key one more time, 'what's it matter?'

'Just get this friggin' heap of scrap goin'!'

The car bursts into life and jumps forward, raring to go. Ginger takes his foot off the clutch and quickly does a three-point turn.

'Where to?'

'Where we got him from.'

'Wha'?'

'You heard.'

Ginger stops the car at the junction of the cul-de-sac and a small, equally abandoned street. He turns to Kenny, with opened mouth and closed mind.

'You coddin'?'

'No, I'm not coddin'.'

'For fuck sake, Kenny!' exclaims Eddie, unsure exactly what Kenny intends to do with their prize. But to take him back to where they found him means crossing a main road in the light of day and that's stupid.

'I don't want any arguments!'

'Why not just give him the message here an' dump him in the Conn?' cries Ginger in a tone that rises in pitch until it becomes a screech as sharp as the gulls.

'This 'un isn't gettin' the message.'

In the silence that follows the only sound is that of metal against metal as Kenny draws his revolver from his belt. If they're going to argue they'll argue with a gun stuck to their heads.

'Wha'? You goin' t' give us the message instead?' asks Ginger in his high-pitched screech.

'Aye, I will if you don't do as I tell you to.'

Does he think he's still in the British Army? Did he do this sort of thing to the men in his squad when they were out killin' some poor fuckin' natives in the jungle somewhere? Ginger would like to reach out and grab hold of the pistol, but he knows by looking into Kenny's eyes that he'd be a dead man.

'The worst thing you can do is question orders, Ginger. So just do the drivin'.'

He does think he's still in the British Army.

'How's your man back there?'

'Out for the count.'

'You all right, Tommy?'

'Aye.'

'Good man.'

Ginger curses and curses again as he drives off through the warren of streets, now bathed in sunlight. He goes along half a dozen streets before seeing any signs of life and then it is a drunk stumbling home, using the sills of windows for support.

'No surrender!' screams the drunk as the car races past.

'Your man's had a rough night by the look of him,' says Eddie as coolly and as normally as possible, but his eyes are on Kenny's right hand. He's rather pleased to be letting this particular Taig go.

'He looks happy enough, doesn't he,' says Kenny.

'Probably came from the club,' says Eddie.

'Another happy customer,' says Ginger.

They brace themselves as Ginger turns a corner and mounts the pavement.

'If you crash the fuckin' car with your man in the back we'll all be finished.'

'You're a mad bastard, Kenny. We should dump the bastard an' get offside pronto!' cries Ginger, spitting out of the car window to show his disgust. If he has anythin' t' do with it the Fenian's goin' where all Fenians belong.

'Ye didn't believe his fairy stories, did ye?'

'Na.'

'Then why're ye lettin' the cunt go?'

'He's not IRA.'

'So what? He might join after what we've done t' him.'

'He's got a family waitin' on him.'

'M' heart bleeds for the cunt.'

Ginger furiously twists the steering wheel round to the left and the car skids around a corner, smashing its rear end into a parked car as it goes.

'I told ye t' take it easy. So take it friggin' easy.'

'Ach, your man's family'll be wonderin' where he is. I

want t' get him home in time for a nice breakfast, you know?'

'Aye, I know.'

Ginger shifts down a gear as the main road comes into view. The car slows to the edge of the broad thoroughfare. Ginger puts the handbrake on and turns to Kenny.

'Go up the avenue an' turn at the baths,' Kenny tells him. 'Pull over an' we'll chuck 'em out. Any questions?'

Ginger does not answer, but he stares into Kenny's eyes without blinking. Then, 'What the friggin' hell's got int' ye, Kenny?'

'Nothin'.'

'You sure it's nothin'?'

'We're lettin' him go. He's not IRA. We'll hit that bar next week.'

'If we're not in the Kesh by then.'

'We won't be in the Kesh.'

'He's seen our faces!'

'So what?'

'So what!'

'Aye?'

Ginger is in a paroxysm of rage and he twists and turns in his seat.

'I'm tellin' ye now I want the cunt finished off!'

'An' I'm tellin' ye we're lettin' him go!'

'You've no right t' risk it, Kenny!'

'He's okay! He'll tell the cops nothin'.'

'How the fuck do you know?'

'Just take it from me.'

'I'm not takin' anythin' from ye, Kenny. You can wave your gun about all ye want, but I'm not riskin' thirty years in gaol for a friggin' rebel!'

'Drive the car.'

'Look, Ginger, why –'

'Eddie, stay out of it,' orders Kenny.

Eddie rests back in his seat and emits a worldly-wise sigh. He'll drive the friggin' car himself, just so long as they don't sit where they are any longer: they're sitting ducks. Anyway, what's up with Kenny? Has he gone soft in the head? It's the first time he's scrupled over whether a rebel should get the message or not. Yet he hopes Kenny wins. Eddie has never actually pulled the trigger, though he doesn't mind people thinking that he has; and now the thought that he may be called upon to do the dirty deed makes him uneasy. Let the poor bastard home to his family so that they can get to their beds. It's been a long day and he is exhausted. He has fought God knows how many fights, thrown God knows how many stones, bottles, bricks. Suddenly he realises where he has seen the Fenian's face before! Yes! The wee man he'd hit with a milk bottle the evening before and chased up the avenue. He'd kicked him about the street a bit and then let a couple of other fellas have a go! He jerks forwards, the words in his mouth, but something causes him to think again and he rests back in his seat. He's had enough for one day. Let the poor bastard home to his family.

'Are ye drivin' the car, or what?'

'Na.'

Kenny's fist drives into the side of Ginger's freckled face and he is flung back in his seat.

'Are ye drivin'?'

'Na.'

Again the fist drives into the side of Ginger's face, this time causing his nose to bleed profusely; he emits a gasp of pain and surprise. The blood starts to drip into his lap and he cups a hand under his nose in an ineffectual attempt to keep the blood off his trousers. His thin face, normally so pale, is smudged with blood.

'You want any more?' asks Kenny.

'I'm not drivin' the friggin' –'

His sentence is cut off by a jab on his chin.

'If you don't drive –'

Eddie shifts uncomfortably. 'Kenny, I'll drive!'

'Shut it! If ye don't do as I tell ye to, Ginger, I'll have ye in the back room an' you'll get thirty years of kickin' in one night.' Kenny has spoken softly, understandingly, and he now lifts Ginger's head with his hand and looks him in the eye. 'Understand?'

He does not reply, merely knocks away Kenny's hand from his face.

'Come on, Ginger, do as you're told.' Eddie leans over to

182

offer his friend his handkerchief. He is distressed to see him so demoralised, crushed.

'I've got one of my own,' says Ginger, pushing away the proffered handkerchief.

'You've got five seconds, an' then I'm goin' t'drag ye out of the friggin' car an' kick your head in.'

Kenny starts counting and Ginger starts to clean his face of blood.

'Ginger, have some sense, for dear sake.' Eddie clenches his fists as he waits for Kenny to stop his counting.

'Well?' asks Kenny.

Ginger turns to Kenny.

'If we get caught it'll be your stupid fault.'

'Aye.'

Ginger depresses the clutch and shifts into first gear. He eases the car out on to the main road and immediately sees an armoured vehicle slowly coming towards them. The vehicle seems to be eyeing the Ford as if making up its mind to pounce.

'Fuck,' says Ginger.

'Keep goin',' says Kenny.

'Fuck,' says Ginger.

'Don't speed up.'

'Fuck.'

'Take it easy.'

'Fuck.'

'We're out on patrol just like them.'

'Fuck.'

'No problem.'

The armoured vehicle roars past, finally uninterested in the car, even though it is packed with men dressed almost exclusively in black. They sigh a collective sigh of relief. Ginger's is the loudest and the deepest as he expels a little of his humiliation; he emits a sardonic, told-you-so laugh and thumps the steering wheel! He was right and Kenny will pay for it, in some way.

'The bastards are probably asleep!' cries Eddie, shaken badly by the close call with the British Army.

'I wouldn't be at all surprised!' exclaims Kenny.

'Christ, were we lucky!' exclaims Ginger.

'You're tellin' me!' exclaims Eddie, in a warm tone that

attempts to rebuild some semblance of their former friendship. 'I have t' admit it, Kenny, but Ginger's right; it's a bloody dangerous thing t' do.'

'Ach, it adds t' the excitement. The experience will harden ye. Won't it, Tommy?' Kenny turns in his seat to smile at the lad in the back of the car. Tommy's face is drained and his eyes stare out as if he doesn't know where he is.

'Are ye with us, Tommy?'

'Ach . . .'

'We're droppin' your man off an' then headin' home for our breakfast. Okay?'

'Aye,' says Tommy sharply, as if he has just woken from a dream, or nightmare. He sits up straight and fixes on the empty road ahead.

'Get ready, everybody. Ginger, pull int' that wee street just before the baths. Eddie an' Tommy, youse two get your man out. How is he?'

Eddie gives Liam a shove with his foot and Liam responds with a moan.

'He's okay.'

'Right.'

'Right,' says Ginger. He doesn't have to check for oncoming traffic so he puts his foot down on the accelerator and takes the corner into the avenue as he would like to take all corners, with screeching tyres.

THIRTY-SEVEN

THE SUNLIGHT IS strong and hot, it washes over the slate roofs and brick walls of the houses to lend them colour and life. Kathleen, with her brother precariously under her control, walks slowly down the broad street towards her home, indifferent to the warmth of a new day on her cheek. She feels nothing. Her emotions, so wrung out by the night's events, have drained away. Her steps along the pavement are slow, leaden, as if she were already walking behind her father's coffin.

At the corner to her street Michael appears before her. She comes to a halt.

'Where 're you goin'?' he asks her.

'Home.'

'Not goin' down t' Father Connor's house?'

'No.'

He backs away and shuffles from side to side. His thumb reaches up from his left pocket and brushes the revolver that's now pushed into his trousers.

'He's 'phoned the peelers an' the Brits, but there's no sign of your da, Kathleen.'

'Aye.'

Again his thumb reaches up and strokes the revolver sticking noticeably out of his belt. What's the use of having a gun if nobody sees you with it? Is she impressed? He sees that she has indeed noticed his revolver.

'Where'd ye get that?' she asks, slight aggression sounding in her voice.

Michael pulls the gun from his belt to look at it before shoving it back; he smiles at Kathleen's pale, red-eyed face, then realises that she isn't impressed at all. He runs a hand through his mop of curly black hair, and then scratches the back of his right thigh where he has been bitten by a flea in the night.

'I was given it,' he answers.

'Who gave ye it, Michael?' she asks, sounding superior.

'Ach, never mind,' he replies, attempting to put her down.

'Did ye steal it?'

'No!' In fact he has borrowed it without permission. He'll get it back to its owner before the man wakes to find it missing. Anyway, he tells himself, if he's the only one not asleep he has a right to some protection.

'What d'ye want it for?'

'Ach, don't you be worryin' yourself about that.' She is only a wee girl after all.

'There's been enough shootin',' says Kathleen softly, passionately; strength begins to seep back into her voice. For a second or two she thinks of snatching the gun away and throwing it down a nearby drain.

'There'll be a load more shootin', Kathleen. An' a load more bombin'. It's the only way t' get things sorted out!'

'Get what sorted out?'

'A united Ireland!'

'Wha'?'

'A united Ireland!' says Michael; the words have a magic sound, everything will be better in a united Ireland. 'A united Ireland!' exclaims Michael fervently, as if he were spreading the good news. 'A united Ireland!' cries Michael with delight, as if he had discovered the answer to all his problems.

'Ach, what 're you talkin' about?'

'It's what the men are talkin' about!'

'Let 'em talk!' What does it mean to her? Her mind is concentrated upon getting Liam home and finding him some food. Then after that? After that there is nothing. She takes a firmer grip on her brother's shoulders to turn him away from Michael and Michael's gun.

'You should've seen them Orangemen scatter when big Pete Leary opened up with his rifle!' He laughs.

'I couldn't see anythin', Michael: I was hidin' in the kitchen most of the night.' His laughter seems deranged; she wants to get away from him as soon as possible, but

186

when she attempts to push Liam in the direction of home she finds that he has turned the full weight of his body against her.

'Let's see your gun, Michael.' Liam holds out a pale white hand, turned orange by a narrow shaft of sunlight coming from between two right-angled rows of houses.

'Never you mind the gun, Liam!' She reaches out and drags his arm down to his side. 'Come on!' It becomes a tug-of-war. His resistance is mute, but unyielding. He digs his heels in and twists his wrist in an attempt to free himself from her two-handed grasp.

'Will you come on!'

'No!'

'Do as I tell ye, Liam!'

'No!'

Michael yawns as he looks on at the struggling pair; he is tired, but even his tiredness can be borne in the exciting new world. A world that has infinite possibilities for improvement. He yawns for a second time and thinks to himself what a bossy girl she is, always tellin' people what to do. It's because she has no ma, and is really English. He scratches the back of his head. Wasn't she born across there? They're all the same. His own two older brothers boss him about when they come home from Manchester. Come home from Manchester to tell him what a great place it is; tell him how easy it is to work, make money and spend it. They come back less often every year and he knows that some year they'll stop coming. Why did her father come back here to live? Nobody comes back to live. Nobody at all. Doesn't make sense. Her da's an eejit. A coward, too. Why hadn't he gone out to help fight the Protestants when the men went knocking on his door? A frigging coward. Michael wouldn't have missed it for anything: the sight of the bastards running for their lives. Never again would they come into the area to smash windows and beat people up; never again would they treat him and his people like filth. He pulls his torn black trousers up and scratches the back of his thigh. He shoves the revolver back into his belt. What is he going to do with her and Liam?

'Will yez stop the fightin'! cries Michael, stepping forward to divide brother from sister, but they will not be divided.

'Mind your own business, Michael.'

Kathleen's warning is enough to dissolve his resolution and he meekly steps away to lean on a lamppost at the curve of the pavement. Michael grabs hold of a dirty white nylon swing-rope tied to the lamppost he has played round with other children not so many years ago.

'Up to yourselves,' he says, a false indifference in his voice.

'Are ye comin' home with me, wee boy?' says Kathleen glaring down at her brother.

'I'm not goin' t' m' bed 'til m' da comes home.'

'All right,' says Kathleen.

In the silence of the deserted streets Kathleen's sigh of acceptance sounds as loud as the click of a car door opening somewhere nearby. Michael turns his head: a man is backing out of a car parked by the baths, like a boxer stepping from a ring. His first thought is of the revolver and he unravels his hand from the rope to check that the gun is available.

'Are you hungry?' Kathleen asks her brother in a warm tone that tries to disguise her ulterior motive.

'Aye, I am,' answers Liam in a matter-of-fact way, knowing he is about to be offered a bribe.

'Then come home an' I'll get you something to eat.'

'I thought ye didn't have any food?'

'The shops'll be opened soon.'

Michael walks away from Kathleen and Liam, out into the middle of the rubble-strewn road, his gaze fixed upon the car and the men now standing round it.

'I'm not goin' t' bed.'

'I don't care if you never go to your friggin' bed.'

Kathleen can see Liam's thoughts register on his face as he makes up his mind.

'All right.'

Kathleen holds out her hand and Liam takes hold of it. She gives his hand a reassuring squeeze and pulls him towards her as they begin to walk down their street.

'Kathleen,' calls Michael softly from the middle of the road.

She stops immediately and lets Liam's hand fall. She turns back to face Michael. His tone of voice has told her all she needs to know.

THIRTY-EIGHT

WHAT IS THE man doing? Has he gone off his head or what? Standing in the middle of the fucking street with his arm around the piece of Fenian filth? Dear Christ! Trembling with anger, Ginger reaches across to get his pistol from the glove compartment. Dear Lord! What next? Is the fucker going to leave him home? Make sure he gets to his door safe and sound? The man needs to see a doctor! The man needs a frontal lobe lobotomy!

Ginger cocks the old .45 and checks that the safety catch is on. 'For Christ sake, somebody's got t' do the right thing!' he hisses into the contained silence of the car.

He climbs out into the little street. A dog sniffing at a lamppost raises its head, doesn't like what it sees, and goes scampering off with a whimper. Eddie stands by the bath house railings, arms folded and a roll-up on his lip; he unfolds an arm and gestures to tell Ginger that he should obey Kenny's instruction to stay back. He sees that Ginger hasn't got the message and immediately puts himself on guard in Ginger's path.

'Wha's goin' on?' says Ginger in a fury.

Eddie grunts and shrugs his shoulders.

'Fuckin' ridiculous!'

Eddie shrugs again. He peers down at Ginger's pistol and wonders if he intends to use the thing.

'They'll shove 's in the Kesh and throw away the key,' Ginger announces in a loud whisper, hoping Kenny will take the hint. To reinforce his point he clicks off the safety catch on his American Second World War pistol: how can he fail to hear that?

Kenny has heard and he glances back just enough to get a fix on Ginger, Eddie and the kid, Tommy sitting unhappily

190

on the kerb with his head in his hands: he had been wrong to bring him out.

Just let the wee shite try something – it's about time he was put down.

'It's a bad business, Liam,' says Kenny, turning back to an old friend. 'You all right?'

'No.'

'You'll survive.'

'Suppose I will.'

'You took it well. I was surprised.'

'Aye,' answers Liam. Is he paying him a great compliment?

'I'm just sorry it had t' be you.'

'So am I.' He glances up to see if there is an ironic smile on his torturer's face, but there isn't.

'Can you manage?' asks Kenny, removing his arm from the back of Liam's waist.

'Aye.' Liam tenses his painful joints to stand more erect. He must be strong enough to make it across the road and through the straggling barricade to safety. Should he just walk away? Should he say goodbye and cross the avenue? The barricade seems so close. Will he be allowed to reach it? Is this the final torture? Seeing his own safe streets before being shot in the back like so many others?

'We don't want to hurt non-combatants, Liam, but these fuckin' bombers have to be put out of action.'

He wishes he had a bomb right now to blow them all to oblivion. Since when have men like Kenny McIntyre cared who they hurt? They'll kill anybody who kicks with his left foot, anybody! Who started the bombing? Who blew up McGurk's? Who shot the first policeman? Who fired machine-guns into the homes of innocent people to keep them down? But is he going to start an argument with him now?

'No decent Christian would leave bombs in restaurants and shops, Kenny,' says Liam.

'Aye,' sighs Kenny, letting him know by the depth of his sigh that he has seen too much to want it to continue. 'Aye,' sighs Kenny again, letting him know that he sentimentally wishes none of it had happened; that things had gone on in the same old way. 'Listen, this didn't happen: understand.'

Liam understands all right, Kenny doesn't have to spell it out, but he knows he will: Protestants have no subtlety; they're a dull-minded lot with the imagination of sheep.

'For our own sake, for your family's sake: forget it happened. Okay?'

'Okay. It's forgotten. All I want is my bed.'

'Now you're talkin'!'

All he wants is to be treated like a human being.

'I could sleep for a week,' is what he says.

'Sorry you were given such a hard time.'

'Are ye?'

In the silence he stares into Kenny's face searching for irony or mockery, but he can see only sincerity on the thin, unshaven and pale face he knows so well: Kenny hasn't changed a bit. Memories of days spent hunting for scrap metal in amongst the bomb sites, to earn a few pence for chocolate or the cinema, come back into his mind. Memories of long chases through streets, fighting, shouting, screaming. Memories of playing football with rolled-up shirts and jumpers.

'All we want is what you want, Kenny,' says Liam quietly.

'Is that right?'

'If we can't get it here isn't it natural that some people want to look elsewhere?'

'Across the water, you mean?' says Kenny in a sharp, edgy tone.

'If you like,' replies Liam, aware that he may have opened his mouth too wide.

'What some of your people are askin' for isn't on offer. Never will be so long as there's a drop of blood in our veins, Liam.'

Same old answer. Why not? Who has ever made them an offer giving them more than they already have? It'd be a waste of time, anyway. They're unyielding. No good trying to talk to them: like holding a conversation with a parrot.

'We'll see the country in ruins before we accept Dublin's rule.'

Same old stuff, but Liam believes him. Anyway, how much bread will Dublin's rule butter?

'All we want is to live our own way,' says Kenny mechanically. 'We were gettin' along just dandy before all this started.'

We get along just dandy so long as you know your place.

'Aye,' says Liam.

Now they can hear the buzz of traffic coming from the main road a couple of hundred feet away to their left. The morning air is warm and already stale. Sunlight pours through the avenue's trees to blotch the tarmac road with the broad shadows of sycamore leaves.

Does Kenny want him to agree that the punishment he has received at their hands has been necessary, understandable, even *just*? Or is he seeking to apologise in some way? Liam turns his head to the left to listen to the traffic, somehow it brings him a little comfort; real people are about in the world again and soon they will come this way to bear witness to his suffering. He cannot feel his legs, he doubts if they will carry him across the avenue; he has no control over them, no means of saving himself. He must stand and wait and hope strength returns soon.

He glances over his shoulder, in response to the certain feeling that he is being weighed up like some animal at the gates to a slaughter house. A small, fragile-looking, red-haired man in a bomber jacket stands at his back with a large pistol in his hand, scowling.

'Ach, never mind your man,' says Kenny, lightly and with a pat on Liam's shoulder as if the gun in the scowling man's hand were a toy. 'I'll take care of him.'

Yes! Kenny will take care of it. Kenny had always taken care of things! Hadn't he? Hadn't he? Yes! Had Kenny ever broken a promise? Never! Liam smiles gratefully. Should he say goodbye now and cross the avenue? Should he shake Kenny's hand? Suddenly he is sure it is a dirty trick and that Kenny will laugh as the red-haired fella finishes him off.

'You all right?' Kenny asks him.

Liam searches Kenny's face in a desperate attempt to know the truth. Kenny's face is pale, expressionless, inscrutable.

'It's a friggin' waste,' says Kenny.

193

What's a waste? His own coming death? He shuts his eyes and hopes he has got it wrong. Hopes that soon he can go home in peace.

'All a waste,' repeats Kenny with the same disgust sounding in his voice.

Yes. Kenny means him no more harm. He understands now. He goes to speak, but the words die in his throat; he clears his throat and tries again: he must say something, desperately needs to say something.

'Aye,' he finally squeaks.

Kenny offers a thin little smile and his head jabs the air, nodding for Liam to be on his way.

'Safe home. Look after yourself, Liam; these are desperate times.'

Safe home? Yes! He means it! Or does he?

Feverishly Liam's gaze wanders over the unruly, dirty blond hair, pale blue eyes, long thin nose, bloodless lips, hollow cheeks and unshaven chin, trying to assure himself that Kenny means what he says.

Yes! Yes, he means for him to reach home safe and sound. Yet something still prevents him from leaving Kenny's side to walk the dozen or so yards to the barricaded street; he feels safe where he is and the dozen yards seem like a dozen miles. He glances back at the man with the gun and a sharp, piercing dread grips his heart.

It is a long walk to the barricade.

'Never mind him, I'll settle his hash,' says Kenny in a soft tone.

Yes, Kenny can be trusted. Kenny is dependable. Kenny is a fair man. All he has to do is to take the first step, Kenny will watch his back.

His right foot goes out, then his left; he feels himself start to fall.

'All right?' asks Kenny.

'Aye,' answers Liam, staggering.

'Good man. Take it easy.'

Kenny's steadying hand is removed and Liam is alone again, sanctuary in front of him. He gathers up the last of his strength and takes a step into the avenue, every muscle in his body aware of the eyes boring a hole in the back of his neck.

'Fenian lover.'

'Wha'?' Kenny turns to Ginger.

'Fenian lover,' Ginger spits again.

Kenny allows his gaze to drift from the white, ice-cold face down to the pistol levelled at his midriff. A Fenian lover? Him? Yes. Maybe. Why shouldn't he get the same treatment others have received for fraternising? Treatment he has handed out on half-a-dozen occasions. How can he excuse himself? By saying the obvious, that he makes the rules? Out of the corner of his eye he can see a worried Eddie stepping towards him.

'For dear sake, Ginger, let's get the hell out of here!'

'Shut your fuckin' gob,' suggests Ginger out of the side of his mouth, without taking his eyes off Kenny.

'Fenian lover,' repeats Ginger.

'He's no Fenian, Ginger: he's an oul friend,' says Kenny with a smile that is meant to convey an indifferent, superior irony. He watches Ginger's gaze wander to look past his shoulder and out to the avenue. Ginger knows he should take his chance now, but does not move. Soon he will have to run out into the avenue to get in a decent shot with the powerful but wildly inaccurate pistol.

'Da!' breaks into the stale morning air and causes Ginger to drop his arm a little and turn in response to the cry's naked, undeniable pain. Pain that seems to fill the surrounding streets with its pleading. 'Da!'

'Go on, Ginger, shoot the wee girl's da,' says Kenny with mocking casualness and a nod of the head. 'You're a bad enough bastard t' do it an' all.'

'Da!'

'I've a family t' think of m'self!' Ginger says.

'Da!'

Ginger tosses Kenny a contemptuous glance as he strides past him, out into the avenue.

'He's goin' t' do it an' all,' says Kenny.

'Aye,' sighs Eddie, glancing at Kenny with confused concern. Kenny has to sort it out.

'Da!'

Fenian lover? Him? It's nothing to do with loving the enemy, it's a matter of discipline, says Kenny to himself, allowing himself a sleight of mind that maintains the necessary morality.

'Da!'

The wee shite's out of order.

'Da!'

'Please,' says Liam as softly as he can. His watery eyes stare into Ginger's hard, greyish-green eyes and he feels himself starting to fall.

'Da!'

'Please.'

I've a family, too, Ginger tells himself.

Each second stretches.

'Da!'

Each second stretches.

'Please.' Tears start to flow as Liam kneels on the pavement.

'Da!'

I've a family, too. Ginger grips his gun with a renewed, forced determination to carry out what he knows to be the only sane action, the only right action.

'Please.'

'Da.'

The shot cracks dully hollow. Ginger half turns in surprise before dropping his gun and falling to the tarmacadam of the road.

'You're lucky I don't put one in your fuckin' head,' says Kenny. He releases a kick in the direction of Ginger's leg. 'Never disobey me again, cunt.'

Ginger lies back on the road and watches Kenny's revolver hover above his body as if it were sniffing out a good place to evacuate another load. The bullet has torn a muscle, making his right leg agonisingly useless. He closes his eyes to the morning sun and listens to the running feet coming to witness his humiliation.

'Pick the eejit up,' orders Kenny.

With a single motion Eddie reaches down and lifts Ginger off the road.

'I can walk,' says Ginger, anxious to salvage something.

Eddie releases him from the cradle of his arms and Ginger gingerly starts to limp his way towards the car. With every step he takes he audibly fights back the pain.

'Sorry about that,' says Kenny with a smile to the huddled Liam as he bends to retrieve Ginger's pistol.

'Thanks,' mutters Liam softly as he fights to sit up. For a second their eyes meet and then part as he begins to rise.

'Ginger!' cries Eddie in real distress, 'why don't you let me give ye a hand?'

'Fuck off!' shouts Ginger, between gasps of pain.

'You asked for it.'

'Did I?'

'Aye!'

'I'll get the Fenian lovin' fucker back someday,' says Ginger with an intensity of hatred that causes even Eddie to come to an abrupt halt.

'What's the wee gobshite slabberin'?' calls Kenny.

'Nothin',' replies Eddie, wearily, hoping to act as a buffer.

'Better be nothin' or he'll get more of the same.'

'I'll get ye back, ye cunt!' screams Ginger, twisting himself around in the middle of the road. 'Fenian lovin' bastard!' Is there a greater insult he can fling? For a second Ginger tries to find one, but fails. His tight, smooth, almost boyish cheeks crumple as tears of pain and rage flow out. For a moment he resists collapsing again, but the physical pain and the pain of humiliation are too great. Eddie moves to help his friend, but Ginger waves him defiantly away.

'Tommy! Come an' pick this friggin' eejit up off his fuckin' arse!' shouts Kenny, seemingly indifferent to Ginger's pain, or Ginger's threats.

Slowly Tommy rises from the kerb, stumbling as if he were struggling with some terrible weight. His step is sluggish, as if he has just woken from a night's sleep. His brain is numb, frozen; he dearly wishes to be in his bed and waking to find that the night has been a dream.

'Da!' The running feet cease and little gasps of relief and gladness brighten the morning. The three men standing exposed in the middle of the road turn from their injured comrade to look on at the huddled reunion taking place on the nearby pavement. They listen to the girl's muffled sobs, each of which seems to strain her voice to breaking point;

they listen to her father's responsive words of comfort like lapping waves. They watch as Liam gets to his feet, buttressed by his children.

Eddie is even more glad that they let the Fenian go.

'Get Ginger int' the car,' orders Kenny, 'we haven't got all day.' His last word breaks slightly with emotion and he looks away from his comrades, towards the car standing in the middle of the tiny side street. He can feel the heat of the coming day on his cheek and it makes him think of the seaside, Helensbay, Crawfordsburn or Bangor.

'I'll look after m'self,' says Ginger with absolute determination to go his own way, no matter what.

Tommy steps aside but with a sudden rush of compassion Eddie steps forward, grabs hold of Ginger, ignoring his protests, curses and half-hearted blows, and lifts him on to his feet. Finally Ginger allows himself to be helped towards the car. Eddie is as much committed to re-establishing Ginger's pride as Ginger himself; later he will seek to ameliorate Ginger's situation by agreeing that he was probably right and Kenny way out of order. Though if Kenny ordered Eddie to stand on his head and sing a rebel song Eddie would do it.

'Okay, kid?' Kenny asks Tommy.

He receives a nod of reply.

'Ach, it's all over. Time t' get somethin' t' eat. My gut thinks m' throat's cut, so it does.' Kenny smiles a watery smile of experience and takes the young man's arm, moving in the direction of the car.

They are within a few feet of the car when a panicky, pleading exclamation stops them. Danger has entered the avenue. They turn in time to see the girl reach out and catch hold of the back of a fella's jacket.

'No!' she cries.

'Fuckers!' screams the fella as he removes a revolver from his trouser belt.

'Who the fuck is he?' asks Kenny softly, checking that his own revolver is where it should be. Is he about to have a shoot-out in the middle of the avenue? The thought brings a smile to his face. Utterly ridiculous, but so many ridiculous things have happened in the past few years. A young fella is heading his way with a revolver: is he going to be intimidated by a boy?

'Fuckers!'

'Michael, no!'

'Fuckers!'

'No!' her voice quavers with an emotion that seems to be pure anger; her voice rises cleanly above the murmur of traffic in the surrounding roads.

Kenny watches as the couple carry out a sort of farcical dance on the other side of the avenue, which is now bathed in an intense high-summer light. Michael tries to go forward, perhaps merely because the girl wants him to go back, and he is brought up with a jerk by her tenacious grip. Michael half turns and with his left hand slices downwards in an attempt to free himself from her interference. She starts to walk round him and then pull him back to the pavement. He seems almost ready to comply but suddenly he grabs the tail of his jacket and tugs it away, elbowing her in the chest repeatedly.

'Will ye let me go!' screams Michael. His eyes are fixed upon the tall fella standing on the opposite pavement with his hand inside his black jacket. 'Fuckers!' If only he could get in a couple of shots, he's sure they'd turn tail. What a story that would make! 'Fuckers!' Is the Protestant bastard smiling? 'Will ye let go of me, Kathleen!'

Kenny turns to look at the car, and at Eddie standing by its open rear door, who shakes his head to express his confusion. What is he to do? If he and Tommy turn their backs on the fella they'll be vulnerable. He knows the fella hasn't a clue how to use the Webley, but he might get in a lucky shot before they can drive off. Eddie shrugs his big shoulders and removes his revolver from his belt. Kenny turns down his offer with a sharp shake of the head. Too many witnesses.

'Shoot the little Fenian fucker an' let's get out of here!' screams Ginger from inside the back of the car.

Kenny steps into the road. He has to try something and not just wait to see if the wee girl wins the fight. He is annoyed, and under other circumstances would take

Ginger's advice. Any rebel with a gun in his hand is a legitimate target.

'Away home to your ma, mucker!' cries Kenny, not getting too close to the fella in case he provokes him into taking a pot shot; if he were to be shot he'd die of embarrassment before he'd die of the wound.

'Fucker!' cries Michael, narrowing his focus upon Kenny.

'Michael!' shouts Liam Kelly from the pavement a couple of yards behind his daughter and Michael, 'for Jesus sake leave it!' He is a helpless bystander, unable to intervene. Young Liam wraps his arms around his father's waist and looks on, wishing the fight between Kathleen and Michael was over and they could go home; they have their father back, that's all that matters, surely.

'Away home to your ma, mucker!'

'Fucker!'

'Away home, wee boy, before ye get yourself hurt,' says Kenny, aware that their verbal duel has descended into a playground banter.

'Fucker!' says Michael, unaware of the repetition. He half-heartedly points the revolver in the smiling fucker's direction, but Kathleen ensures that his aim is hopeless. He spins round to face her, his fist clenched by his side. He will have to deal with her, or live with his humiliation for the rest of his life.

'Michael!' cries Liam from the pavement, 'will you leave it!' He starts forward in a desperate bid to intervene, but his exhausted legs give way and he collapses to the pavement, his son landing by his side.

'Fuck off,' spits Michael, sending a shower of saliva into Kathleen's face.

She steps back in disgust and hurt, wiping her face with her sleeve. Why should she bother? What's Michael to her? Did she ever like him? He is an eejit, a gobshite; not worth tuppence. Let him go and get himself killed, she won't get in his way. It's what he wants. They deserve each other. Let them get on with it.

As she turns away she sees the manic hatred fade from his face to be replaced by a gentle, honest, concern. Michael's fist unclenches and reaches out towards her as if he were offering to shake her hand, but then his hand stops in mid-air. She looks into his eyes, his tremulous eyes, and thinks she can see his confusion being fought out behind them.

Kathleen puts out a pale, nail-bitten hand to reassure him; she releases a smile that seems to draw Michael towards her and eases his busy thoughts. Taking hold of his forearm she guides him back to the sunlit pavement.

'That's a-boy,' says Kenny in a harsh, mocking, infinitely condescending voice, 'away home to your ma before ye get yourself hurt.'

Kathleen has time to see the re-establishment of hate in Michael's face; time to see Michael's right hand jerk up; time, unthinkingly, to step forward in front of him.

The shot sounds dull against Kathleen's body; the bullet strikes her ribs before ricocheting into her spine. She gasps more in surprise than pain, and falls, her eyes pleading to her father.

'Da!' she cries.

Liam picks himself up and stumbles to her.

'Ach, Kathleen, Kathleen,' he mutters, taking her head in his arms and hugging her body to his own as her life bleeds on the kerb and down it into the road.

Michael stands rooted to the spot, unable to speak with shock. Then he seems to unfreeze and he falls backwards to a garden wall.

'Michael,' says Liam in a voice that is strong, 'away an' get the ambulance.'

'Aye. Aye,' says Michael. He sets the revolver on the garden wall and with a burst of speed runs up the avenue towards a telephone box, glad to be allowed to leave the scene. He has gone only a few yards before he decides that her shooting had nothing to do with him, that it was her fault, and if not her fault, then the fault of the Protestant fucker who had provoked him.

Liam looks up from Kathleen as he detects Kenny's presence.

'Anythin' I can do?' asks Kenny, a few feet away.

'No, nothin'. She's gone.'

'I'm sorry.'

'She's gone,' repeats Liam softly, but with clear-eyed

finality and firm emotion. Extricating his blood-soaked legs from beneath Kathleen's body he lets her rest gently on the pavement. Standing, he removes his coat and lets it fall over her face. He turns away from her and reaches out to take his son in an embrace. Young Liam does not speak, or acknowledge his father's presence; he stares down at his sister's body, feeling utterly cold, abandoned.

'Is there anythin' I can do?' asks Kenny again, in a soft, respectful, graveyard voice.

'Kenny!' shouts Eddie from the middle of the road, seeking to warn him of the danger approaching. His eyes are fixed upon the bottom of the avenue and the metal pig slowly creeping towards them.

'I'm terribly sorry, Liam,' says Kenny.

'So am I,' says Liam, slowly shaking his head, a sharpness entering his voice.

'Kenny!' cries Eddie with greater urgency.

Quite suddenly Liam's expression changes and a bitter, bottomless grimace of repugnance grips and twists his face. He goes to speak, but no words of hate come out; instead he turns away from Kenny and gazes down the avenue at the approaching car.

'Sorry,' says Kenny, before turning away. He runs to the car and jumps into the passenger seat.

The armoured car starts to whine, as if it has seen its prey. It comes to a screeching halt in the middle of the avenue and its big steel doors swing open and a little fat soldier leaps out followed by his comrades.

Eddie, never having learned how to drive a car properly, curses as he juggles the gear lever. In his nightmares he has dreamt of such a situation, of being chased and being unable to escape as if his feet were sunk in wet cement.

'Come on, Eddie,' urges Kenny.

'What a friggin' mess,' mutters Ginger.

'For Christ's sake!' shouts Eddie.

He releases a lungful of air and relaxes enough to look down at the gear stick, he sees his mistake and makes one more try to get the big car going: if it won't move he's going to get out and leg it: every man for himself.

'Come on!'

'Move it, for Christ's sake!'

'I'll do it!' cries Ginger from the back, leaning over the passenger seat to take hold of the gear lever. 'Clutch in!' Ginger shoves the car into gear and it roars off down the street.

All turn their heads to look back at the soldiers kneeling in the street with their rifles pointing towards them.

'They won't shoot. Might hit some oul doll in her bed,' says Kenny with some authority and his fingers crossed for everyone to see.

Banging into a couple of cars, Eddie manages to get round a corner and into the maze of tight little streets, where they all feel safe. They sigh a united sigh and rest back.

'Where to?' asks Eddie.

'Ann's,' replies Kenny. 'Get this joker fixed up.'

'Right.'

'Drop us off, then go an' get rid of the car: torch it.'

'Hey!' exclaims Ginger.

'Did you pay for it?' asks Kenny, from the passenger seat.

'No.'

'Torch it.'

'Right,' answers Eddie.

'Go thieve another somewhere.'

A silence is established and they all concentrate on the road ahead, hoping that they will not bump into the Army again around some little corner or other.

'You all right, kid?' asks Kenny, leaning back to give Tommy a shake.

'Aye,' mumbles Tommy, his whole body sunken, withdrawn. In his mind's eye the girl's beautiful green eyes are staring at him, her lips are parted and her face is screwed up in eternal pain.

'What happened back there? Did your wee girl get shot, or what?' asks Ginger, fixing his injured leg into a better position. In a way Ginger is becoming rather proud of the wound. He has, after all, been proved right. It will count against Kenny, he knows that for certain.

'She's dead.'

'Dead?' asks Ginger, as if he couldn't care less, and

he couldn't. 'Well, that's another one where they all belong.'

'You bad wee bastard,' mutters Kenny.

With an electric hatred Tommy dives at Ginger's throat and starts to strangle the life out of him. Kenny does not intervene for a few seconds but rests back, enjoying the changing colour of Ginger's face. Tommy emits a whining noise as if his attack were being driven by an internal motor.

'For Christ's sake stop the man before he kills him,' says Eddie, putting his foot on the brake, stopping the car.

'Let him do it,' says Kenny.

'Hey! Tommy! Don't listen to the wee bastard!' shouts Eddie as loud as he can.

Kenny reaches and inserts his strong hands between Tommy's and begins to prise them free of Ginger's throat. Ginger falls away and gasps for air. Tommy drops back into the seat and sobs.

'Ach, you're all right, Tommy,' says Eddie in an attempt to give comfort.

'This is your fault an' all!' cries Ginger, between gasps. 'I never wanted the fucker to come with us.'

The back door clicks open and Tommy is running down the deserted street, his shoulders bent; he does not look back to the car to see if he is being followed. In a few seconds he has entered an alleyway and is gone.

'Is he away to the police?' asks an indignant Ginger.

'Ach, Ginger, don't talk nonsense! The fella's upset!' exclaims Eddie, turning round to grab hold fiercely of Ginger's bomber jacket and give him a good shake.

'Not youse two now!' cries Kenny. 'Cut it out! Eddie, get movin'!'

Eddie turns around and depresses the clutch before twisting the ignition key, but the starter motor turns over without the engine firing. He tries again, but has no luck.

'What's wrong with this friggin' thing?' asks Eddie.

Repeatedly Eddie attempts to start the engine, but fails to get a response. He thumps the steering wheel and curses.

'The friggin' thing is out of petrol!'

No sooner has he made the discovery of the empty petrol tank than he is staring into the face of the chubby little soldier. Looking past the soldier he sees the metal pig turning the corner.

'Fuck it,' hisses Ginger.

'Nobody move a finger,' warns Kenny.

The car door opens and the chubby soldier's smiling face is shoved into the car.

'Morning, gents, having trouble with the car?'

'Aye,' says Kenny. 'You couldn't give's a push, could you?'

''Fraid not, mate, but we'll give you a lift.'

'No, thanks,' says Ginger.

'Get out of the fucking car,' says the chubby little soldier, shoving his rifle into Eddie's ribs.

THIRTY-NINE

FIGHTING THE NAUSEA in the pit of his stomach, fighting the tremor in his left hand, fighting a headache that makes his brain seem like a lump of ice inside his cranium, fighting the desire to rise and stumble back to his bed, fighting the urge to push away his plate and drop his fork, James eases a morsel of scrambled egg on to a triangle of dark brown toast and closes his thickish lips over both. He forces the food down his throat and wishes he had not drunk so much.

'It's quite incredible,' says Steven, with a nod towards the television. The young man glances at James to see if he has managed to keep the food down, and smiles a thin superior smile when he sees James's difficulty. How the hell is the old fool going to get through the morning? The camera sees through everything.

'Hum?' hums James, eyeing him across the starched white damask linen table-cloth.

'Quite incredible!' says Steven again. 'I suppose we can take some satisfaction from the fact that they spoke English while taking the first giant leap!' His voice is unnecessarily loud, as if he were talking to a Chelsea pensioner.

'Yes,' replies James with a belch, his eyes momentarily on the silver-grey television image of the moon's surface. A soft, assured American voice coming from the Moon informs Earth that everything is just great. 'Why isn't the damn thing taking off?'

'Perhaps they dropped the ignition key on the lunar surface, sir?' says Steven; he smiles and smoothes down his short blond hair, hoping now that his facetious tone will be excused.

'Hum,' hums James as he gives his aide a sharp admonishing look. 'It is a quite remarkable feat.'

Steven forks a chunk of scrambled egg into his mouth.

206

'Delicious eggs,' he says. He spears a sausage up off the central platter and quickly devours it. 'Delicious sausages.'

'Steven, my boy, you eat like a bloody pig,' says James.

'I'm a pleb, sir,' says Steven with an impish grin on his fresh, small-featured face: it makes him look ridiculously young.

'I hardly come from a privileged background myself, Steven, but even in our Manchester slum my mother made sure I knew how to hold a knife and fork,' says James in a pompous tone.

Steven inwardly curses James for being a silly sod. How can he be sonorous, dressed in a dressing-gown and slippers, suffering a headache and bad breath? Steven sits himself up straight and holds his knife and fork properly; he begins slowly, genteelly, comically, to cut up another sausage.

'Silly bugger,' mutters James.

'What you need, sir, is the hair of the dog,' says Steven, smiling his most childish smile which has long helped him get away with all sorts of cheek.

'You will never make a civil servant, Steven,' says James, lightly. He regrets having asked the young man to join him for breakfast, but at least he is someone to talk to.

'Thank you, sir,' says Steven. 'Actually I'm waiting to enter politics.'

'God help your constituents,' says James. 'Will you stand for the Jesters' Party?'

'Actually, sir, I'm apolitical,' says Steven with a loud ironic laugh. 'I'll jump aboard any charabanc that will get me where I want to go.'

'Where is that?'

'To as many parties as possible; and as the Tories throw much grander parties and their women are better looking I'll plump for them.'

'You wouldn't be the first to enter politics for the chance of leading the good life. Haven't you enough young women in London?'

'I so rarely get to London to see anyone I've forgotten what the place looks like.' A touch of self-pitying longing enters his voice. He spears a grilled tomato from the dish and dumps it on his plate. 'As far as I'm concerned the only good thing about this God-forsaken dump is the rather sumptious breakfasts.' He takes a slice of soda bread. 'It's obvious that we should set a date to quit and let them sort it out for themselves.' He adds a rasher of bacon. 'Or shoot all the known gunmen.' He spoons a little more egg on to his plate. 'That's the way the French would do it.' He looks into James's face and laughs.

'Perhaps, Steven, you should ask for a new job out of the province?'

'*Entre nous*, I have a couple of times, but they don't like it, sir. Letting the side down, all that nonsense.'

He attacks his food.

'You have the appetite of a navvy.'

'Thank you again, sir,' says Steven, setting his knife and fork down on the plate at the six o'clock position and taking up his napkin to give his greasy lips an overly delicate pat.

'How do you stay so slim?' asks James with considerable envy.

'Hard work, sir.'

'Hum,' hums James, sipping his coffee.

'Did you know, sir,' begins Steven as if he is relating some incredible fact to his father after school, 'that they say –'

'Who says?'

'Some army chaps. They say they could bump off –'

'Bump off?'

'Kill. They could bump off every single IRA man in a single night. They know where they all live and hide out. Simple matter of putting them against the wall.'

'Hardly our style: the rule of law and all that. Not even the French would do *that*, Steven.'

'Yes,' continues Steven, brushing aside James's grown-up objections, 'but wouldn't it make everything simple?'

'No.'

'Perhaps not,' says Steven, 'but it comforts the Army chaps, and me. It's such a silly mess. We're here by an accident of history. Making things impossible by the historical baggage we carry in this country. Actually, I'm on the side of the rebels, not merely because I'm a Catholic myself, sir, but because I think their cause is just, don't you?' Steven gazes straight into James's eyes and waits to see if he has managed to goad the old boy into an angry reply.

'If you are attempting to rile me please remember my delicate condition and forbear,' says James.

All his life he had been unafraid to listen to younger men, a new generation.

'I would never dream of disturbing your breakfast, sir.'

'Good,' says James, eating a little more egg; he reaches out and picks up a rasher of bacon with his fingers; he, too, can ignore table manners. 'If their cause is so just why do they constantly demean that cause by their acts of atrocity?'

'Why indeed, sir! Why indeed!' says Steven, mingling an undergraduate levity with a rhetorical musicality.

'Steven, is there something wrong?' asks James.

'Nothing out of the ordinary, sir,' replies Steven, reaching out for another sausage.

'I have no doubt whatsoever that the divisions in this society will only be solved by a cessation of violence, the passing of time and the growth of a mutual need that makes division illogical.' James picks up his coffee and wishes he weren't so hammy.

'Undoubtedly, sir,' says Steven, biting into the sausage to deflect his urge to laugh. Does the old bastard think he's addressing the House? Or the cameras? He wouldn't really care a damn if the good people of the island murdered each other 'til the cows came home, so long as London wasn't footing the bill.

James begins to feel uncomfortable as Steven continues his unblinking, cold stare; he feels as if a clear-eyed member of the audience has refused to suspend his disbelief and at any moment will declare that the king has no clothes, that the whole show is a fraud.

'We have a difficult task, Steven,' he continues 'a task for which we'll get no thanks and all the blame, whatever happens. History will give us a footnote if we're lucky. He shifts in his chair as he sees Steven raise an eyebrow at his mention of history. 'But we have to do the right thing and I do think we are doing the right thing. Aren't we?'

Steven shrugs.

'We are the only power strong enough to bring about a final resolution. We can't walk away with washed hands,' James changes his tone, stops addressing an audience and starts to talk to a man who is probably far more intelligent than himself. 'We carry out a policy. No change unless it's through the ballot-box.'

Steven sits forward, about to offer a quote about war being politics by other means when he decides against it: it is, after all, over-used, trite. Instead he forks up a small piece of bacon and pops it into his mouth.

'The violence is merely storing up insurmountable problems for future unity. They have made a terrible error.'

'Terrible error indeed, sir,' Steven repeats complacently. 'Actually, I read into the problem on the 'plane over, sir. I think I understand all the complexities of the situation, but really the reason why there is so much violence is that these people are a nasty, brutish, stupid bunch of bastards who won't take the sensible course.' He stares into James's face, waiting for the anodyne rebuff, but hoping he has ruffled a few feathers.

'Would you be any less brutish if the Germans occupied Kent?' asks James, flustered into the first answer that comes into his head and immediately aware that it is from a newspaper, a newspaper Steven has also read.

'Not in defence of Kent, sir. Though I might vote the Germans out of the Cotswolds.'

'I admire your taste.'

'Quite frankly I prefer the quick solution of having all the gunmen, from both lots, shot.'

Steven's gaze drifts, with a slow, deliberate, intention away from James, fixing itself upon the television screen.

'Looks as if something is happening, sir,' says Steven as a clock face begins to count off seconds.

'Is it away this time?'

'Seems so.'

The two men wait, with growing tension, as the seconds go by and the soft voice in the small, sunlit dining-room reassures them that everything will be well.

'Apparently, sir, they have poison pills in case they get stuck up there.'

'My God, really?' says James. 'They'll make it, fingers

crossed.' He crosses his fingers and holds them up for Steven to see.

'One loose wire.'

'Thirty seconds . . .' says the voice from the television.

'Strictly a flag-waving exercise. No real need to send them up there in the first place.'

'Twenty seconds . . .'

'But *what* a flag-waving, Steven.'

'Masters of the universe,' sighs Steven, with a hint of sarcasm and envy. 'I suppose we can claim, as they say, to have been Athens to their Rome.'

'Hum,' hums James.

'Fifteen seconds . . .'

'Ironically enough, it was a son of Ireland who began the whole thing.'

James glances at the young man, wondering how irony came into it.

'Ten, nine, eight . . .'

'Oh, this is ridiculous!' cries out James in protest at the tension clamped down upon his head.

'Five, four . . .'

A soft knocking is heard on the heavy panelled doors.

'Come in!'

The door opens and a podgy soldier with a stripe on his rolled-up sleeve and a thin folder in his hand enters the dining-room with his mouth already forming his first word.

'Shut up!' Steven tells him.

Silently the silver-grey object breaks in two and the return module rises in the black lunar sky sending debris and dust fluttering across the Moon's sterile surface. All three men greet the success with applause.

'You don't think it was all done in a studio somewhere?' says Steven, regaining his cool.

'Well, it was all strictly Hollywood . . . but I think not.'

'Sir, last night's incidents report,' says the podgy soldier in a thick Glasgow accent.

'Ta, Fontanelle.' Steven takes the folder and signs his name to a piece of paper.

'Glad it got off, aren't you, sir?'

'Very,' says Steven.

211

'My knuckles are white!' cries James, holding up his hands in the air, hands that had gripped the chair tightly. 'Let's hope they don't put us through that again!'

'Next stop Mars, sir!' says Fontanelle, about to leave.

'Before you go, corporal, switch off the box, will you?'

'Yes, sir.'

Fontanelle crosses the dining-room and clicks off the television set just as a talking head begins to give its expert opinion. Fontanelle turns, re-crosses the carpet with reverential care, and leaves the room as if it were a sleeping child's bedroom.

'Here you are, sir,' says Steven, holding up the folder he has quickly scanned, 'last night's traffic accidents.'

'Traffic accidents?' queries James with raised eyebrows, always ready to listen before he condemns.

'The killings have become so routine they're beginning to seem as inevitable as car pile-ups.'

'I don't like the joke, Steven,' says James, displaying the thuggish anger he is known for. 'It isn't smart.'

'No, sir.'

James flips open the folder and is immediately aware of why the young man is behaving badly.

'I'm sorry, Steven. Why didn't you say?'

Steven shrugs and rises to his feet, ready to leave.

'I didn't think I should claim any special attention.'

'Nonsense.'

'I'll tell O'Reilly to clear the table, shall I?'

'You were at university with Lieutenant Clark, weren't you?'

'Yes. We had completely different backgrounds, of course; but we got on extraordinarily well. He was fantastic fun.'

'His father is a friend of mine.'

'Yes, he mentioned that,' replies Steven.

There is a silence between the two.

'I'll 'phone his father. Try to get to his funeral.'

Steven gives a little nod of acknowledgement.

'Apparently he died instantly. Single shot in the head. A sniper in some ghastly block of flats. He liked this place, and its people. God knows why. For me it's not worth the life of a single one of our men.'

'I can't agree with you.'

'Obviously,' says Steven. He shows his indifference to what James thinks by turning his back on him and leaving the room. James scans the rest of the single sheet of A4 paper. At the bottom of the page his eye is caught by a four-line report of another shooting. Nothing unusual for the times, a Catholic girl apparently shot by a gang of Protestants. A shiver of disgust and anger passes through his body and he drops the folder on to the breakfast table.

'Bloody awful country,' mutters James as he gets to his feet.

He has to prepare himself for the day ahead. What can he do to help these people? Nothing much, he decides. Except to make the law work. The formulaic words he will use to condemn the previous day's violence start to echo in his mind. What is the use of putting real anger, real feeling into what he says? He is ignored by the zealots. It's all been said before. His brief appearance on the scene won't change a thing. Steady as she goes. Things could be worse.

He slaps his hand down on the door handle and for some reason the image of a dying girl soaked in blood comes into his mind and he feels physically sick. He rests against the door and wills the image away.

What a waste, but it's up to them, he tells himself. The sooner they get sick of it the sooner they'll get round to sensible politics and away from fascistic nationalism.

He opens the door and steps into the corridor.

FORTY

THE WAD OF banknotes feels heavy against his thigh and Tommy is sure it is visible to all and sundry; he will have to hide it in a safe place. His father had asked no questions when told that Tommy wanted to go to England. His father had merely nodded and gone out to the bank. His mother had been less stoic, but had calmed down and admitted that given the terrible violence it was best if he got out, for a while. Looking down at the churning waters as the ferry's propellers start to turn Tommy isn't sure if he'll ever come back. The last rope is dropped from the bollard into the greyish-black water and hauled aboard as the ferry slowly eases out of its berth.

The early evening sun is brightly orange, but unable to warm the sharp autumnal winds coming down the valley to the west. The low-rise city spreads over as much of the valley's land as has been found fit to build on. It is a non-descript, anonymous, straggling, workaday city planted beneath brooding hills which somehow seem to threaten it. The river and the lough it flows into are dirty, frigid; a means of waste disposal and transportation, otherwise ignored as a nuisance that has to be crossed by five plain bridges.

He turns away from the side of the ship and pulls open a steel and glass door to the large lounge; he steps in just as the bar's shutters are being rolled up. It will be a heavy night's drinking for the hundred or so young men crowding the bar, shouting orders at the half-dozen barmen. The men are all dressed in a similar fashion, jeans, printed shirts, cheap jackets of one kind or another. They have come from every corner of Belfast and the surrounding towns and for the first time they find a common cause in getting a drink and seeing out the night. They glance at each other suspiciously, attempting to place each other in the old framework, now slowly disappearing at their backs. Gradually they realise that they are all on the boat for similar reasons, that they are all refugees. They elbow forward to get a drink, to deaden their nerves, emotions, fears.

Looking about the low-ceilinged lounge, Tommy decides to wait for the crush to thin out a bit before going to the bar. He dumps his holdall in one chair and sits in another by a small round table. The engines work hard to change course, vibrating the whole ship, making Tommy feel slightly queasy.

'Tommy!' cries Joe, quickly crossing the cheap blue carpet with his hand held out. 'What about ye!' They shake hands and Joe dumps his father's old army kit-bag into a chair. 'Where 're you headin'?'

'Sheffield.'

'Ye got family over there?'

'Aye.'

'Ach, you're lucky.'

'You?'

'Liverpool, can't afford anywhere else. I'm goin t' join up.'

'Join up what?'

'Army. Or anybody else that'll take me!'

'Ach, what about the Salvation Army, Joe?'

'Ach, get away with ye!'

'Do ye want a drink?'

'Do I want to live?'

Tommy gets to his feet with his hand in his pocket.

'Tommy,' says Joe, grabbing hold of Tommy's wrist, 'you couldn't lend's a few spondulicks?'

'No problem.'

'I'm wrecked.'

'No problem.'

Tommy turns away and joins the queue. He pats his back pocket and takes out the slip of paper on which is written the address of his aunt and uncle's house; he attempts to memorise the address in case he loses the paper. He folds it and slides it in beside his wad of money. The nervousness that grips his stomach, bowels and mind starts to relax and he almost enjoys the excitement now rising in the swaying lounge. As he draws near to the bar counter he takes out a five-pound note and grips it tightly in his hand.

'A double vodka an' coke, an' a bottle of orangeade for the lad,' says a man directly in front of him. The man turns and smiles at Tommy.

Tommy turns in panic and attempts to escape, but Liam grabs his wrist and pulls him back.

'Ach, where're ye goin'?'

Tommy tries to shake his wrist free, but is unable to escape the tight, almost painful, hold.

'What will ye have t' drink?' asks Liam, looking into the young man's eyes without hatred or malice. 'What will ye have t' drink?' he asks again, twisting the lad's wrist so that he is forced to return to the bar.

'Will ye get a move on!' cries a man from the back of the queue.

Tommy thinks about making a run for it and jumping over the side of the ship, but he can't swim.

'Now I'm only askin' ye t' have a drink with me,' says Liam, strongly, kindly. 'All that's over with,' says Liam, with a nod towards the receding coast. 'Nobody's fault.' He does not believe what he says, but he wants to calm the lad's nerves. This fresh-faced, gentle, quivering boy has done him no harm.

'I'm gettin' a drink for a friend,' is all the words Tommy can find.

'Well what's he drinkin'?'

'Harp.'

'Right. An' yourself?'

'Pint of double,' says Tommy.

Tommy's head hangs down as Liam turns back to the barman and orders the drink. He forces himself to look up at the man he had seen so close to death, but who now seems so strong, alive, powerful.

'Cheer up, son,' says Liam. 'Where're you goin'?'

'Sheffield.'

'Ach, an awful bloody place. London's where you want to be.' Liam turns back to the bar to pay for his drinks. He hands Tommy the two pints of beer. 'Here you are. Look after yourself.' What else can he say? For a second he wants to punch the lad in the face, but the thought passes.

'Thanks,' says Tommy, receiving the drinks, so frozen by fear and surprise that he is unable to think of words that could possibly express his sense of shame.

They step away from the crowd until they are amongst the tables. Liam sets his glasses on a table and turns to face Tommy.

'I'm terribly sorry, Mr Kelly,' Tommy mumbles, feeling his lower lip quiver. He stares down at the floor.

'So am I, kid. So am I. You look after yourself across the water.'

Liam's warm tone of voice causes Tommy's head to come up.

'I will that,' says Tommy.

'England's all very well, but never forget where you belong, son.' Liam reaches out and squeezes the young man's arm as he gives him a weak smile.

Liam picks up his drinks and walks quickly across the lounge to where his son sits gazing out the window at the gulls sweeping over the ship and at the thin strip of land becoming thinner every minute. Tommy returns in a daze to the small table. He sets the beer down and takes a seat, oblivious of Joe, his thoughts still concentrated upon his meeting with Liam. How could he have been so kind? He stares across the lounge and watches Liam and his son get up from their seats and disappear round a corner. Tommy wants to run after him, but what can he say? There's nothing to be said. He remains in his seat.

'Ach, Tommy, it's a great wee country. God's own,' says Joe into his pint of lager. 'I'll miss the oul place.'

'Aye,' says Tommy, not listening.

'I'm sorry I have to leave it,' says Joe between sips of beer.

'Aye,' says Tommy. He turns to face Joe and his stout; he lifts the glass and quickly sees off a third of the pint.

'What's it like?' asks Joe.

'What's what like?' replies Tommy; he sets his glass down.

'Across the water.'

'The same as Belfast,' says Tommy.

'Aye?' says Joe, sceptically.

The two young men drink their beer and the sea gulls

screech over their heads. The ferry begins to roll and pitch with the swell of the open sea. The coast of Ireland disappears under the shadows of night and the ship heads on out across the sea with another load of emigrants.